D0398164

SOLITARY PLACES

McKenzie County
Public Library
19930
43400

SOLITARY PLACES

Joan Vannorsdall Schroeder

G. P. PUTNAM'S SONS NEW YORK

This is a work of fiction. While some of the scenes are based on actual events, the characters and their lives are the invention of the author. Any similarity to actual persons, living or dead, is entirely coincidental.

Copyright © 1994 by Joan Vannorsdall Schroeder
All rights reserved. This book, or parts thereof,
may not be reproduced in any form without permission.

Published by G. P. Putnam's Sons
200 Madison Avenue
New York, NY 10016
Published simultaneously in Canada

Library of Congress Cataloging-in-Publication Data

Schroeder, Joan Vannorsdall, date.
Solitary places / Joan Vannorsdall Schroeder.
p. cm.
ISBN 0-399-13987-7
1. City and town life—Fiction. I. Title.
PS3569.C5333M53 1994 94-11297 CIP
813'.54—dc20

The text of this book is set in Aster.

Designed by MaryJane DiMassi
Printed in the United States of America
1 2 3 4 5 6 7 8 9 10

This book is printed on acid-free paper.
∞

Thanks to Monty Leitch and Renée Crackel, for their support and encouragement; to Jeanne Larsen, for jump-starting this book; to Ron Goldfarb, for taking care of business; and to Faith Sale, for making it a better book.

I am grateful also to the staff of the Virginia Center for the Creative Arts, where a substantial portion of *Solitary Places* was written.

For Mark, who has always believed,
and Matt, Olivia, and Jordan, who have taught me much

I love all waste
And solitary places; where we taste
The pleasure of believing what we see
Is boundless, as we wish our souls to be.

PERCY BYSSHE SHELLEY,
Julian and Maddalo

1

THE LIE OF THE LAND

LUCY McCOMB

I feel the wind across my face. It comes out of the north, wild and mean; it howls about my gravestone and reaches deep among my bones. It means something, this wind.

Down from Canada, across Lake Ontario, it cuts through upstate New York forests and snatches the leaves. It howls through Pennsylvania strip mines, tatters Union flags flying at Gettysburg and Antietam. Like a serpent, it moves down the Shenandoah Valley, tearing budding apple blossoms from trees and stealing topsoil from freshly turned fields.

Up and over the Allegheny Front the wind rushes, leaving in its wake a cold as deep and black as sin. The people of Collier take in the plants from their front porches and spread extra blankets atop their sleeping children. They sigh and long for a gentler spring.

The wind finds its way inside my house, beneath the curled edges of the tin chimney flashing. It plumbs the bricks and pushes into the corner of my closet, finds the shoe box hidden there and riffles the postcards within. The house shakes and moans as the storm strikes it open-handed, straight on. My rose trellis gives way; the wisteria vines release their hold on the porch railing.

Sarah Rose McComb, my niece by marriage, sits at the kitchen table, listening to the strange music of the storm, worrying about her husband and money and their sheep. She's forgotten to latch the porch screen door at the store, and all night it bangs like rifle shots.

In his cabin high on the ridge, Sarah Rose's brother, Berkley Paxton, sleeps close to his twelve-year-old son, as if he could keep him safe forever. Jesse is scared by the freight-train force of the wind and welcomes his father's comfort. He thinks about school and his mother, the chest of her things that Berkley has forbidden him to touch pushed far beneath the bed. Now Jesse sits up, works to catch his mother's scent. But he cannot; Sharon has been gone seven years.

Reba Walker loses a shutter off her house. It hangs for an instant on bent hinges, then falls to the ground against the underside of her porch, where it blocks a mother cat from her nest of kittens. They cry for one another, but their sorrow is lost in the wind.

Reba knows none of this as she works her shift at the nursing home, where my friend Edith Halsey lies silent as stone, staring into the wild night outside her window, wishing she were dead. When Reba comes, Edith turns her face away and shuts her eyes. Still, Reba speaks to her, though she knows there will be no answer. Their understanding is fragile and lies beyond words.

The wind takes the flowers from my grave and goes on, never ends. All this, I see and know.

REBA WALKER

The wind picked up late in the afternoon, throwing around the skinny trees in front of Stoneleigh, playing through the screens like they were Jew's harps. The old people were jittery, calling out for God knows who, pushing their help buttons over and over until I turned off the main switch and hoped nobody would die because of it.

Edith Halsey was quiet, of course. She hadn't said a word for three years; she just lay there in bed breathing, staring at the ceiling. We got her to eat and drink only enough to keep her alive. Her bones poked through her skin like tent poles under canvas. Bobby Halsey had all but quit coming to see his grandmother after his daddy, Russell, died. I couldn't blame the boy, since Edith paid no attention to him. With the dump going at Lucy's place under Bobby's supervision, Edith wouldn't have had much good to say to him if she *had* been talking.

For my part, I always spoke to Edith as if she answered back. "Big wind out there, Edith. Could freeze again tonight. Yeah, I put in my peas and lettuce today. Got my tomatoes and peppers started on the kitchen table this morning. Just the tomatoes and peppers—don't want to rush things." Someday Edith was going to surprise everybody and start in talking again, and even if she didn't, I figured she needed to hear a human voice say her name now and then.

I had a soft spot for Edith, and not just because she was quiet and trouble-free at the nursing home. A long time before, when I was younger, Edith would drive past my house every evening to sit on Lucy McComb's porch. I'd be outside, maybe working in my garden, or fiddling with my broken-down car, or chasing after my kids, and Edith would slow down and wave at me with a big smile on her face. That might not sound like much, but it was more than most did for me then. And now here she was, as good as dead. I smoothed the sheet over her skinny chest and turned out her overhead light.

When my shift ended, I left Stoneleigh and drove through Collier toward home. At the courthouse, I saw that somebody'd left the flag raised; it flew straight south, tight against the wind. The traffic signals danced and twisted on their cables and made you look twice to see whether to stop or go. But then, it was the kind of night those rules don't much matter.

As I came onto the interstate, a blast of wind hit my

truck and shoved it over into the left lane. A car horn blew, and I jerked the steering wheel, then felt my left wheels rise off the pavement. I slowed down to forty-five, switched on my brights and the radio. The wind would blow all night, the man announced, and gust to forty miles an hour, bringing Canadian cold behind it. "Cover up those plants, bolt the door, and snuggle up with your honey!" he advised. "Here's some music to love by."

"Ha, ha," I said. "Me and the cat'll keep each other warm."

A cardboard box skidded across the road. I braked but hit it anyway, catching a flap on my bumper and dragging the box a hundred yards. Newspapers held on to the guardrail and then flew high in the air like kites. The night was alive and nasty, black as hell's basement, pushing around anybody who dared to be out in it.

Coming up the exit ramp by the Jackson School, I thought about Lucy McComb teaching us in the fourth grade. We'd practiced our public speaking by memorizing poems, Lucy pairing us up and assigning two poems to each pair. We'd done recitation in front of the class every Friday.

Sometime that spring Sarah Rose and I got handed a set of poems about wind. One was called "Zephyr," and it was decorated with a picture of a beautiful long-haired woman breathing gently on flowers and leafy trees. Of course Sarah Rose took that poem. She colored the woman's hair yellow, her lips bright red. She added flowers and birds to the scene, and up in a corner she drew a great big yellow sun with rays reaching down through the words of the poem. That Friday she wore a gauzy green dress and tied scarves on her arms to look like her wind-woman. When Sarah Rose finished reciting, Lucy told her she had a voice as sweet as spring's west wind.

That left me with the other poem, "Old North Wind." My picture showed a balloon-headed old man with fat pursed lips puffing misery down on shivering children and animals. I wore out my blue crayon making everybody look frozen.

I knew I couldn't compete with Sarah Rose's pretty performance, so I stuffed my blue sailor dress with newspapers and covered my head with a stocking from my sister's drawer. I carried our oscillating fan to school in a pillowcase, and when it was my turn to recite I turned the fan on high. I blew all the spelling tests off Lucy's desk and messed up Sarah Rose's hair. Lucy told me I made a very convincing North Wind.

I pulled into my driveway. Patsy Cline was sitting in the front window looking for me, her round cat body outlined by the light from the table lamp. She was better than a man; she ate canned food without complaining, didn't throw her clothes around, and never said a word about how I looked.

The wind howled all night. Danny walked through my dreams naked, stinking of sweat and sulfur from the paper mill. "Put some clothes on—the kids'll see," I said, and he answered, "You're making them into damn prudes, like you." Then the wind moaned—or was it me?—when Danny hit me on the face and arms, and I told him to stop, begged him not to kill me, because Angie and Tim needed a mother. The dream was in black-and-white, and when I woke, before dawn, the whole world was just as colorless. I was shaking, and it wasn't until I looked around the room and saw my face in the mirror that I remembered Danny'd been gone thirty years, and that blood doesn't come in black-and-white.

The sun shone lonely and cold the next morning. After two days of blowing, the wind had left behind a strange quiet that begged to be filled. I cleaned my drawers, took out all the socks without mates. ("Never throw away those single socks," my mother used to say. "If you do, you'll never get married.") I looked at the pile of socks, thought about my dream, and dumped the whole mess in the trash.

I sat down with a cup of coffee and the Collier *Gazette.* A big picture of an uprooted tree lying across the roof of a house stared up at me. "It was an ill wind . . ." the caption began. The story listed the damage the wind had caused—a collapsed roof, two car accidents, roads blocked by downed power lines. I read the last paragraph out loud: "Sheriff John Anstett says that Cedar Creek Churchyard is littered with loose trash from the nearby dump. He suspects that vandals are responsible for several overturned monuments in the cemetery." I had a strong feeling that one of those stones would be Mama's.

I threw on a jacket and drove the half-mile to the church. It was worse than I'd expected. The big cedar by the road, dead for more than a year, lay at the foot of the steep stairs leading down into the cemetery. The tree had taken the wrought-iron entrance arch with it, and pressed the scrolly lettering into the soft ground.

Among the gravestones and along the fence, newspapers flapped like ghosts. I picked one up—it was in some kind of foreign language. Magazines and catalogues with curled-up pages huddled against the church steps. *Gardener's Eden,* one of them was called, "For the Gardener in Everyone." Thousands of small paper squares dotted the grass: blurred Jack Daniel's labels, somebody's mistake at the factory.

In the back corner by Cedar Creek, where fifteen Civil War soldiers rested, the statue of Thomas Isaacs lay facedown on the wet ground. The barrel of his granite rifle had broken off and rolled up against Russell Halsey's headstone.

And there was my mother's granite cross flat in the grass, raw dirt like a cut where it had stood. Seeing her stone pressed into the ground, just where her face and chest would be, I felt the weight of it push down hard on my bones. It was as if she'd died all over again. I got down on my knees and tried to right the marker, but I managed to move it forward only a few inches.

I sat beside her toppled stone. Around me lay the graves of Ambrose County's earliest settlers: Carpenters, Lewises, Pendletons, Kanes; Paxtons, Halseys, Rules, Deatons. And the McCombs—Lucy's grave was in the front corner near the low wrought-iron fence, as close to her homeplace as she could get. Benjamin Lee and Deborah Rose, Sarah Rose and Hunter's two babies, rested next to her, their graves marked with sad-eyed stone lambs. All of them buried anew in the stinking filth blowing from the dump that used to be Lucy's home.

I took a white plastic sack from beneath a rhododendron and set to filling it with trash. As I worked, I thought about how Sarah Rose was to blame for all of this, despite what she and Hunter told everybody about having been lied to. Sure, we had to have somewhere to put our garbage, but why here—at Lucy's place, so near the church, so near my house? "You always did get everything you wanted, Sarah Rose," I said. "Hope you're satisfied now!"

When I'd filled the sack, I dumped the rubbish near the church steps, being careful to avoid the daffodils sprouting up around the foundation. I filled the sack over and over again, until my back and legs hurt too much to bend anymore.

My pile of trash stood waist-high, papers moving in the slight breeze as if they were alive. I picked one off the top: the New York *Daily News*, March 15, 1989. "Hope Fades for Missing Bronx Baby," the headline read. I used it to sit on, leaned up against the biggest oak tree, and looked up into the branches. Their tips were swollen, ready to leaf out. Three shiny crows strutted around in the grass, feeding on fat white grubs and whatever else they could find. The sun warm on my belly,

I closed my eyes, tired as I was from my broken sleep.

I started at the crows' scrawing. One of the birds perched on Benjamin McComb's stone, its claws wrapped tight around the lamb's head. The other two fought over a styrofoam tray stained brown with meat juice. They had been at work on my pile and had spread the garbage all around the grass.

"Damn you!" I jerked my shoe off and threw it as hard as I could, but missed the birds. They flew into a cedar tree and made fun of me with their ugly noises. The churchyard was filthy as back-alley Richmond again, as if I'd not even been there that morning. It would take every Boy Scout troop between here and there to clean it up right. "Look at all this shit!" I screamed. The crows scattered and flew off toward the dump.

Sick at heart, I climbed up the cemetery bank to the road. Six years of Ambrose County trash had left Lucy's place a sorry sight. The house had lost most of its paint, and the grass was long gone. A few sad clumps of crocuses bloomed by the maple tree. Bobby Halsey had brought in a couple of bulldozers and a dump truck, and the workers were digging a huge pit, pushing the dirt tight against the foot of the mountain behind Lucy's house.

A truck roared past me and rolled up the driveway; QUAKER STATE TRANSPORT was painted on the back in big red letters, and its license plates reflected the morning sun. Another truck followed close on its tail, this one from New York. I watched more trucks come: one from New Jersey; another from New York.

Then it hit me like a slap across the face: the trash that was blowing around our cemetery wasn't ours. The newspapers and magazines had sat on somebody's pretty end table up North for a few days, and now they were scattered across my mother's grave. The meat off the styrofoam trays and the coffee from the fancy bags had gone into northern guts, and now we had the leftovers. The balled-up disposable diapers held Yankee shit. And all of it was stinking up our churchyard something awful.

I crossed the road and hid behind the big walnut tree. A couple of truckers stood on Lucy's porch like they owned the place. The Halsey boy walked out the front door, handed the drivers sheets of blue paper, and pointed to the men working the garbage.

One of the drivers jumped off the side of the porch and walked to where Lucy's berry bushes used to be, next to the summer kitchen. He fumbled around a little at his crotch and then he pissed right in plain view, like a male dog marking his territory. When he finished he went to stand with Bobby Halsey. Together they watched the workers unload garbage, poking the bundles with sticks and rolling them until they dropped off the truck into the chewed-up dirt.

I recognized Berkley Paxton, Sarah Rose's giant brother, working in the garbage. You couldn't miss him; nobody else in the county was near his size, or walked the way he did, with big sloppy steps as if his joints were about ready to come loose. Bobby and the truck driver were laughing about something and wouldn't have noticed me if I'd jumped right into their garbage pit. But Berkley, he looked straight through the walnut tree and saw me. The way a deer senses a hunter in a blind, he knew I was watching.

I stayed for more than an hour, sick over what I saw: eight trucks roaring in a line up Lucy's driveway, all tractor-trailers, all from up North. One stopped outside the entrance gates to let an empty truck leave, and dark water leaked out its rear end and pooled on the gravel. The raw gash of Mama's tipped headstone fresh before my eyes, I threw a rock as big as a baseball and made a dent in the side of the truck. I didn't stay to talk to the driver.

SARAH ROSE McCOMB

I sat by the window in the dark, listening to the high March wind in the trees and Hunter's fumbling in the kitchen, and I wished mightily I'd shot Wesley Ferris six years earlier. But I'm not that kind of woman.

He came into the store on a still, heavy August afternoon, Bobby Halsey trailing behind him. Ferris looked past everything and straight into the center of my heart. I held the collar of my white blouse closed and looked down at the counter, astonished by his hard boldness.

"Hey, Sarah Rose. What you got cold to drink?" Bobby said. Next to Ferris, he looked like a little boy, pink-faced and sweaty. Ferris tipped his fancy cowboy hat and turned around to look in the ancient cooler. He and Bobby spent a long time bent over the drinks, as if choosing the right one mattered more than anything in the world. Then Ferris straightened up and fixed his eyes on me again, his cola bottle dripping dark spots on the warped floorboards.

I walked around the counter and started picking the bad grapes from the box in the cooler. The bittersweet fermented juice stained my fingers, and yellowjackets hovered over my hands, which were made clumsy by Ferris's strange stare. Bobby might as well not have been there.

Bobby laid some money on the counter. "Hot, isn't it?" he said. I nodded.

Ferris rolled his bottle across his forehead, and the water dripped down his face and onto his pressed tan shirt. His eyes never wavered; they were the pale, translucent blue of skimmed milk, cold as ice. Then he pushed the bottle against the metal edge of the counter and opened it with a quick downward jerk of his wrist. He drank until it was empty.

"Sarah Rose, Wesley is looking for some land up this way," Bobby said. "I thought you might know of something, with all the people coming in and out of the store. Maybe something that isn't officially on the market."

"Can't say that I do," I said. The few farms left around here didn't trade hands but once in a blue moon—unless someone needed the money bad enough to sell.

Bobby leaned against the counter. "Yeah, well, I was just wondering." They both stood there, waiting, and in the thick August heat the silence pressed against me like an iron weight. I prayed for Hunter to come in through the back and rescue me.

"You might try over in Lexington. Hunter says they're selling out to horse people right and left," I told him.

"I'm not in the horse business." Ferris smiled, showing perfect white teeth. "They're bad investments—a broken leg and they're dog food."

"Wes is a developer. He builds houses," Bobby stated.

I opened my cash drawer and began counting the change, for something to do. "There's not much need for new houses around here. Not many people looking, with jobs as scarce as they are."

"We went by Lucy's old place," Bobby mentioned. "Hunter still own his aunt's land?"

I nodded. "But you couldn't build houses on it. It's all mud from the springs running off the mountain."

"Wesley'd be interested in talking to Hunter about it."

I scooped up a handful of pennies. "He won't sell."

Ferris walked around, looking at everything as if he'd never been in a store. He spun the magazine rack and smiled at the rusty squealing as if it pleased his ears.

"Lucy's land is just sitting there pushing up weeds," Bobby said.

"I guess that's our business, not yours." The pennies jangled in my trembling hands.

Ferris reached into the crate of green apples by the door and took a big bite of one. I waited for him to spit it out—the apples were good only for pies or frying up with sugar, sour enough to turn your mouth inside out—but he didn't, he just kept on biting and chewing, and when he was done with the flesh he popped the core into his mouth and ate that, too. I could taste the almondy bitterness of those seeds in my own mouth.

I began stacking the nickels and dimes. The two men watched my fingers move through the silver coins. The fan whirred overhead, the chain tinkling against the center light.

Before leaving, Ferris bought three cartons of Marlboros, a half-bushel of tomatoes, and all the peaches I had. It doubled my bank deposit for the day.

Just after they had pulled away in Bobby's red convertible, the heavens let loose. The windows rattled with thunder, and water hit the tin roof like flying gravel. How many rains had washed over that roof and made the three worn porch steps slick as ice? Three generations of Paxtons had run the store, and I'd be the last. Hunter and I were childless; my brother, Berkley, would shrivel and die if he had to work inside every day. I drew a deep breath and took in decades of fruits and vegetables, spicy sausage, sweat and dust. And over it all, Bobby Halsey's sweet cologne hung like a dark cloud.

I locked up early that day, wanting very much to be with Hunter. We went to bed early, and our lovemaking was frantic. I was hungry for his solid weight, and I took him within me eagerly. I closed my eyes and tried to will away the shadow that Wesley Ferris had cast over us.

Two days later, at bedtime, Hunter handed me a box, wrapped in white paper and tied with a thin lacy ribbon. Inside was a ring, a gold filigree band with the biggest diamond I'd ever seen, set high on prongs to make it look even larger than it was.

I sat on the bed and stared at it. "Where'd this come from, Hunter?" I looked into his handsome face.

"Carter's. I bought it yesterday," he said.

"I mean, where'd you get the money for it? I don't imagine the McPhersons paid you this much for hay."

He sat down next to me. "Forget the money. You like the ring?"

"You know I do." I kissed his cheek, dearly loving the salty taste of it.

"Put it on, then."

The band was tight on my heat-swollen finger. The stone sparkled in the lamplight like blue ice. Like Wesley Ferris's eyes.

"Lord, Hunter. You didn't sell Lucy's land. Not to that friend of Bobby Halsey's—"

"I couldn't say no to that much money, Sarah Rose. It was the right thing to do. We still have our place. That corner of land wasn't doing anything but breeding mosquitoes." He talked fast, and his hands worked nervously in his lap.

"Lucy wouldn't have cared for him, you know that."

"Lucy's dead," Hunter said flatly. "Ferris had the money in hand. It's just a piece of dirt, damn it!" He stood and looked down at me, the light from the cut diamond playing across his face.

We didn't speak again that night. We went to bed with our backs to each other. Long after his breathing slowed and deepened, I lay awake and wondered at his calm sleep, knowing my own, when it finally came, would be shaken loose by dreams. I believed that dreams pointed you to the truth: that you could sit up nights and think for hours, trying to force sense out of what happens in the real world, but sooner or later the heart of your life would come to you in sleep if you let it.

I'd always been a rich and wild dreamer, from my earliest days in my mother's womb, and that was all right. To dream meant you were still alive and thinking, even in the deepest sleep places, even when your breathing slowed down to almost nothing and you were as close to death as you were going to get before The Day.

But that night my visions would have knocked the

devil off his perch in hell. I saw and heard and smelled unspeakable things. I saw a young Lucy McComb change before my eyes into an ancient, shedding skins like a snake, the ruby pin she'd worn glittering on her breast. She drew steaming waters from underground rivers and bathed in them, her body shriveled, then bloated. She ate apples and tomatoes from the garden and cried out for more.

I woke the next morning exhausted, afraid to touch my husband, the weight of the ring he'd given me too much to bear. I put it in my bottom dresser drawer.

Now, almost six years later, Hunter sat at the window, watching the night and humming a tune I didn't know, in strange harmony with the wind.

"It's late. Come on to bed." I touched his shoulder and he flinched, struggling to come back from somewhere far away. "Hunter—"

He turned then, took my hand, kissed it. My heart jumped high in my throat, and I thought for a moment that everything could be as it used to be, before Wesley Ferris and the ring, before the trucks came and dumped garbage all over Lucy's place, before the veil fell across Hunter's eyes and left him quiet and alone.

I looked at my husband's handsome, empty face, and I knew better. The chill that gripped me then wasn't from the wind blowing outside.

JESSE PAXTON

I lay on my bed thinking about the fight and about Amber McPherson. My whole body ached, and the place above my eye began to bleed as if it'd just been hit.

I caught the iron smell of fresh blood mixed with my fear and their hate of me, and it all stank. I'd made a mistake leaving the store with Ford and Ricky hanging around on the porch; of course they'd followed me, waiting until Sarah Rose wasn't looking to jump the railing and trail me through the weeds. They'd caught me where they had a few months earlier—on the far side of the cemetery, in the woods where no one could see them.

They said, "We're letting you off easy this time, runt, we're in a hurry. Count to fifty before you stand up, or we'll do it all over again." And the whole time they were hitting me, all I could see was their big dirty Nikes with fluorescent yellow laces. My blood spattered on Ford's shoes, and I was glad.

Now, lying on my bed, I imagined Ford going home and walking into his kitchen, and his mother staring at the blood on his shoes and asking, "What happened to *you*?" And Ford would think for a minute, and then his eyes would get real narrow and mean-looking, and he'd lie, say something like, "A kid had a nosebleed today in gym," and his mother would get down on her hands and knees in front of him and scrub until there were only pale little dots left on the white leather, like maybe he'd just spilled some chocolate milk.

My blood on Ford's shoes. He hated me, and that's why Ricky hated me. Ricky didn't matter; he did whatever Ford did; it was that simple for him. Ford was the puzzle. There he was, living with a mother and father who made themselves part of things. He had older brothers and sisters who came to visit; half the kids at school were related to him. He lived in a real house surrounded by smooth grass and other houses that looked just like it. He knew how to say things so they made sense to his friends. Girls watched him when he walked down the hall in those shoes, those fancy shoes that now were dotted with my blood.

Here I was, living on top of a mountain in a run-down place that didn't even belong to us. When the sun fell just right on the west side of the cabin, threads of light showed where the chinking had pulled away from the chestnut logs. That was the best it got: winter was a whole lot worse. We had hard-packed dirt for a yard and got our water from a spring pipe sticking out of a rock wall. I had no brothers or sisters or cousins, at least that I knew about. And my father did all he could to stay by himself, away from everything. He talked only when he had to.

I was nothing up against Ford, nothing at all.

Thinking about Amber made me hurt less. I remembered her scent, a straight, clean horse smell in English class and then school-soapy after gym. Her legs were nothing in jeans, but when she wore shorts or maybe a skirt you saw how strong she was from riding her horse, why she was the only girl in the class who ran the mile as fast as the boys who played basketball.

She sat next to me in math. One day she'd looked at me for a while and then asked, "Are you going to be big as your daddy?"

"Maybe." I made it sound like I hadn't thought about it before.

"He's a real giant, isn't he?" She said it like she only wanted to know for herself, as if it didn't really matter much.

"He might be. Berkley's big."

"How come you use your father's first name? My parents would kill me if I called them 'Bill' and 'Karen.' It feels funny even thinking about them like that, like they were regular people, with names and secrets."

"Don't you think they are? Real people, I mean."

"Not to me they're not," she said. By then the teacher was staring hard at her, and Amber stretched her neck tall to look at the blackboard, then pretended to write on her paper. When the teacher turned her back, Amber talked some more.

"I dreamed about your dad last night. It was so weird.

He was riding a Clydesdale, you know, a Budweiser horse. They were coming down the road toward me, and all of a sudden they just took off into the air and disappeared. Your father was like a knight or something."

"He'd probably love that," I whispered back. Berkley, the knight, hidden away safe and sound in a dark, heavy iron suit.

I'd wanted to ask Amber more about that dream, but she got moved to the front of the room. The rest of the day I thought about what she'd said, about why she would bother to dream about my father at all, and especially on a horse, and I hoped that she might someday decide to dream about me, too, the way I dreamed about her almost every night.

I thought about Berkley and Sharon, tried to remember what it was like to see them together, but it was a long time since my mother had left. Berkley had thrown out all the pictures of her. This much I could remember: the black braid snaking down her back, and her eyes dark as night in her smooth round face; her blue clothes, always blue, and dangling bead earrings that begged me to touch them. For months after she left, we found her things around the cabin: a lacy blue sock under the bed, hair clips in the corners, a thin silver ring in the woodbox. Berkley would grab them up, stick them in his pockets, and later he'd lock them up in the chest under the bed. He wore the key around his neck; all I could do was slide the chest out and shake it, imagining the shapes and scents held tight inside.

Every month it became harder to remember Sharon. Her stories lost their details, until the only thing left for me was the shadow of her words. She'd talked to me about things while she drew, told me the stories behind the pictures in her art books, about gods and goddesses and men and women, as if they were real to her, and maybe they were.

One of the stories I remembered more than the others.

It was from when Sharon was young, up North, about a big painting from the Civil War. She said the picture was displayed in a big round building that was always dark, and you had to pay to see it. She would save her allowance and buy a ticket, beg the ushers to let her stay between showings and look, and they let her, finally, when they saw she wasn't going to give up and go home until they did.

"The fighting—it was thousands of men tangled up, dying everywhere you looked," she told me. "You could smell the smoke coming off the canvas, and the heat from the fires and the red sun would wrap you up tight like a blanket and make you sweat." She'd take on a faraway look and she'd get quiet.

That was the most I could bring back of my mother: bits and pieces and a few words from the dark hollow of my past. And the strange feeling that she had made Berkley happy in a way I never could.

The library was quiet in the back corner, where I liked to sit on the floor and look at books. It was late enough that most of the kids had gone home for supper, so I wouldn't be bothered. Old J.W. was sitting by the magazines reading. He liked to hang out at the store with Sarah Rose. She said he could have been eighty or more; nobody knew for sure. He'd shown up in Ambrose County a few years back and everybody took care of him, giving him odd jobs and feeding him. Some people thought he was magic, could see into the future. But I didn't. He was just an old guy who listened to the talk going on around him and had plenty of time to think about things. I knew all about that.

Over by the display case, a lady spun the paperback rack; it tipped a little, but she kept on spinning it until she found a book she liked. When she turned to look at the clock, I saw it was Mrs. McPherson, Amber's mother. She looked pretty old to have a twelve-year-old, more like a grandmother, really. Amber called herself a change-of-life baby and said she was lucky to have been born normal. I thought she was better than normal.

The only other person in the place was the librarian; he was eating pizza in his office as I walked past. I found the Civil War books and took a stack into my corner. They were mostly boring, without enough pictures, and the ones that were there were scratched up and gray. I found one book that had paintings in it, but they were all of single people, men standing with their swords or riding prancing horses. I went back to the shelf and got another stack.

"Please don't reshelve. I'll take care of it." The librarian wiped his hands on his pants, then leaned down and picked up some books. He had tomato sauce on his face, and he smelled like a restaurant.

"Maybe I can help you with what you're looking for," he said.

"That's okay, I can find it." My face got hot, the way it always did when somebody talked to me, and I hid behind a book.

"Usually you come in here and just look around, pick something off the shelf, and read. You must be searching for a specific book today." He sat down on the floor next to me, grunting a little.

I flipped some pages and didn't say anything.

"Helping people is what they pay me for," he said. "The rest of it, checking the books in and out and keeping the budget, that's just paperwork." He took the book out of my hands. "You're interested in the Civil War, huh? Is this for school?"

I shook my head. Mrs. McPherson stood at the desk waiting to check her books out, but the librarian ignored her. "You ever hear about the reenactments? When people dress up like soldiers and camp out, shoot blanks at each other? I do that. Bought the full uniform last year, it cost me more than three hundred dollars."

I grinned at him.

"Yeah, I know, I don't look much like a soldier. But it's fun pretending. So how come you're in here poring over these books so late? You should be home eating supper." He stuck out his hand. "I'm Douglas. And you are—"

"Looking for something about the big round painting from the Civil War. From up in Pennsylvania."

He thought a minute. "You mean the Cyclorama. In Gettysburg. It's wonderful." Mrs. McPherson hit the bell over and over, staring at Douglas. Finally he pushed himself up off the floor. "I can get you a booklet about it. Come back next week and I'll have something for you. I'll even let you try on my scabbard. If you don't know what that is, find out."

I left my books for Douglas to put back, as he'd asked me. J.W. had fallen asleep, his chin on his chest. The magazine had fallen out of his hands onto the floor, and I picked it up. *Soldier of Fortune,* the desert issue.

Going back up the mountain, I saw lights in the cabin and knew Berkley was home. I hoped he'd have washed off the stink of the landfill, which most nights hung on him like a leech. And I hoped there'd be something hot for supper, which usually there wasn't.

SARAH ROSE McCOMB

The nurse left with Hunter, and the doctor sat writing about him in the chart. "Physically, your husband's in good shape, aside from somewhat slow reflexes," he told me.

"He's losing his mind."

"What do you mean by that?" He capped his pen and leaned forward.

"I mean, there are times he'll just start talking nonsense, about things that happened a long time ago. It's happening more and more. But other days he's fine." I chewed the inside of my mouth to keep back the tears.

"Does he sleep?"

I shook my head. "Some nights, not at all. He'll wake up and wander the house until I'm about crazy with it. He talks to himself, whole conversations."

The doctor let me talk, writing notes and not looking at me. "How long has this been going on?" he asked when I'd finished.

"Hunter's been like this for a few years. Since sometime after they started dumping the garbage." I worked my hands in my lap and watched myself from elsewhere in the room. I told the doctor about Bobby Halsey and Wesley Ferris, how they'd promised Hunter they were going to build houses on Lucy's land and then turned around and contracted with the county to take its trash. How things had started slowly, a truck or two a day dumping near what had been Lucy's garden, then more and more trucks. How the garbage sat out in plain sight of the road, and how Hunter would drive there and watch.

"He blames himself for ruining his aunt's place," I said. "The talk is we got rich off the land, knew all along it was going to be a dump. How could we have known that? We were lied to."

The doctor looked so clean in his starched white coat and pressed shirt. "Mrs. McComb, are you saying you think your husband's problems are the result of his selling this land to the wrong people?"

"It seems that way to me."

He looked at me with tired eyes. "What's bothering your husband is more than depression over the land. It's an illness. What do you know about Alzheimer's disease?"

I stood up. "You can call it what you want. But I call it a broken heart."

He handed me a prescription form. "I know this is hard for you. Let's try some medication and see what happens. He'll at least get some rest, which should help you out, too."

"Hunter doesn't take pills." I opened the door to leave.

The doctor touched my arm. "Sarah Rose, why did you bring your husband to me?"

"The nurse practitioner said I should. I didn't know what else to do."

"Then you don't have much to lose by having Hunter try some medication. I know this is hard on you—"

I left so he wouldn't see the tears spilling down my cheeks. In the reception area Hunter sat watching *Days of Our Lives* on the little black-and-white TV. If you hadn't known better, you'd have thought he was just another husband waiting on his wife.

I heard Reba's loud voice out front in the store when Hunter and I came through the back. "A god-awful mess, J.W.," she said. "It's insulting is what it is."

J.W. had been minding the store and seemed glad to see me. He was dressed up as always, wearing a suit much too big for him and a wild red tie. "You go by the cemetery?" he asked, combing his hair straight back and patting it.

"I didn't take the time. We had to wait an hour to see the doctor." I hit the cash-total button on the register. J.W. had taken in more than forty dollars in two hours. Almost enough to pay the doctor bill.

"You really should run by the churchyard and see what the wind left us," Reba said.

"What do you want, Reba? Just come out and tell me what you mean." I wasn't in any mood for her cat-and-mouse way of saying things. I began restocking the chip rack.

"I mean that the garbage from Lucy's place is lying all over the cemetery. My mother's stone and two others are lying on the ground—and it wasn't the wind that pushed them over."

I let a bag of potato chips fall to the floor, the clip snapping on air. "Who are you saying *did* push them over?"

"I guess I wouldn't know," she replied. "Maybe it was kids, riled by the wind. Or maybe it was those Yankee truck drivers, thinking they might as well keep busy while their garbage is being spread out all over Lucy's place. Let's ask Hunter—"

J.W. made himself small behind the counter. Nobody said anything for a minute or more. I saw Hunter's blue shirt moving between the curtains and knew he'd heard Reba.

"That dump's quite the family affair, what with your brother working there and the money from the land fattening your bankroll," she continued.

"Make sense. You know if we'd been told what Lucy's land was going to be used for, we'd never have sold. You just come in here—"

"I got to go." J.W. picked up the bag of food I'd packed for him in trade for watching the store.

Reba walked him to the door and pushed open the screen with her foot. "Don't forget the meeting Tuesday," she told him loudly. "Hold up a minute and I'll drive you into town." He sat down on the porch and opened a box of crackers.

"What meeting, Reba?" I asked.

She picked up her purse and a six-pack of Coke. "Some of us concerned citizens are getting together at the Methodist church to discuss the dump problem. Come if you want."

"I don't guess I can miss it," I said. "There'd be no end to the talk if I did."

Reba shrugged and pushed open the screen door, almost hitting two men. They had the stiff-legged walk of long-distance haulers; their rig idled noisily by the road. While they picked out some snacks, I pretended to wash the front window and watched Reba and J.W. circle the truck. Reba tore a corner off J.W.'s grocery bag and wrote down the license plate number, then moved to the other side of the truck, fishing around in her purse for something. She stooped beside the rear tires and J.W. stood by her, keeping guard.

"Ready to check out," one of the men called to me. He set a package of doughnuts and a bottle of fruit punch on the counter, then added a Snickers from the candy rack. "One for the road," he said.

I handed him his change. "Where you headed?"

"North—Massachusetts. We'll be back day after tomorrow." He uncapped his drink and took a long swallow. "Made good time last night, with that wind pushing south." He moved aside to let his friend pay.

"What're you hauling?" I asked carefully.

"Solid waste."

"Garbage," his friend corrected. He looked young, no more than twenty, and wore a white "Save the Earth" sweatshirt. His black hair was slicked back into a ponytail, and a small gold earring shone bright against his dark skin. I rang him up: two apples, a bunch of bananas, a pint of buttermilk.

"I hear the wind blew a lot of trash into the churchyard last night," I said.

The older man bit into a doughnut and shrugged, his beard whitened by powdered sugar. "Huh."

"It was a mess. They need a fence up there or something." The younger man ran his fingers across the scrolled brass top of the register. "Nice store—I like places like this." He walked over to the bulletin board and read the lost-and-found notices.

"It's damned expensive," his friend said. "I pay twenty cents less for this same juice at Food Lion."

"You don't get homemade rolls like these at Food Lion." I pointed to the tray on the counter.

"Don't guess you do," he replied. "Give me a half-dozen, and ring up a package of bologna with it. We'll eat lunch here." The two of them went out on the porch and made themselves sandwiches.

When they'd finished, the younger one put his head in the door. "Good rolls. See you next trip."

The truckers weren't so happy when they came back in to call Angle's Garage. It seemed somebody'd stuck a nail file between the rim and the rubber of their left rear tire and left them with a flat.

"I'd like to know who the hell fooled with our truck," the older driver said.

"Forget it. We'll be on the road soon enough." His partner picked up a red bandanna and gave me two dollars for it. "I'm Rastin," he said, sticking his hand out. I couldn't help but like him.

They stayed in the store and looked at my tape rack while waiting for the garage truck. "Maybe I can fingerprint the nail file," the older driver joked. Rastin laughed, said it was probably some kid doing it on a dare from his girlfriend.

I could have told them who owned the nail file. But there was no reason to volunteer trouble when neither of them thought to ask.

LUCY McCOMB

Look closely at Sarah Rose as she tucks the crocheted afghan around her husband. He stirs, and she touches his cheek tenderly. Though she is terrified of what their future holds, no one can doubt the fullness of her love for Hunter.

Is there anything original that can be said of love?

Little, indeed. The wonder is that anyone continues to search for some newly turned phrase, some startling metaphor, some stunning revelation that will leave its hearer awed and humbled. And search they do: soap-opera addicts, romance-novel readers, tabloid scanners, Peeping Toms and marriage counselors, teenagers and middle-aged men, Avon saleswomen and musclemen, men of the cloth and women of the night. It is love that sets them in motion and exerts the certain pull of their orbit. Love is the bedrock of our economy, the stuff of our dreams and our worst nightmares.

Why, you ask, should you listen to an old-maid schoolteacher hold forth on love? What might she know, never married, wearing a rut between her shut-up house and the dusty school, with side trips to the library and the church and, once a week, the market?

I know that is what people thought of me. Someone—a former student, perhaps—would meet me on the sidewalk, holding her son by the hand, and stop to chat. Always it was, "And have you been well?" as if the only activity I might enjoy was staying healthy, however one manages that. The child might interrupt, wanting to get on with things, and she would hush him, push him behind her back, as if she were afraid his presence would sorrow me, remind me of my childless state and what she assumed was loneliness.

It was her lack of imagination that made her behave so. My life was rich and full, more varied than anyone will ever know. And I did not die a virgin.

I had time enough to observe the faces of love, and I am here to testify that many are contorted in pain. "Every lover is a warrior, and Cupid has his camps," wrote Ovid. Such a metaphor begs for conclusion: If love is war, death and pain and great suffering will accompany it.

But listen to me: I am as windy as March, huffing and puffing and making grand, empty noise—what I most sternly warned my students against. If you write of love, you must give it a face and a body, a taste and a scent. And yes, you must give it a name.

Reba loved my nephew Hunter from the fourth grade on. She was a large child, developed early, stood a full head above her female classmates. Coupled with a shrewd intelligence, that size served to get Reba her way. Her classmates learned that she would ask once for what she wanted—and then she would take it.

As September cooled into October the year Reba and Sarah Rose and Hunter were sixth-graders, it became clear to me that the best I could do for Reba was teach her respect for others. The girl was well ahead of the rest in her learning, but she was a lost soul, alone most of the time, her classmates finding her bossiness tiresome. (It is part of a teacher's duty, I believe, to give each child a space in the order of things.)

One morning, after recess, Sarah Rose announced that she had made sugar cookies for the class. The tulip-shaped sweets were elegant: she had painted them with a wash of egg white and sprinkled them with large crystals of colored sugar.

Most of the girls just nibbled at the edges of the leaves, and only fingered the delicate, sugary blossoms. The boys gulped their cookies down like hungry dogs, caring not at all about the artistry being devoured. Sarah Rose's cheeks flushed with pleasure when I tied a ribbon around my cookie and hung it from the window latch as a decoration.

Two cookies remained in the tin when Sarah Rose finished passing them out. Reba asked for another, having eaten the first with great gusto.

"These are for Hunter. I'm taking them over to his house after school," Sarah Rose said as she put the lid on the tin. He'd been out for several days with the chicken pox, having escaped it at a more tender age.

Reba nodded and picked up her speller.

That afternoon, when Sarah Rose gathered her things for dismissal, she discovered that the tin was empty. "No one will leave here until the cookies are returned to Sarah Rose," I announced. "Or until someone confesses to having eaten them. All of you, put your heads down on your desk—you needn't be ashamed to admit your mistake, for no one will be looking."

The room fell absolutely silent as the red second hand of the classroom clock moved around the dial one, two, three times. The final bell rang. One girl began to cry. "Quit that, baby," Reba whispered. Another two minutes passed. The Sanders boy raised his hand. "I have to go to the dentist this afternoon," he said. "My mama'll kill me if I'm late. She told me to come straight home." With his face down, I couldn't tell whether he was telling me the truth or not—he was one who couldn't look you in the eye with a lie coming out of his mouth—but either way I had to dismiss the class or deliver twenty-six children to their homes by myself.

"If the guilty party confesses right now, the penalty will be light," I said. "If it goes until tomorrow, there will be trouble." After another minute I opened the door and lined up the children, looking them full in the face, one by one, as they walked out the door. Sarah Rose was the last in line.

"Here," I said, untying my cookie and wrapping it in paper. "Give this to Hunter—maybe it will stop the itching." She smiled brightly and hugged me. I stood at the window and watched her run down the street, the white package held gingerly to her breast.

The next morning, I watched as Sarah Rose waited for Reba in the coatroom. "You took the cookies," Sarah Rose shouted. "And you told Hunter that *you'd* made them for him!"

Reba narrowed her brown eyes into slits and pushed her face into Sarah Rose's. "Maybe I did. Here's the napkin." She stuffed it in Sarah Rose's pocket.

I stepped between them. "You girls must control yourselves." (Control, don't you see, is what I had to have if my students were to learn anything in my classroom.) "Reba, you will apologize now to Sarah Rose and receive your punishment later from Mr. Bowles."

Reba smirked at Sarah Rose. "Sorry you were so slow getting to Hunter's house with your cookie." I glared at Reba; she relented. "Sorry."

"For what?" I prompted.

"That Hunter likes me better than you, Sarah Rose. He told me so."

"That's a lie!" Sarah Rose flew at Reba's face, raking her nails down the girl's left cheek. I myself incurred injury as Sarah Rose's hand caught in my hair and pulled a fair amount loose.

"Sit!" I ordered. Sarah Rose moved away, aghast at what she had done. Reba looked oddly satisfied.

For her deceitfulness, Reba was made to sweep the playground with a heavy push broom every afternoon for a week. Sarah Rose was so contrite that she asked to stay after school, helping me prepare for the next morning by washing the blackboard, clapping erasers, and dusting the chalk ledges. She cleaned the windows within her reach with vinegar and water, polished them wonderfully with newspaper. She stood on the radiators and watched Reba move about the playground two stories below, pushing the broom without enthusiasm.

If Sarah Rose had been a more spiteful person by nature, she might have gloated. Instead, she simply allowed her used newspapers to drop from the windows, thereby adding to Reba's work.

For most of the years I taught at the Jackson School, I was given the dubious pleasure of chaperoning school dances. I suppose that extracurricular duty fell upon me because I did not play field hockey or have the voice or demeanor of a cheerleading coach. Perhaps, too, Principal Bowles felt a certain confidence in my spinsterhood, and assumed that my saintly presence would dampen the possibility of any sexual hanky-panky. His strategy did not succeed.

As Reba and Sarah Rose passed through the grades, they went in very different directions. Reba became a handsome but far from beautiful girl, with broad shoulders and strong legs. She took a job at the C&O Diner after school, smoking Chesterfields on her breaks. Her studies fell off, and she was a regular in the backseat of Danny Walker's '39 Ford. Other boys noticed her large breasts and easy ways, and might have asked her for a date if they hadn't been so scared of Danny, whose reputation as a bully was rivaled only by Reba's.

Danny and Reba were unlike any other teenaged couple at the Jackson School. Their heads were never seen bowed close together in the corner of the hall; Reba sat with her friends in the lunchroom, and Danny with his. Did she mind not having his heavy class ring hung around her neck like a dog license? If she did, she wouldn't have confessed to it.

Sarah Rose remained petite and soft-spoken, looking far younger than her years, a sharp contrast to her younger brother, Berkley, who at age twelve stood nearly six feet tall and kept to himself. Sarah Rose volunteered as a candy striper at the Ambrose County Hospital and put great effort into her studies. Her time with Hunter was limited and, I am certain, virtuous.

My nephew overcame the chicken pox and grew into a striking young man. No one ever questioned what route Hunter would take. Although he was a good student, he never considered college; he begged to leave school his junior year to work the family farm. He seemed obsessed with learning how to do all that farmers must do, as if he knew that his father, my brother, would be dead at forty-three, pinned beneath his overturned tractor for two hours before Hunter rode into the far field and found him. The following summer, a week after their graduation from the Jackson School, Hunter and Sarah Rose were married at the Cedar Creek Presbyterian Church.

One late-April afternoon I chose to walk home along Cedar Creek. It had been an especially wearing day; my students were so restless that they no longer even pretended to pay attention. What sustained me was the thought of corn and tomatoes and peppers waiting to be planted, and the vision of my planned dinner: a leaf lettuce and cress salad dressed with vinegar and oil, and fresh bread.

As I stooped beside the creek to pick cress, I was startled to see Reba sitting on the far bank, leaning against a big cedar with her eyes closed.

I thought to leave as quietly as I'd come, knowing she wasn't the kind who craved company. But she heard my shoes knocking on the river rocks and sat up, her eyes red and swollen. She had been crying.

"Do you have the afternoon off from the diner, Reba?" I asked.

"I'm taking it off." She tossed a rock into the creek.

"Are you ill?" I dangled my fingers in the water, watching the minnows approach and gape at them.

She shook her head. "Just didn't feel like being inside."

I nodded. Above us, in the churchyard, the gravediggers' shovels struck a steady rhythm in the dirt.

"It's Parris Keckler's grave they're digging," Reba said. "Mama says he floated himself there on a river of whiskey."

"That's an interesting way of putting it," I said.

The men laughed at something; one of them cursed as his shovel hit rock. They stopped their work, and all fell quiet. The noise of water over rocks filled our silence. Reba closed her eyes again and appeared to be asleep.

"Are you and Danny going to the senior dance?" I asked finally.

She snorted. "He doesn't want to go. I wouldn't go with him anyway." She crossed her arms over her breasts.

I decided to gamble. "Reba, would you like to take tickets with me? I could use the help."

She stood and brushed off her skirt. "Hell, no! That'd be the limit, just the limit, going to my senior dance with an old maid—" She clamped her mouth shut.

"That language isn't acceptable," I said.

"Acceptable? What difference does it make to be acceptable around here? The only way I'd go to that dance is with Hunter McComb. And we both know that's not going to happen." She strode up the hill and headed toward town.

The gravediggers resumed their work in rhythm. One of them began to sing tunelessly, grunting each time his shovel bit into the heavy clay. I took my cress and cut through the cemetery to my house.

It was the first time I'd been called an old maid in my presence. That the label was untrue was known by only a few, and the injustice of it brought angry tears to my eyes.

REBA WALKER

The day of the landfill meeting I paid a visit to Richard Andrew Kane III, our state legislator. I parked my truck next to his silver BMW and waited until his secretary left for lunch. Then I slipped through the back door and walked down the long, dark hall toward his office.

I passed what used to be the kitchen of the Kane family home, a large brick house in the middle of downtown Collier. A year after his father died, Richard Kane converted the house into offices and built himself a mansion on the side of Warm Springs Mountain. People said he could see all over the valley from the picture window of his living room. And we sure could see his place, since he had cut down most of the trees and flew the biggest American flag south of Washington, D.C., in the front yard.

Kane's offices took up most of the first floor. In the center hallway a chandelier hung from the high ceiling and threw pieces of light on the dark Oriental rug and paneled walls. Stained-glass patterns—bluebirds turned one way and then the other, with their wing tips touching—ran along the tops of the windows. The small waiting room was furnished with a dark red leather couch and matching armchairs. Watching me from the far wall were Richard Andrew Kane Senior and Junior. Whoever painted those pictures must have been paid royally to make the Kanes handsomer than they ever were in real life. If you took away their nice clothes and jewelry, the Kanes were homely people, with poor hair and teeth too big for their pursed-lipped mouths.

The secretary's desk, as tidy as her voice, stood guard by the front door. Kane's appointment book lay next to the phone. How many times in the past week had his secretary told me over that phone that Mr. Kane was out of the office, out of town, not available, in conference. I was certain that the pink message tablet had never felt *my* name run across it, regardless of what Kane's girl told me.

I pressed my ear to the main office door and listened. I recognized Kane's deep, slow voice right away; another voice, higher and more excited, sounded like a young man's. The appointment book showed nothing scheduled for noon, and I didn't figure it would be long before Kane finished up his business. From the looks of him, he wasn't one who skipped lunch very often. I stretched out on the leather couch and tried to get comfortable, but the seat was humped and slick.

I flipped through a *Southern Living*, my stomach

growling as I looked at the color photos of Easter hams garnished with apricots and cloves, bright green asparagus steaming in a bowl, rabbit-shaped bread with raisin eyes, golden-brown in a wicker basket. You were supposed to believe that the smiling woman beside the table had cooked the food with her own perfectly manicured hands, in her spotless starched white apron with an Easter basket stenciled on the bib. But anybody who's ever made a big family dinner knows the cook sits down at the table shiny-faced from the stove heat and stinking of grease. This woman didn't fool me one bit. She had a colored lady in the kitchen doing all her work.

I was getting ready to read something about the five up-and-coming beaches on the Gulf Coast, when Kane walked out of his office. Bobby Halsey followed behind.

I stood up and nodded to Bobby. "Mr. Kane, I want to talk to you a minute."

"I'm on my way out for lunch." He checked me over from top to bottom, clearly hating the sight of my old gray Reeboks on his Oriental rug.

"We need to talk." I looked at Bobby, who was easing toward the back door. "On your way out, too, son? You ought to stay—this is about your landfill business."

"Bobby, you run along."

Bobby didn't even say good-bye as he left.

"Sit down," Kane told me.

"In there?" I started for his office.

"Here—out here." He sat down in one of the leather armchairs and pointed at the other.

"This is cozy. Real nice." I grinned, but Kane just looked at me and waited. "Do you remember me?"

He smiled now. "Of course I do."

He didn't know me from Adam. He'd left the Jackson School after eighth grade and gone to boarding school up North. The last he'd seen of me was in the all-school chorus, where we'd both sung alto and I'd stood a good six inches taller than he did, despite my being two years younger.

"You remember me?" I smiled big. "What's my name?"

He didn't miss a beat. "You haven't changed at all. It's Sarah, isn't it?"

"Sarah Rose? Sarah Rose Paxton, you're thinking? I don't believe it!" And truly I didn't.

"I'm pretty good with names and faces, especially women's," he said.

"Not this woman's. I'm Reba Walker—used to be Allert—and I'm guessing that name doesn't ring a bell with you."

He frowned as I propped my feet on the dark, shiny coffee table before me. "Certainly I remember you, Reba." I liked that, how he repeated my name to fix it in his mind. They must have taught him that up North.

"Uh-huh," I said. "Maybe you remember me from when I had my husband declared legally dead after he deserted me, so I could get on with my life. Or from when my son was in court for his third drunk-driving charge before he left for Florida. Or from when my daughter was picked up for shoplifting some watches. We're well-known in your circle."

He was good. He didn't even raise an eyebrow at what I told him.

"Listen, Richard, we need to talk about the dump near my house. I guess you're familiar with it, seeing as how Bobby Halsey was just here," I said.

"Halsey's Drugstore has been a client of mine for a long time. Bobby was here on legal business."

"Uh-huh." I pulled my chair closer to his. "I'm wondering what you're planning to do about the dump Bobby's managing, you being our representative in Richmond and all."

Kane picked some lint off his jacket. "There's nothing

illegal about operating a landfill. They secured their permit, and the land was properly zoned."

"There's nothing illegal about dumping garbage across the road from the dead and letting it blow all over, stinking to high heaven?"

"I don't know every technicality of dumping," he said. "But I do know they went about opening their business legally."

"You do? Then maybe you need to make sure they're running it legally. There's garbage lying uncovered for days at a time up there, and it's not even our garbage. They're bringing it in from all over the Northeast."

Kane stared at me. "How do you know that? What you're telling me is hearsay."

"Dick," I said, enjoying the sound of his nickname, "this isn't hearsay. You'd have to be blind and senseless not to know what's going on up there. Two days ago, upwards of forty trucks went into that dump. I watched them from my porch, and not one of those trucks carried plates from south of the Mason-Dixon line. That's not right, and it can't be legal!"

Kane stood up. "Ms. Walker, I understand your being upset. You need to talk to the Solid Waste Management people in Richmond if you have problems with the operation of the business."

"Then come to our meeting tonight and tell the people that," I said. "You're our legislator, and we elected you to protect us. We've got plenty of questions for you. Seven, in the basement of the Methodist church. We'll expect to see you there."

He looked at his watch. "I have a prior commitment. I'm sorry."

"What? What do you have to do that's more important than protecting your district?" I leaned toward him, my elbows on my knees. "Don't you have an election coming up in November?"

Kane looked at me like he'd just as soon shoot me

dead, which probably wasn't far from the truth. "I'll try to come for a little while."

"You might be interested to know that I called the *Gazette* this morning, and Larry Hopkins will be covering the meeting."

Kane waved me out the door. As I drove out of his lot, I checked my rearview mirror and saw him standing in the doorway, staring at nothing. What was running through his mind was anybody's guess.

I pulled up in front of the Dollar General and blew the horn for J.W. As usual, he was dressed to the nines: a gray sharkskin suit; pointy-toed patent shoes the likes of which hadn't been seen on the streets of Collier for ten years; a tie red as cockscomb, with big black stallions running at a slant.

"Where the hell do you get your clothes?" I asked.

"Salvation Army. Boys, they grow so fast there's no time for them to wear their church clothes but once or twice. I'm a perfect boys' sixteen. Lucky, aren't I?"

"Depends on how you look at it," I said.

"You can drop me off at McComb's. I'm helping Hunter do the rams. If you know what I mean."

"You're castrating sheep in that getup?" I almost ran a red light.

"I'll wear coveralls. I got to look nice for the meeting tonight."

"Yeah, me too, J.W. I'll be sure to wear my finest. You never do know who'll show up at the garbage dump meeting, do you?"

SARAH ROSE McCOMB

Hunter sat in front of the television listening to the news. I bent down and kissed him on the forehead, breathing in his dear, familiar scent, like warm bread wrapped in a clean linen towel. I lingered a moment, laid my hand on his cheek. I wasn't happy about leaving him alone, but he'd had a good day working with the sheep and he seemed peaceful.

Dusk settled heavily as I drove up White Gap Road toward the church, the sun slipping below the top of the ridge. Earlier, the moon had been a curved sliver in the sky; now it sagged on the mountains like a worn-out grin. I realized I'd forgotten to put on the headlights, and in the instant of illumination the darkness thickened around the Dodge so that it seemed as if I were far underwater, or out in space beyond the stars. Was there such a place, I wondered.

I coddled the Dodge up the near side of Wilson's Ridge, taking the curves slowly, pensively working a piece of hardtack candy around in my mouth. Clove was my weakness: I used no coloring in it, so the strong spiciness always came as a surprise. I'd made a double batch that morning, sold five bags to the truck drivers by noon.

From out of the woods, a doe stepped into my headlights, cautious and big-bellied with fawn. I stepped down hard on the brakes and prayed. Loose gravel crunched beneath the tires. In the silence that came when the car finally stopped, I watched the deer move crookedly across the road and plunge into a thicket.

I got out of the Dodge and shone my flashlight into the thick growth of rhododendron beside the road. The doe lay on a bed of brown leaves, her huge eyes reflecting my light. I tried to make my way closer to her, but the tangled branches caught my coat and scratched my fingers. She lay calm and quiet, staring at me as if she belonged there and, of course, I didn't. No sign of blood darkened her smooth brown sides, which moved in and out rapidly with fear. Her swollen belly showed signs of a near birthing; her teats looked swollen and tender. Her legs were folded beneath her, the sharp tips of her front hooves showing in the flashlight beam. "Poor mama," I whispered.

I crept backward out of the bushes and returned to the car, then drove down the mountain to the church, worrying. Had I hit the doe? Was she bleeding inside, her baby slowly dying as the blood pooled uselessly in her belly? I turned on the radio to chase away my thoughts.

I arrived at the church twenty minutes before the meeting was to start, so I walked around back and went into the chapel. The closed-up darkness wrapped tight around me, calmed me, made me sit still and think. Downstairs, chairs scraped across the floor. Someone plinked an off-key piano, sang snatches of a song whose words I no longer remembered. I shut my eyes and hoped prayer would come.

Berkley came instead. He laid his broad, warm hand on my shoulder. "Sarah Rose, it's about time for the meeting."

"Lord, Berkley—you oughtn't to scare a person like that. What are you doing here?"

"I saw your car."

"At the meeting, I mean. You know how people feel about your working at the dump." I leaned against his shoulder and felt the curve of muscle beneath his flannel shirt.

"I figured you'd be here, trying to keep the peace," he said. "And it could get ugly."

"It already *is* ugly. What's happening at that dump?"

He was quiet for a moment. Through the darkness I could just make out his large profile. A heavy brow hooded his deep-set eyes, and his thick hair curled at the base of his neck. His perfectly straight nose was a larger copy of my own, as was his squared-off jaw. My younger brother was a handsome man: there was just too much of him.

"Nothing terrible is going in there," he said. "Household stuff, office wastepaper. The same things people throw away here."

"Reba says it's all from up North, from the cities."

Berkley nodded. "Most of it is. Does that really matter?"

"It does to some. It's as if Fort Sumter's been fired on all over again."

"Does it matter to you?" he asked.

"I don't know, I guess not. I hate seeing Aunt Lucy's place so filthy and torn up, I know that much. And Hunter is hurting in places I can't get at." My voice thickened, and I rested my forehead on my crossed arms. "I don't know what to do."

He held me for a minute, and his wide, gentle touch comforted me. "Go to the meeting. Sit up straight and don't say too much. When you do talk, tell the truth."

We left the chapel, walked around the church and into the basement, through separate doors. I carried Berkley's strength with me and held it close as the meeting started.

At exactly seven Reba showed up, bulky in her white uniform. From where I sat in the back row, I could see just about everyone in the room. Chance Sanders and his wife, Patty, sat with Bill and Karen McPherson—we'd all been in school together. Brenda Campbell stood near the piano and counted heads. J.W. moved around the room, visiting as if he hadn't seen anyone for years. We were friends, but I wasn't sure how far friendship would carry us tonight.

"We've got the social hall for only an hour—the church council meets here at eight," Reba announced. "And I'm on my supper break from work. So let's get right down to things.

"If we liked what was happening at the dump, we wouldn't be here, would we? Or most of us, anyway." She flicked her eyes on me and then Berkley, a twisted smile on her face.

People nodded, exchanging glances and terse comments. It seemed everyone had something to say, but nobody wanted to stand up and say it.

"Quiet!" Reba grabbed a hymnal from the bookcase behind her and slammed it on the table. "Come on, friends, we have a lot to decide on tonight. There's no use rehashing what we already know. Now, I'm thinking we need a name for ourselves. Any ideas?"

"How about a leader?" someone called out. "If we're going to be a group with a name and all, we need officers."

Reba frowned. "I guess we do need that." She glanced at Larry Hopkins, who was sitting in the row ahead of me writing in his reporter's notebook. "A president. Any volunteers?"

J.W. stood up and tucked his red tie into the waist of his pants. "Me. I always did want to be a president." He bowed and sat down.

People laughed. Reba wrote J.W.'s name on the blackboard. "Who else?"

"I'll do it," Chance Sanders said. "Can't be any harder than trying to teach sixteen-year-olds history."

Bill McPherson raised his hand. "Don't elect Chance. Patty never lets him out of the house. Put me on the list, too, Reba."

I raised my hand. Reba ignored me.

"Over in the back," J.W. said. "Sarah Rose has her hand up."

"You volunteering, Sarah Rose?" Reba stared hard at me.

"This isn't how it's done, Reba," I said. "You take

nominations—people give you names and then we vote on them."

"All right," she said slowly, "who do you *nominate* for president of this group?"

"You," I shot back. "You've already taken charge, and you're doing a good enough job of it."

Reba drew back as if I'd slapped her, then added her name to the board. "Any more?"

"Sarah Rose," Berkley said.

Reba wrote my name in small letters at the bottom of the list. "That's probably enough. Let's everybody write down one name on a piece of paper and put it in the offering plate."

Brenda Campbell did the tally. "There were sixty-one votes cast. Reba and Sarah Rose are tied with nineteen each. Chance got twelve votes and Bill ten. J.W., you voted for yourself, didn't you?"

J.W. smiled and tipped his snap-brim hat. "Low man wins?"

"You have a runoff," Chance said. "Vote again, this time for either Sarah Rose or Reba."

I stood up. "Give it to Reba. I don't want to be president."

"No, we'll do it fair and square. Let them choose between us. Just raise your hands so I can see you. Now, who votes for me?" Reba counted the hands twice, then wrote "33" next to her name.

"So I'm president. That means Sarah Rose is vice-president." Reba didn't work too hard to disguise the pride in her voice.

"I decline," I said.

"Suit yourself. I don't need any help, anyway." She erased the blackboard and slammed the hymnal again, calling for order.

Richard Kane slipped into the folding chair next to me. He nodded in my direction and smoothed his hair. "What have I missed?"

"Reba's gotten herself elected president," I told him.

"That's all." Kane looked around the room; he sat up a little straighter when he saw Larry Hopkins.

Reba pointed at Chance. "How about being secretary?"

"I'm not going to be secretary for any woman president. Let Patty do it."

Bill McPherson volunteered to keep the books, and passed the offering plate for donations.

"Thirty minutes left," Reba said over the buzzing talk. "We need to choose a name and decide what we're going to do, real quickly."

"I say we shoot Bobby Halsey and his friend," Patty Sanders suggested. "Then we'll bury them in their own garbage." A few people clapped.

"Maybe we should throw Berkley Paxton into that group, too," someone added. "I don't see why he needs to be here at this meeting, unless he's gathering information to sell to Halsey and his crew."

Berkley walked to the front of the room. The sharp ticking of the walnut grandfather clock filled my ears. Kane drew in his breath and held it.

My brother stood before the crowd and stared. His eyes were murderous, and his huge hands opened and closed in a steady rhythm. Reba hung back, said nothing, cowed by Berkley's powerful silence.

Kane cleared his throat. "Friends, everyone here is in the same boat. If it sinks, we all go down. Let's stay calm."

He joined Berkley at the front of the hall. "The landfill up at Lucy McComb's place was opened legally. I'm here to help in any way I can to see that it stays within the law. Let's work together, shall we?"

Karen McPherson began clapping, and others followed. Smiling, Kane held up his hands to stop the applause. Berkley walked out the side door into the night.

By the time the meeting was over, our group had a name—Save Our Mountain Environment—and more than a hundred dollars in its treasury. "Before we meet again next Tuesday, I want each of you to talk to at least one person about the dump, and tell that person to talk to one other person. I want this room jammed full next week, and everybody ready to get down to business," Reba said.

She stood with Kane at the front of the room, shaking hands. Reba looked happy, her cheeks pink, her eyes free of their pinched, angry look. She didn't seem to be in any hurry to get back to work.

J.W. patted my shoulder. "Need a ride?" I asked him.

He shook his head. "Reba's dropping me off on her way through town."

LUCY McCOMB

My house stands on a rise, across the road from Cedar Creek Presbyterian Church. From my wide, shaded front porch, I had full view of my neighbors' comings and goings: the weddings and baptisms and funerals that drew Ambrose County through the thick oak doors of the church; lovers' trysts in the shadows of the twisted cedar trees at the woods' edge; the quiet grieving, eternal as flowing water, that settled among the granite tombstones outside the churchyard fence.

Much of what I know about the living I learned from my front porch, that shadowy threshold carefully placed between the controllable order of home and the messiness of the world outside. Forty years ago they stopped the practice of building front porches, removing from new houses a place to observe and ponder. Television sets cast blue light into the darkness, and a new generation of people began to think they were learning the truth about life from their overstuffed easy chairs.

I never bought a television set, and I kept my porch as nicely as I kept my parlor.

Edith Halsey knew the pleasures of that porch better than anyone else in the county. A good wife, Edith would lay her supper table neatly and well, and when her husband had finished eating, she would tidy the kitchen and, most evenings, drive up the road to sit on my porch.

Those times remain with me, a gentle blur of words and their absence, a companionable silence in dusk. Much of our talk was idle, lazy, about nothing more than the matters of the home: laundry starch and good drying weather; the best apples for frying and the right spices to use with them; the quality of the latest Reader's Digest Condensed Books volume. Such talk is safety, wherein women find solace from the emotional burdens they bear daily.

One evening stands out in my mind, etched as delicately as frost on window glass. It was September 1959, an especially warm night, and I was at loose ends, having retired from teaching the previous June.

"I feel as if I should be preparing my lessons for tomorrow," I told Edith. "This is the first September since I was six years old that I've spent outside a school building. Yesterday I woke with the scent of chalk all about me, as real as the chair I'm sitting on."

Silence. "Edith?"

She turned to me, and tears shone on her cheeks in the sun's last light. I took her hand and we sat silently, watching night come.

"Russell Junior's seeing someone," she said finally. "Dorothy came to me yesterday in tears, asking me to talk to him. I can't talk to my son about something like that, Lucy. I just can't."

"Seems to me it's his father's place to say something."

She shook her head. "I can't tell him. You know how men are about things like that—"

"No," I said, "I don't know."

Her hand flew to her mouth. "Oh! Forgive me, Lucy. What I mean is, my Russell has always enjoyed the carnal side of marriage, but, well, he finds it hard to talk about it."

"Just what did Dorothy tell you?" I asked.

"That Russell Junior was never home since the baby was born. He tells her that the baby takes all of her time—that between her and the church there's no time left for him. Lucy, she said a woman's been calling the house all hours, looking for him, and when she asked him who it was calling, he left the house and slept in the drugstore for three nights."

"It sounds as if Dorothy may be better off without him," I said.

"I didn't raise my son to be a philanderer, to treat his wife and daughter like they were old shoes to toss in the back of the closet!" She covered her face and sobbed.

"What Russell Junior does has nothing to do with you, Edith. All you can do is help Dorothy the best you can." I brought her some water and waited. I wondered why it was that women so quickly took blame for the wrongdoings of their men.

She took the glass and drank. "It scares me, Lucy. What's next? He can't stay at the store forever. Sooner or later, he'll have to make a decision."

"Indeed he will." I had never liked Russell Junior, a small, ferret-faced boy who had caused much trouble in school but was smart enough to avoid the punishment. It didn't surprise me a bit that he was causing his wife grief and shirking his responsibilities.

Edith and I said little after that. Berkley walked out of the churchyard, bending to fit his huge frame beneath the wrought-iron arch; a string of fish dangled from his loose-jointed hand. He stopped at the edge of the woods bordering my garden, turned and looked at us, and silently went on his way up the mountain, alone.

The soothing roll of Cedar Creek was slower than

usual, the late-summer drought upon us. I listened and rocked, conjuring up the simple, cold clarity of the water, and I wished that our lives could be as simple. "Come on with me, Edith." I slipped a pencil and paper in my dress pocket and together we crossed the road.

It was cool and damp in the churchyard, as the dense cedars held moisture in the earth and the air surrounding. "We're going to get hurt—it's too dark to be down here without a flashlight," Edith said. I took her arm and we made our way among the graves, across the uneven ground to the creek bank, to a place where town boys met for cigarettes and drinking, a place I routinely cleaned up out of reverence for the dead, and for the water.

I reached beneath a spicebush and found a wine bottle half full of muscatel. "Now, Edith, I want you to take this pencil and paper and write down your heart's burdens."

Edith was quiet for a long while. "I can't see your face well enough to know if you mean it," she said finally.

Her fingers traced the curve of my lips. "You do mean it." She sat on a flat rock to think.

Leaning over the creek, I rinsed out the bottle until the smell lingered only in the swollen cork. I wiped the cool glass with the hem of my dress and went to sit with Edith. "Give me your paper. I'll write something, too."

"This is silly," she said.

"Maybe. But there's no harm done." I stuffed the paper in the bottle and corked it tightly.

She touched my sleeve. "What did you tell?"

"I'm not saying. And don't you mention this to a soul, Edith Halsey. Not to anyone—Russell Senior or Junior or even Dorothy."

We stepped carefully across the rocks. I tightened the cork once more and laid the bottle in the water. Then it was gone.

Downstream to the Jackson River it ran, bumping against sodden sycamore limbs, becalmed in deep trout pools, and then onward, to where the Jackson joins the

James, past harvested fields and the tobacco sheds of southside Virginia, bobbing beneath bridges, keeping pace with the coal-laden trains that ran day and night to Richmond. To Richmond the bottle floated, carrying our troubles away, to fall, I hoped, into other hands.

REBA WALKER

We built ourselves a lean-to along the road, straight across from the dump gates. Bill McPherson donated the scrap lumber, and J.W. washed windows and painted the front door at Gilmer's Hardware in exchange for a sack of tenpenny nails and a roll of tarpaper.

We worked for two days. The back of the building stood on four-by-fours above the tangle of scrub pines and brambles on the cemetery bank. We cut no windows in the plywood walls and left the front half-open for light, with a see-through plastic sheet that could be rolled down if the weather blew in. J.W. climbed onto the roof to tack down tarpaper; he looked like a monkey up there, hunched over his work with a mouth full of roofing nails.

After setting a couple of brackets into the back wall, I laid a piece of planed lumber across for a shelf. I drove nails for coathooks and brought three tippy folding chairs from my toolshed. J.W. spread out an old braided rug he'd found in somebody's trash.

Then I took a brush and some red paint, and lettered a sign on the side of the shanty:

SAY "NO"
TO OUT-OF-STATE GARBAGE!
HONK YOUR HORN!

Larry Hopkins came right away when I called him. He took pictures of me and J.W. in the shanty doorway, and then had us stand on either side of my sign and took a few more.

"Come on inside and sit," I said.

Larry looked at the back of the shanty hanging over the bank and shook his head. "What're you going to do here?" he asked from the doorway.

I moved two chairs outside into a spot of sun and gave him one. "We plan to watch real carefully," I said, settling into the other chair. "Now, write this down: 'The members of Save Our Mountain Environment will begin a protest at the Buena Vista Landfill on April seventeenth. They are looking for volunteers and donations. Interested citizens are asked to attend the next meeting of SOME at seven p.m., Tuesday, April eleventh, at First Methodist Church.' "

Larry looked up from his notes. "I'll ask you again: Just exactly *what* will you be doing here?"

I showed him the notebook I'd put together. "We'll keep track of all the trucks coming in and out of this dump. It's gathering evidence. Now, write this down, too: 'President Reba Walker says the group is trying to discover what is being dumped at the landfill.' And you can end with something about stopping the destruction of our environment."

"I can't put that in my paper," Larry said. "We don't know for a *fact* that our environment is being destroyed."

I kept quiet for a second or two, not trusting myself to be civil. "Get your face out of that damn notebook and come on with me." I jumped up and grabbed Larry's arm, knocking over both our chairs. I pulled him across the road and pressed his face against the makeshift chicken-wire fence the landfill workers had set up four days earlier.

"Look, come on, *look!*" I shouted.

Larry squirmed away from me. He backed off and

rubbed his arm where I'd held it. "Settle down, Reba!"

"*You* settle down! And don't be saying such damn ignorant things!"

J.W. put his hand on my shoulder. "Come on, Reba."

"Any horse's ass can see what's happening behind this fence," I said.

We stood and watched a bulldozer shoving piles of garbage into a shallow pit behind Lucy's garden plot. She'd been partial to fertilizing with chicken manure, storing pickup loads of it from the poultry farms up the valley in one of her outbuildings. After two or three years in the shed, the manure became a fine gray powder, which Lucy spread three inches deep on her garden every year about this time. For days after, you could smell that chicken shit. Gradually it settled into the soil, and her tomatoes were the best in the county.

Eight years after her death, that soil was still rich. The garbage tumbled together with the dirt before the wide bulldozer blade, standing out white and hard against the soil's blackness: styrofoam and plastic and paper, ragged and chewed up, stinking of waste and rot.

"Lucy, Lucy, old Miz Lucy, how does your garden grow?" I said. Nobody finished my rhyme.

Larry stuck his notebook in his jacket pocket and hung on to the fence. "So, would you eat anything grown in that dirt?" I asked him.

He shook his head. "Of course not. But that doesn't mean they're polluting our whole environment. This is a landfill, state-regulated. We don't know anything about what's happening to the garbage after it's dumped here. I have to report facts, not opinions."

J.W. snorted. "Son, what more do you need?"

I walked through the open gates and up the driveway to where the men were working the garbage. They stared as I found myself an unbroken mayonnaise jar with a lid and scooped up some stagnant water from where Lucy's springhouse once stood. It stank like the inside of a metal garbage can, like filth from the devil's kitchen, and bitterness rose in my throat.

Bobby Halsey stood by the gates. "You can leave the jar with me."

"I guess I could. But we're thirsty, and I remember how good the water always was at Miss Lucy's place."

He grabbed my arm. "It's landfill property."

"There's plenty more for you up there." I tried to pull away from him, but his fingers squeezed my flesh hard against the bone. I kicked his leg and he held on tighter.

Then Berkley Paxton stepped between Bobby and me, and I was free. Nobody said anything. I turned and walked down the driveway, taking my time and thanking God that J.W. and Larry had been there to see it all.

"You were crazy to go in there," Larry said. He scribbled in his notebook and then took a picture of me holding the jar of landfill water.

"Maybe. Here—drink fact." I offered the water to him. He stepped back.

"Reba," J.W. warned, "he's on our side."

"No, J.W., he says everything's okay here, that all this garbage is behaving itself, lying here in neat little piles and just sort of disappearing, I guess. He thinks what I'm saying is crazy. So he can drink this, and it won't hurt him!"

Just then, Larry had become everybody who'd made fun of me in the past couple of weeks, telling me I had garbage on the brain, disbelieving me, as if I'd made up the trucks and the filth and the noise and this stinking water.

"Leave him be, Reba," J.W. ordered. He took the jar out of my hand.

"Look, I understand what you're telling me," Larry said. "And you may be right. I'm just trying to do my job the way I was taught." He took a couple of pictures of Berkley through the fence and some of the truck unloading near Lucy's garden. As he pulled away, he honked the horn twice.

The sun had disappeared behind a bank of dark clouds. J.W. and I moved our chairs back into the shanty, out of the wind, and sat down.

"You were pretty hard on him," J.W. said.

"I know. But we need to get people seeing red when they go past this place, and they're not going to do that reading timid little articles in our local paper."

J.W. nodded. "The shanty will help. This place feels real good to me right about now." He relaxed in his chair and closed his eyes. A minute later he was snoring softly, his breath coming in little puffs. A car honked as it passed; J.W. started, then settled back into his dreams.

I watched the trucks in the dump, four of them now, lined up like pigs at a trough. The workers had made a wide, flat area to the left of the driveway so the trucks could turn around. Bobby Halsey and another man leaned against the posts on Lucy's porch. Bobby was talking on the phone; the other man turned binoculars on me.

In the corner of the porch, next to the door that had led into Lucy's parlor, sat a big red-and-white Coke machine. A Coke machine! As if Lucy's place were a gas station, or a grocery store.

I picked up the mayonnaise jar and walked across the road to the fence. I raised the container high in the air and grinned. Then I sashayed over to my truck, wrapped the jar in an old blanket, and locked it up in the cab.

Inside the shanty, J.W. slept on peacefully, as if he were stretched out on the softest feather bed in a fine hotel room. If all men were like J.W., I thought, we'd have a lot less trouble in the world. With him, there was no pushing people around, no big talk about what was between his legs. But I'd never tell him that; he'd take it all wrong.

J.W. grunted when I shook him awake. "Why'd you do that? I was dreaming good."

"I've got to go to work. Come on home with me, and I'll fix us a sandwich."

An empty truck roared out of the gates and past the

shanty; the driver stuck his head out the window and shouted something into the wind; I thought I heard my name. Then he threw a Mountain Dew can at us. I wrote his license plate number in my notebook with the others and fixed his ugly face in my mind.

It was hard to concentrate at work. I gave low-salt dinners to three nonrestricted patients, and they complained as if I'd tried to poison them. Chance Sanders's mother, Helen, shoved her tray on the floor and poked me hard with her spoon when I bent to clean up the mess.

"You're getting fat," she said. "You'd better watch your figure, or you'll lose your man. I've got a diet for you I pulled out of the newspaper." She'd been reading those grocery store checkout-line papers again—Patty brought them to her sometimes when she was feeling guilty about keeping her mother-in-law at Stoneleigh. Helen herself weighed ninety-four pounds and refused to eat any desserts; she told everyone that her husband couldn't abide heavy women, which was funny, since he'd weighed so much by the time he died—close to three hundred pounds—that Chance had to ask twelve men to be pallbearers.

"Helen, Danny's been gone for thirty years now—the Lord's been good to me." I took the spoon out of her hand and stuck it in my pocket. "And my figure is my business."

She snorted. "You don't want to end up looking like my boy's wife. Patty's as big as a house! She weighed less than a hundred and ten when Chance married her."

"He doesn't seem to mind," I said. "I'll bring you another tray, and I want you to eat this time."

"I couldn't eat a bite, I know I couldn't." Helen took hold of my sleeve. "Did you know Chance is having an affair? That's how come he tolerates that cow wife of his. It's the only way he gets through his days, and especially his nights, if you know what I mean."

"Oh?" I was dying to ask who it was Chance was seeing, but a good nurse's aide didn't pry. "No. I didn't know that."

"For years. He's been seeing Reba Allert—no, her name is Walker now, she married the Walker boy right out of high school. I know because Chance told me he liked her, he told me that just the other day. He was talking about asking her to a dance."

I stuck my chest right up in her face and pointed to my name tag. "That's *me,* Helen. Reba Walker. And the only way I'm seeing your son is with my eyes at meetings about the dump."

The old woman stared at me. "Reba wouldn't go with him. To the dance. She sat around waiting for Hunter McComb to ask her. She should have said yes to my Chance. Everybody in Collier knows Hunter is seeing that pretty Sarah Rose."

I left, carrying the spilled food scrambled up in the middle of the tray. It served me right, I thought, for listening to her craziness. In my head I knew better than to think my patients made sense, but deep down I believed they deserved a hearing anyway. I smiled at the thought of Chance Sanders asking me to a dance now, and wondered how it could be that so many years had passed since he might have.

At last break I passed up the doughnuts in the lunchroom and drank my coffee black. Tamyra, a kid just out of high school, told me she'd been by our shanty. "What're you doing up there?" she asked, filing her long red nails into perfect curves.

"Protesting, and watching," I said. "We could use some help. Can I sign you up for a shift?"

She giggled. "I don't have time for that stuff. Besides, my boyfriend has an application in at the dump. He's hoping to get on with them so he can quit the mill. He wants to work outside. He says the mill stink makes him sick."

"Huh! He thinks the paper mill stinks—come out to

my truck, and I'll give you a sniff of what's waiting for him at the dump!"

Tamyra looked at the clock. "Naw. Break's over."

I grabbed my keys and pulled her out the back door. Outside, the cold air took hold of my lungs and squeezed them tight. A low fog hung in the parking lot, and mist beaded Tamyra's hair. She squirmed out of my hold but couldn't resist following me to the truck. "I'm getting soaked," she said, and covered her head with her hands. "We've still got two hours of work to go."

"You'll dry." Something hard crunched beneath my thick-soled white shoes. "What the hell's all over the ground here? It looks like ice!"

"It's glass. Your windows are smashed, Reba!" Tamyra pulled on my sleeve. "Let's go back inside. We should call the police."

"Just wait. Stay here for a second." I reached into the passenger's seat and felt for the wool army blanket I'd wrapped around the mayonnaise jar earlier. I touched something sharp, and then came a quick, hard pain.

"Christ!" Pressing my hand against my belly, I felt warm blood through my uniform. "Go get a flashlight and a towel."

Tamyra ran. In the dim light of the parking lot I saw a neat slice across the soft tips of my first two fingers. With each beat of my heart came a fresh draw of blood, which pooled in my palm, then dripped onto my shoes. Tamyra came back with the nurse on duty, who took me inside and made me lie down while they bandaged me.

"They must have poured something in your truck. It stinks like a john," Tamyra said. "I'll drive you home."

"Yeah, and we can drop off the repair bill at the dump on our way." I took a couple of aspirin.

"Listen, Reba. Maybe you should give this protest thing a rest, mind your own business. It's not worth it."

"That dump *is* my business. Yours, too. They're not just up there playing with toy bulldozers like kids.

What's all over my truck is straight out of the landfill. Where the stuff goes after that I don't know. But I plan to find out."

Tamyra patted my arm. "Relax. I'm just telling you, don't take it all on yourself."

"I know what I'm doing."

I stayed up and watched the fog drift through the night: a lonely sight that filled me with sadness, as it had my mother. Weather like this had always brought on her sick headaches. She'd start out being angry, her sharp tongue cutting deep. But worse was when she went up the stairs to her room and closed the door, leaving the five of us to take care of ourselves. Sometimes the silence lasted for two or three days. My father cooked beans that scorched on the bottom of the pan, and baked cornbread that never rose. We took to eating out of the garden when we could.

Once, during an especially wet and gray spring, my grandmother came to stay for a week. She left my mother to herself, ignoring every mention of my mother's name. She washed and cooked and made the house right, and when my mother came downstairs the first day the sun shone, my grandmother turned on her heel and walked out the door. It seemed there wasn't room enough in the house for both women.

My fingers ached beneath the bandages, and a shadow of blood showed through. I had no doubt in my mind that Bobby Halsey was responsible for breaking into my truck; I hoped like hell he'd be satisfied with that. The rain beat hard against the roof, and Patsy Cline moved nervously around my chair, jumping to the windowsill and off again, her tail whipping the air as she went. For the first time since Tim had left home for Florida, I wished there were someone in the house with me. But there wasn't, and that was that. I switched off the light and went to bed.

As I lay in the dark, it occurred to me I'd taken on my grandmother's strength and temper, my mother's fits of sadness. My brown eyes, my cooking, and my housekeeping, these were my father's.

SARAH ROSE McCOMB

For three days straight, the rain fell hard, stopping just often enough to give you hope. It spilled over the gutters along the porch roof and formed deep puddles. The temperature hung above freezing during the day, but the nights turned colder. The trees stood still in time, their branches tipped with fat buds cased in ice. I couldn't bear to look at the daffodils we'd moved from Lucy's place. Their tattered blooms bowed close to the ground, heavy with mud. One morning I found the mailbox door frozen shut when I went to bring in the newspaper.

The rain made Hunter blue; the sound of it on the tin roof wore on him. He'd always been restless when poor weather kept him out of the fields, not being one to find things that needed doing in the house. Each morning I sent him out to the barn to check on the sheep—eleven were ready to lamb. He was gone only a few minutes, then came back into the kitchen, forgetting to take off his boots. I tried not to be ugly with him, but the rain wore on me, too.

Sunday evening I started the bread for the store; the feel of the dough beneath my fingers lightened my spirits, as it always did. Hunter stood slump-shouldered by the window and watched the rain. He'd been in the barn late the night before, pulling a stubborn lamb; although he'd lost the mother, the baby survived and now lay in a box by the woodstove, bleating for a bottle.

"Hunter, feed the baby," I said.

Confusion showed on his face. "Baby? Which one?"

"The lamb. She needs milk." I pointed to the box.

"The babies are dead. Benjamin and Deborah are dead."

"No, Hunter. The lamb. Feed the lamb the bottle."

"I know," he shouted. "I know that! I know what's alive and what's dead!" I handed him the bottle of milk and held him to me. "Sarah Rose," he said. "Your babies died."

"Yes. A long time ago," I whispered into the front of his shirt. "I miss them."

"So do I." He began to cry. Then he pulled back. "Don't talk to me like I'm crazy!" He walked into the front room; the sofa frame creaked as he lowered his weight onto it.

I fed the lamb, then sat with Hunter and eased his head onto my lap. The soft pulsing at his temple kept pace with the mantel clock. My mind idled, making shapes of the faint, long-fingered stain on the wallpaper in a far corner of the room. Hunter had left the tub running one night in January, and the water had overflowed onto the bathroom floor and leaked through the ceiling and down the walls below. He'd repaired the plaster, but there wasn't money for new wallpaper. Now the stains seemed part of the room, like the family pictures, and the clock, and the gilt-framed mirror over the fireplace. I dreamed of how it had been when I could lean on Hunter and not be afraid.

I started at the sound of the back door opening. "Who's there?" I called. The door shut quietly.

I lowered Hunter's head carefully onto a cushion and moved into the kitchen. My nephew Jesse stood by the largest of the covered bread bowls and inhaled the rich scent. His hands rested just above the perfect arc of the dough beneath the tea towel.

"Don't touch!" I said softly. "It'll fall."

Jesse jumped, as people who spend too much time

alone will do at the sound of a human voice. I smiled at him and was glad to see his face relax.

"If you stay for a bit, there'll be a loaf for you and your father," I told him. "You hungry?"

He nodded and sat at the table, saying nothing while I fixed him a sandwich of leftover chicken. His hungry eyes followed me as I moved from the refrigerator to the sink and back again. He was small for twelve, but he bore his father's dark good looks well. I knew Jesse was hoping he didn't take on Berkley's size, and for his sake I prayed for the same.

I set his food on the table and hugged him, surprised at the hard muscle I felt. "Where's your daddy?"

He took a big bite of the sandwich and washed it down with a long drink of milk. "Out someplace."

"In this rain?" I refilled his glass and cut him a piece of apple pie. "He in town?"

"Don't know. He's just out."

"You all right?" I asked.

"Mostly," he said.

"You stay here tonight."

Jesse kept his eyes on his plate. "I've got school tomorrow."

"I'll drop you off after I open the store. You sleep here."

He shook his head. "When he comes home, he'll worry that I'm gone."

"You came all this way in the rain just for a meal?" I looked hard into his eyes. There was fear and a great deal of loneliness gathered there. What was my brother thinking of, leaving his boy on such a night?

The lamb woke and struggled to her feet. She peeked out of the box, deciding whether to jump free or stay put. Jesse smiled and went to her, picked her up, and carried her to the table. He cradled the lamb like a baby, his fingers buried in the curly wool above the tail.

"What should we call her?" I hoped the lamb was strong enough to bear naming.

Jesse shrugged, but his eyes shone.

"You go on and pick a name for her," I told him.

"I already have."

"What? Tell me, so I can call her by name when you're not here."

He rubbed the lamb's ears. "Sharon."

I let them sit together for a while. From the front room Hunter cried out in his sleep, then fell quiet. The lamb tried to struggle free. Jesse set her on the linoleum and smiled at her shaky steps.

"Don't let her mess my floor." I sprinkled flour on the counter and punched down the bread dough. I spread it with the flat of my hands, then divided it into quarters and shaped each into a loaf.

Jesse got down on his hands and knees and played with the lamb, laughing when she searched his belly for a teat and standing her back up when her legs went out from under her. He didn't hear the door when his father came in.

Rain dripped from Berkley's hair and beard, and puddled on the kitchen floor. His denim coat hung from his huge shoulders and his overalls clung to his legs. Jesse looked at his father, waiting for him to say something. I put a chair by the stove and told Berkley to sit.

"What're you doing out in this?" I draped an old quilt around Berkley's shoulders and rubbed his hair with a dish towel. Jesse brought the lamb over to the stove and sat at his father's feet.

Berkley shook his head. "I been around."

"And him?" I nodded toward Jesse.

"He's old enough to take care of himself for a time." Berkley's huge hand rested on Jesse's head.

"You should've brought him to me," I told him.

"He found his own way here."

I turned my back on them and worked the rest of the dough into bowknot rolls, knowing better than to push Berkley when he didn't want to talk. Though I'd never feared for my safety around my brother, he had a temper, which, coupled with his size, gave him the reputation of a dangerous man. The stories that circulated about him—that he'd killed a dog with his bare hands, that he'd broken a man's collarbone by squeezing it too hard, that he could lift a full-grown man with one arm—weren't true. Berkley wasn't one to fool with, but I'd never seen him hurt anyone.

Berkley opened the stove door and added wood. He stretched his hands toward the heat, and the light played across his face and Jesse's. Their occasional quiet words joined with the popping of the fire and the rhythmic beating of the rain. Things seemed right and good with them there.

I thought of Jesse's mother, gone seven years. Sharon had come down from Pennsylvania, just arrived one day in the post office asking for work, a skinny girl no more than twenty, with a coal-black braid down her back. She and Berkley found each other right away, and she moved into his cabin with her backpack full of books and drawing things. He was happy those years Sharon stayed with him, happier than I'd ever seen him.

She drew and painted, put up curtains and made braided rugs for the floor, planted her garden by the almanac. Lucy and I taught her to quilt, and she worked hard at it, studying Berkley's old baby quilt and practicing until her fingers bled, until her stitches were twelve to the inch and Lucy said all right to them. Sharon went at everything hard, with all her being, and then a voice inside her must have said, "Enough." I think her love for Berkley was like that, too.

One morning she walked in the back door and announced to Hunter and me that she was four months pregnant. You couldn't have known, with the loose shirts and big sweaters she wore. But I'd suspected it for weeks, every time I looked at her flushed cheeks and dark-circled eyes.

Watching Berkley now at the fire, I remembered the

way his face looked when Sharon was near: clear and open, as if a breeze had come along and pushed the clouds away. He would have died for her.

Of course folks talked about them, but they never married, even after Jesse was born. Some said that was Berkley's mistake, but Sharon would have left even if they'd been man and wife. She wasn't a woman to feel bound by words on paper. She was hungry for something—I never knew just what—and Berkley, then Jesse, satisfied her for a time. But just a time.

I didn't hold it against Sharon that she left. I missed her, and I knew that Berkley was hurting bad, but there was no need to hate her. She was a stranger here, and her roots, her deep roots, were someplace else. People discussed her for months: they said that she'd used Berkley, that she was standoffish and acted as though she was above the rest of us; a leftover hippie, they called her, just looking for some new, different thing. But I ignored all the gossip and did what I could to make Berkley feel better.

I slid the rolls into the oven and checked on Hunter. He was still asleep on the couch, his face smooth and free of trouble. Berkley came up behind me. "Why can't he be right again?" I whispered. "He's a good man. He doesn't deserve all this."

"Neither do you." Berkley patted my shoulder, and I took his hand and pressed it against my cheek. His skin smelled of earth, smoke, and rain.

"We're going home," he said.

"Let me drive you. No need for you both to be out again in this."

We said little in the car; the darkness put all of us in separate places. The wipers pushed aside the rain in a steady beat; in the backseat Jesse matched their rhythm with the flat of his hand against his leg.

Reba's house was dark as we drove past, splashing through potholes. The road had gotten rougher with all

19930
McKenzie County
Public Library

the tractor-trailer rigs roaring into the dump. Their double wheels had broken off the edges of the blacktop and loosened the hastily laid cinder patching. In front of us the sky glowed from the floodlights that had been run into the dump the week before.

Berkley stared straight ahead, and Jesse's hands fell quiet. "Go slow here," Berkley said as we approached the landfill fence line. The car sloshed through water sheeting the road.

I braked and the wheels locked. The back end of the Dodge slid toward the wide ditch just outside the landfill and came to rest against the walnut tree where Lucy's mailbox used to hang. The headlights shone into Reba's shanty and caught her broad shape in the doorway.

She walked over to the car and peered inside. "You all okay?"

I nodded. "It was like I hit ice."

"Mud. It's all over the road along here." Reba leaned farther into the car and shone her flashlight in Berkley's face. "Come look at something with me," she ordered. He ignored her.

"You, then, Sarah Rose." She opened my door and pulled me out. The wind had picked up, and the rain fell out of the north at a slant. We walked into it; water dripped off the hood of my rain jacket into my eyes. The mud slid beneath my shoes, and I fell to one knee, catching myself with my hand.

I didn't hear the water running until we came right up on it. Reba shone her flashlight into the ditch. A stream of brown water a foot deep poured out of the dump and rushed along the road. "Smell it," Reba yelled over the wind. I bent down and scooped up a reeking handful. My stomach churned, and a bitter taste filled my mouth. In the flashlight's beam, Reba's face was twisted with anger and not a little hate. "Take a guess where it's going from here," she said. "Water flows downhill."

"You're saying this is all my fault!" I shouted. "I don't like it, either."

She stuck her face close to mine. "Then help us do something about it." She spoke slowly, using her words like weapons.

"I've got all I can handle, with Hunter and the store and the farm." I turned to walk to the car, and saw that Berkley had pushed it back onto the road.

Reba took my arm. "They're poisoning the water. You can't ignore that!"

I pulled away from her and ran to the car, my shoes heavy with mud. Berkley and Jesse were gone; their flashlight bobbed up the side of the mountain.

As I drove slowly down the road, I worried about Hunter. Most likely he was awake now and confused to find me gone. Somewhere far away the lamb cried for her mother. Just then I wished that I'd not brought her in my house and fed her; letting her die would have been kinder.

I looked in my rearview mirror in time to see Reba grab a handful of earth from the ditch. It made a sickening splat against my rear window. I knew she stood her ground well after I drove around the bend toward home.

LUCY McCOMB

Spring comes late to the mountains, and each year I wait for it with longing. Sudden storms spread dark patches of ice on twisting roads that do not see the sun until well into afternoon. In the mountains, all one can do is wait, knowing that winter will eventually end, just as it always has.

One year—it must have been 1943, the year of the

twenty-five-inch early-March snow—the Jackson School stayed open through most of June, which was unusually hot and humid. Most of the boys had already left for the summer, needed in the fields by their fathers or pretending to be. But the girls, among whom sat both Sarah Rose and Reba, attended dutifully to the very end, happy to be free of housekeeping and gardening chores.

One of those last days, just after we'd finished lunch, I became very light-headed and overheated, going as I was through the change of life. When I stood to write some names and dates on the blackboard, I lost all sense of where I was and fell to the floor; I hit my head on the corner of my desk and opened a cut above my eye. There was a frightful amount of blood, and in the back of my mind I heard screaming and the scraping of chairs being pushed away from desks. *Get up!* I ordered myself. *There are students needing you.* But half blind from the blood, sick and dizzy, I could not rise.

Then I felt hands and heard Sarah Rose's voice: "Miss McComb, lie still. We'll get someone." She raised my head and had Reba slip my chair cushion beneath it. Reba must have been scared enough by the sight of me to take orders from Sarah Rose. The two of them stayed near, Reba pressing a wet handkerchief to my cut, Sarah Rose offering water. When Principal Bowles arrived to drive me to the hospital—he carried me all the way to the backseat of his navy blue Ford—Sarah Rose and Reba moved apart as if repelled.

That was perhaps the only time the two of them ever worked together peaceably at anything. I am flattered no end by that thought, and wish heartily that children might now care as much about their teachers.

All their certain protests to the contrary, Sarah Rose and Reba are cut from the same cloth. They are out of this land as surely as I am beneath it. You see them now, and you say, "There is Sarah Rose, keeping store and a clean house, delighting in the feel of bread dough beneath her fingers, sick with worry over Hunter. She is fresh and lovely at fifty-nine, her hair still dark and smooth. She takes care to keep herself neat."

And then you say, "Now think of Reba. Heavy and clumsy and mannish, she doesn't give a fig about her house or the coarse gray in her chopped-off hair. Her daughter won't call home, and her son is in jail in Florida—though she won't talk about that. She walks through life as if she were angry with God and all His people."

Surface incidentals. Sarah Rose and Reba are both steadfast women, sprung from the flinty soil of Ambrose County. Generations of Hawkinses and Tolleys and Cahoons harden their bones. That they will persevere and find some state of grace I have never doubted.

Berkley Paxton will be blessed with the same, though his redemption will be hard-won and late in coming. Berkley is a good man—he has lived honestly, doing harm to no one. But the heavy silence that surrounds him obscures the truth, makes it difficult for him to hear voices other than his own. His choices have been disastrous, none worse than taking the sorry job at the landfill.

I watched Berkley grow up in the deep shadow cast by Sarah Rose, his uneasy awkwardness an odd contrast with her friendly graciousness. Eleven years younger than his sister, Berkley was born too late to enjoy an enthusiastic upbringing by youthful parents; both of them died before he finished high school, leaving him in Sarah Rose's care.

Berkley turned to the woods for solace, as lost children will. For that is what he was—only a boy—despite his standing six and a half feet tall, broad-shouldered and thick-limbed, his final year of school. Sarah Rose did the best she could for him, tangled as she was in a web of grief for her dead son. Berkley didn't make it easy for her; he missed school at every opportunity and helped with the sheep only when Hunter insisted. It must have been with some relief that Sarah Rose watched her brother slip away from the store and climb the mountain to be alone.

I remember seeing him in the hallway of the Jackson School on a bright Friday in June, shortly before he graduated. Although dozens of students swirled around him, Berkley seemed blind to everything.

"Berkley," I called. He moved through the sunlit double glass doors as if he hadn't heard.

I worked my way through the crowded hall and caught up with him at the edge of the road. "Can we talk for a bit?" I asked.

"What about?" His eye was on the mountain.

"About your plans, what you'll do after graduation. Sarah Rose said—"

"I know what she told you. She wants me to take college classes up in Blue Ridge. She says maybe forestry, so I could get a job at the paper mill."

"You're bright enough. You're going to need some training. Jobs are hard to come by without it."

"Hunter didn't go to college. Neither did Sarah Rose, or our father. I'll find something." He looked at the ground.

"There's nothing here for you, Berkley. You know that," I said softly.

"You came back after the University. What was here for you?"

"I had a house waiting for me, as well as a job. And that was a very long time ago."

"What does it matter to you?" He turned his back and started walking.

I hurried after him and pulled him to a halt. "Berkley, you're my nephew, even if it's by marriage. I want to see things work out well for you, and that's going to be difficult if you stay here."

He stopped and looked down at me for what seemed

like a very long while. "It'll be all right." I stood alone at the edge of the road and watched him disappear around the curve.

Late in the day, I went to the store and got Berkley; we climbed the mountain to the cabin. Although the Forest Service had bought the land years earlier, the cabin was mine in perpetuity—the only condition I'd put on the sale. It had been well over a year since I'd been up the mountain, and I was surprised to find the place in better repair than I'd last seen it. The chimney had been rebuilt, the porch jacked up. The window glass was new; the latch had been restrung so that the door stayed squarely closed.

Out back, Berkley cupped his hands beneath the spring pipe and took a long drink. He straightened up and wiped his hands on his pants, then walked to a corner of the cabin and ran his fingers across the chinking, frowning at its looseness. He felt along the edge of the roof for curled shakes, and used his sleeve to wipe away the lemon-colored pollen that streaked the two small windows.

"It's your place now," I said.

He nodded. "I'll keep it up."

"I know that. Mind you, I'm not saying this is where you ought to stay forever, Berkley. But for now, until you know more, it will be good enough."

He removed a cocoon from the door lintel with a stick. "What I said this afternoon about your coming back here—it was none of my business."

"I didn't consider it prying, Berkley. To be honest, it pleased me that you'd even thought about me as having a life." I took a deep breath. "We need to be going. The path will be hard for me any darker than this."

As we descended the mountain, Berkley took my arm and walked beside me in silence. His contentment was evident, and although he never thanked me, so was his gratitude.

2

THE DAILY NEWS

REBA WALKER

I poured some coffee, then pushed the kitchen curtains to the side and looked in the backyard. Finally the bad weather had moved out, and the sun shone bright in a spring-blue sky. Leftover rain glittered in the grass and sparkled on the new leaves. In the garden the overturned clay was balled in heavy clumps, and along the far edge water pooled like a reservoir.

I'd slept in fits and starts, dreamed of being buried in mud, of filthy water filling up my basement and seeping through my carpeting. I dreamed in shades of brown and curdled green: unhealthy colors that you could never see through in a thousand years.

The coffee burned my mouth, but I didn't mind, because it meant I was awake again. I wondered: Had I also dreamed what I remembered of the night before—the stinking water rushing down my road and the mud slick beneath my feet? Sarah Rose coming along in her car late like that? Berkley and the boy climbing the mountain in the dark?

What was happening to my life? I was here, watching the trucks loaded with tons of city filth pass my house, roll by my mother's grave. I could hear them, and see them, and I sure as hell could smell them. But I couldn't stop them. I'd done small things—called a couple of meetings, gone to see Richard Kane, talked it up, written truck license plate numbers in a notebook. And who cared?

We'd built a shanty, for what—so we could have a place to watch the trucks from when the weather was bad? Nobody had to tell me how old and worn-out I looked; I hadn't even taken the time to get my hair fixed in more than a month. I was snappish with everyone at work, hardly looking at the residents as I delivered their dinner trays. My house was filthy, my garden only half planted.

What was it all for? Nothing was changing, and my life was falling in big, wet chunks around me. I felt sorry for myself, even sorrier than I did when Danny left me with a broken-down truck and two kids to raise. If I'd been one to cry, I'd have pushed my face in my hands and let loose.

Along the scalloped edge of my aluminum awning, drops of water hung neatly spaced, heavy-bottomed, like brimming tears. I couldn't stand to see them clinging like that, as if they were afraid to fall.

I began to think of those drops of water as people, dangling from third-story windows above a busy street and calling for help. Most of them would be thinking, "Dear God, I can't let go of this life. I want to live forever, see my children grow up. It's impossible that this is happening to me."

But at least one of those people would be thinking about the fall. She wouldn't want to die, but there'd be this little corner of her brain wondering what it would feel like, just for those few seconds, to be airborne and know that you'd had guts enough to let it all go.

I imagined the people watching from the sidewalk. They'd be thinking, as we all do, that someone *else* was taking care of things up above, that they could simply go about their business and watch things happen. "Thank God that isn't me up there," they'd say to themselves.

The way I saw it, we all dangled from window ledges sometime in our lives. We could choose: either hang there kicking and screaming, or just let go, knowing then that you'd done at least one perfectly straight thing in your life.

I opened the storm window and ran my finger along the awning. The raindrops fell in a rush into the window box and were gone, just like that. And then I dialed the governor's office.

The receptionist answered the phone on the second ring, her voice cool and efficient.

"This is Delegate Kane's office, eleventh district, calling for Governor Andrews," I said.

"The governor is unavailable. If you'll tell me the nature of your call, I'll connect you with someone who can help you." She sounded like a recorded message. I didn't believe her for a second.

"Let me check Delegate Kane's notes here and see." I grabbed the newspaper, turned to the Virginia section, and ran my finger down the columns until I found the legislative calendar. "Delegate Kane needs to talk to the governor regarding his vote on . . . redistricting. You know, how it could change the party balance?" I shut my eyes and waited.

Silence.

"Hello?" I thought she might have hung up.

"Governor Andrews will be in touch," she said finally. "He appreciates Mr. Kane's interest." And she hung up on me.

I'll bet he does, I thought. Maybe Richard Andrew Kane didn't pull as much weight in Richmond as he led everyone to believe. I called her right back and let the phone ring and ring.

"Hello again. Mr. Kane is on his way to address a Democratic breakfast meeting. And he'd like to be able to mention the governor's ideas on this matter. You know, to help the cause."

Dead quiet. This woman was top-notch at bossing people around with silence. I'd have to work on that myself. She told me to hold while she checked the governor's other line, and—miracle of miracles—it was free. I was talking to the governor.

"Dick. What can I do for you?" His voice was rich as mud pie.

"This is Delegate Kane's secretary, sir. He asked me to call and see what could be done about the landfill here in Ambrose County. It's a real mess, with them taking in all that northern garbage and it blowing everywhere, and after all the rain we've had lately, the water is pouring out of there, stinking to high heaven. You just can't imagine what it's like—"

"Yes, well, I'll have someone check into that. It sounds terrible. Connect me with Mr. Kane, please."

I jiggled the dial on my phone to make it sound as if I were pushing some buttons. "Can you believe it? Mr. Kane just slipped down the hall to use the restroom. While we're waiting, he asked me to get the name of someone who could check into this landfill water problem."

"Dick Kane knows full well that landfills are licensed out of the Department of Solid Waste Management. If it's a water-quality issue, call Angela Finnerty at the Water Control Board. Who the hell is this?"

He had my number now, so to speak, and I knew I'd better get off the phone before anyone traced the call. "Just somebody who thinks you'd better get your ass down to this landfill *now* and take a look at what's going on." And I hung up.

I was on a roll. I called the Richmond operator and got a number for the Solid Waste Management office. Whoever answered the phone made it clear that she thought I was crazy when I told her about the landfill. It was uh-huh and yes, she'd look into it—no questions, and she didn't take my name and number. So I called the Richmond paper.

The switchboard connected me with a George Candler, who sounded half asleep until I told him I'd just spoken to the governor. "He didn't seem too interested in what I had to say," I told him. "In fact, he sort of yelled at me. I'm just wondering about why—"

"Give me your name again. And where you're calling from."

I told him. "I want your paper to come down here and see this mess," I added. "And bring a camera."

"We'll check into it." He coughed a few times—a smoker for sure. "We don't just hop in a car and drive three hours unless we know there's a real story."

"Oh, we're real down here." I told him about the trucks blocking traffic on the bridge and the garbage lying half covered, about the records we were keeping at the shanty, about Bobby Halsey and Wesley Ferris setting up camp in Lucy's house and putting a Coke machine on her front porch. "Guess what they do with the cans and the rest of their trash?"

"I couldn't say."

"Just guess."

"I don't know, I suppose they toss them in the dump?"

"Unh-unh, no. They put them in plastic trash bags, and the county trucks come along and pick them up and take them to the Bent Mountain Landfill. Can you beat that—hauling garbage from one dump to another?"

He laughed, and I knew he'd be down.

I called Karen McPherson and Patty Sanders and asked them to meet me at the shanty. Karen mumbled something about having plans to change the beds that morning, and I told her the laundry could go to hell, it wouldn't go on her headstone that she slept on clean sheets. Patty said she'd just given herself a permanent and wasn't about to leave the house with her hair frizzy.

"You're worried about your hair being too curly for you to sit across the road from a garbage pit?" I shouted into the phone. "This isn't a goddamn beauty contest we're engaged in here, Patty. It's a war." I liked that last part, so I said it again, and she hung up on me. I got myself dressed and walked through the cemetery to the shanty.

J.W. was already there. Everything looked sorrier in the daylight than it had the night before, and the road was a slick of stinking mud. The dump sat like a scraped-open scab at the foot of the mountain, garbage heaped in gray ragged mounds. Deep gullies ran willy-nilly in the red clay, as if some huge animal had run its claws down the cutaway hill. Water pooled in the deep ruts left by the trucks.

During the night, dump water had run into the shanty and left the plywood floor warped and muddy. I sent J.W. across the road to pick up a plastic bottle from the ditch and then down to Cedar Creek to collect water. He came back shaking his head. "Things aren't right. Fast as that water's running today, there oughtn't to be the scum that's there."

I walked down the hill with him. The creek was running fast, as he'd said, and it was full of brown filth that coated your hand like cold gravy. The patches of cress that had grown by that creek for as long as I could remember were poor-looking, skimpy and yellow. I'd always used the cress in my salads, thinking about the bones of the cemetery folks that fed it and how I was making them part of me again. Now I'd no more eat it than I would tomatoes grown in what used to be Lucy's garden.

"J.W., follow the creek on down to Breckinridge's Pond and see what it looks like." I scooped up some stream water in a bottle.

Karen and Patty, loaded down as if they were on a picnic, yoohooed at us from the shanty doorway. By the time I'd climbed the bank, they'd eaten half a package of Sarah Rose's sweet rolls; now they sat in the folding chairs sipping coffee and sharing a cigarette. A Randy Travis tape played on a boom box stuck in the corner.

The two of them had been best friends since they were kids. Karen was as quiet and plain as Patty was loud and flashy, opposites who just seemed to go together. Chance and Bill liked each other, too, and the four of them took vacations together every year. I was a little envious.

"How in heaven's name can you two sit there and have a tea party in the middle of this god-awful mess?" I said.

Patty shrugged. "The mud'll still be here whether we have a cup of coffee or not."

I bit my tongue to keep from saying anything about her hair, which was every bit as frizzy as she claimed. The cozy cinnamon smell of the rolls made my mouth water and reminded me I'd had nothing but coffee for breakfast.

"Mind if I tack this up here?" Patty unwrapped a Willie Nelson poster and hammered it on the wall next to me. "I don't care what you say about all the pretty new boys singing now. Willie's my man."

I took a big bite out of a roll. "He might as well be—he's probably been married to everyone else on earth and has a hundred kids. The IRS is after him for tax evasion. I wouldn't touch the man with a ten-foot pole. He's going to go totally bankrupt any day now."

Patty stood and wiped the crumbs off her shirt. "Well, you know, I believe God makes one particular man for each woman on earth. Some of us find each other early, and others it takes a while. Willie'll be along for me someday." She licked some frosting from her lip. "Sarah Rose should close up that old store of hers and open a bakery, good as her rolls are." She reached for another.

Karen snorted. "Patty, you keep eating like that and Willie Nelson won't know you from a cow in the field when he comes to town."

"I don't know why everybody makes such a fuss over being thin. Chance says he likes me soft and round."

I smiled, remembering what Helen Sanders had told

me about her daughter-in-law's size and Chance's having an affair—with me. Husbands who said things like that to their wives just weren't looking at them close enough anymore to see what was in front of them. I mean, really see.

"So what're we supposed to be doing here?" Karen asked.

"Turn down the music and we'll talk." I told them we'd work together, all of us watching the trucks coming and going, being careful to write down license plate numbers and times accurately and, if we could, descriptions of the drivers. "The more information we get on these guys, the better."

Karen walked out to the road. "It's not the drivers' fault, y'know. My cousin hauls long-distance, and he hooks up his cab to whatever trailer his boss points to. He's just doing his job."

"They're not all like your cousin, Karen. The other day one of them threw a can at me. And you know what happened to my truck window. We're not going to put up with that kind of stuff. Next time I'll call the police. And if we're going to get the law after somebody, we'd damn well better have the information we need to make our charges stick."

Patty took a deep breath and threw back her shoulders. "Manners, ladies. We're talking civilized behavior at this landfill."

"No, Patty, we're talking assault."

"Since when did you become a lawyer, Reba?"

"Since thirty-five years ago, the first time Danny gave me a fat lip. I didn't like it then, and I'm sure as hell not going to take it from some cracker-assed trucker—"

"Leave me alone. Your life isn't my fault, and neither is this mess!" Patty shoved me against the Willie Nelson poster, and if Karen hadn't pulled her off she'd have gone for my face.

Patty backed out of the shanty, running a hand across her mouth and smearing her lipstick. She straightened out her sweatshirt, which had twisted above the waistband of her jeans to show soft belly. Her hair stuck out like steel wool. Just then I felt sorry for her. She was doing the best she could, like everybody else.

"Go home, Patty," I said tiredly. "We've got work to do here, and I can't be wasting my time catfighting with you."

She turned and pointed down the road. "Forget what I said. You'll need the help."

I looked. Five trucks snaked around the turn, grinding their gears as they climbed the hill.

"It's like they've been waiting in a bunch somewhere down the road," Karen said.

"They have." J.W. walked into the shanty and sat down. He carried a knotted plastic bag and dropped it in the middle of the floor. "Out by the interstate, at Truckstop of the Americas. Halsey radios from the landfill when his men are ready for more trucks, so they don't lose any time. I been out there and heard it." He helped himself to some coffee. "Look at what's in this bag—"

But the three of us were out in the road with our notebooks, taking down information as the trucks moved through the landfill gates.

George Candler didn't need to tell me who he was. He stepped out of his beat-up green Honda, clutching a small notebook with a cigarette jammed in the spiral binding.

He came over to Patty. "Are you Reba Walker?"

She jerked her head my way. "Over there." She and Karen checked him out: his saggy pants and wrinkled blue shirt and the loaded plastic pen-holder didn't make it with them.

I stuck out my hand; my eyes were level with his. "You're from the paper. Glad you found us."

"It wasn't easy," he said in that smoker's voice. He stamped his left foot a couple of times. "Long trip. Leg goes to sleep driving the interstate."

We walked across the road to the landfill fence. "My

God. You ladies have yourselves a real mess." He took notes while I talked. I pointed out the washed-away face of the mountain and the National Forest boundary. He took pictures of the bulldozer and trucks moving around.

From Lucy's porch, Bobby Halsey stood watching us. I made sure George got a close-up shot of him. "That's H-A-L-S-E-Y. He's the manager. He's local, but he's partners with somebody named Ferris, that's F-E—"

"I know how to spell that one." He took lots of notes, turning pages with quick flips of his wrist. A little color came into his cheeks. I was sure we were front-page news. "Anyone else covering this story?" he asked.

"Larry Hopkins," I said.

George looked up. "What paper's he with?"

"Ours. The Collier *Gazette*."

"I mean anyone from Norfolk, or Washington? Nobody's been doing regular stories on this thing?"

"I called your paper because you folks always seem to be after the governor for one thing or another, being right there in Richmond and all. I thought you might listen to me."

George put his notebook in his back pocket. "Is there a phone I can use?"

"There's one down the road at Sarah Rose's store. Or you could drive me back to my house and use mine—long as you don't run up any long-distance bills." We started toward the Honda, George rooting in his pockets for his keys.

"Hold on, Reba. You'll want to see this," J.W. said.

"We'll be back. He needs a phone," I told him. George opened the car door for me, and I eased into the front seat, thinking how long it had been since I'd had the luxury of a man's courtesy. Patty and Karen waved their fingertips, smiling tight little smiles. George was no Randy Travis, but at least he was a gentleman.

"Don't go making any phone calls until you look at what's in this sack." J.W. emptied his plastic bag onto the side of the road. George stared at the ground and didn't move a muscle. I slid across the seat and looked.

A pile of fish lay in the dirt, their pale undersides iridescent in the noon sun. "From Breckinridge's Pond," J.W. said. "There's plenty more floating there, belly-up."

SARAH ROSE McCOMB

It was all in the Richmond paper the next morning. Splashed across the front page was a full-color picture of J.W. beside the shanty, staring down at some dead fish. Reba got herself on page seven, looking like a gym teacher, with her clipboard and sunglasses. The picture was from a good angle and more than did her justice.

She came into the store and set a stack of papers next to the cash register. "Can I leave these here? They're free for the taking—courtesy of George."

"George?" I polished the glass-front case and glanced at Reba. Her cheeks flushed and she stuck out her chin.

"George Candler. The reporter. He says we all should read what he wrote, so we'll have the story straight. There's more rumors flying around than there are rats in a dump, if you get my meaning."

I flipped through the paper. "This is a good picture of you, Reba. You look sort of official, in charge."

She stared at me, as if waiting for the other shoe to drop: for me to finish my statement with something nasty. I was too tired to worry about such sparring.

"I mean it," I said.

"Well, George brought a *real* photographer back with him today. They're going to climb the mountain and get pictures of the whole landfill from above. He's writing a special story about us for the Sunday magazine. He'll be wanting to talk to you and Hunter, I expect."

The bell over the door jangled and in walked Rastin. He wore his red bandanna, its creases still sharp, tied neatly around his head like a pirate. He winked at me, pretended to tip his hat. "Good morning, fair ladies." He took a cassette from the tape rack. "New shipment—less dust. I'll take this Whitney Houston and a couple of ham-and-mustards to go."

Reba watched me fix his sandwiches. "You're one of our best customers up at the dump. Let's see, your rig is blue, with Massachusetts plates, right? You know who I am?"

He handed me his money. Reba stepped closer and repeated her question. Rastin smiled.

"All right, sure, I know who you are. You're one of the dump ladies—this one here." He picked up the paper and found Reba's picture. "Reba Walker. Hi. I'm Rastin Keyser." He offered his hand.

"I don't shake hands with criminals."

Rastin kept his hand extended. "I'm a trucker, that's all. A human being who drives a truck, you know? My job isn't who I am."

Reba spit on his shoe. "As far as I'm concerned, you're about as good as a murderer."

"Reba, stop it," I warned.

"Listen to you defending him! You're part of it, too, Sarah Rose. Selling sandwiches and supplies to these people. You ought not to have a thing to do with this boy, not a *thing*." She tossed two quarters on the counter, took a drink from the cooler, and headed for the door.

"Hold on," Rastin said.

"Like hell I will." She put her free hand on her hip and stared him down.

Rastin unwrapped one of his sandwiches and took a bite. "Okay, Reba, listen. See this piece of plastic wrap? It's trash, right? I'm going to throw it into the can on the porch when I leave here. And what do you think is going to happen to it?"

Reba shrugged. "I'll tell you what should happen to it. I'd like to load it in the back of your truck and ship it north. You could dump it on *your* land—if you have any left up there."

"Let's be serious. You know and I know that trash is trash, whether I'm at home unwrapping a sandwich or down here. We've all got to work together on this."

"*We?* I don't want to listen to your save-the-earth crap. We take care of our own garbage, and you should do the same!"

"Settle down, Reba." I prayed that someone else would come into the store. "Get out of here if you've done your business."

"Oh, I have, Sarah Rose. And as long as you're in bed with these truckers, I've done the last business I'm going to do with you!"

"Don't you talk to her like that. She hasn't done anything to you. Lady, you're as weird as the guys at the landfill say you are." Rastin glared at her, then turned to leave. "See you in a few days, Sarah Rose."

It happened so fast I didn't have time to do more than scream at him to look out. Reba grabbed a sack of potatoes from the shelf and caught him square across the shoulders, knocking him forward against the candy rack. Her face twisted with fury, as if she'd been possessed by a vengeful demon.

She'd have hit him again if Hunter hadn't come from behind the curtain and grabbed her wrist. "Quit!" It was the deep and certain voice of the man I'd loved as a young woman. He took the bag of potatoes from her and put it back on the shelf. "Reba Walker, you're crazy. Get out of here," he told her.

"*I'm* crazy? *I* am? That's the pot calling the kettle black! Hunter McComb, you don't know your own wife half the time. You know why you're losing your mind?

I'll tell you why. You sold Lucy's place to the devil and now he's stealing your soul, piece by piece. You're being punished, and rightly so."

"That's enough. These people don't need your crap. Get out of here." Rastin pushed her out the door and locked it.

I wrapped my arms around my husband and held him tight against me, stroking the back of his neck. His scent and feel: he was eighteen behind my closed eyelids, and sure enough of himself to do anything, anything. Having a glimpse of that Hunter made me hungry for more; I wanted desperately to believe he had been returned to me, that the past months were someone else's bad dream. I didn't open my eyes, even when I heard Rastin leave through the back door. I held on to Hunter the way a mother clings to her son going off to war, certain that if she holds him close enough she can keep him from all harm.

When Berkley knocked on the door and pressed his face against the window to see in, Hunter broke away and looked at me with a stranger's eyes. I saw plainly that he was balanced on the edge of his life, and that I stood too far away to be of any help. "I'll be going home now," he murmured.

"I'll drive you. Berkley can mind things here."

He refused, saying he wanted to walk. I let him get as far as the post office and sent Berkley with the car. Then I sat on the porch, my head in my hands, and cried at the sight of my husband being coaxed into his own car like a runaway child.

What had my life come to? I had a break-even store and a farm that was crumbling around my ears. My neighbors looked at me as if I were as fragile as bone china. Reba was on the warpath, and she considered me the enemy, just like the landfill people were. Each day I wondered how many more customers we'd lose because of her badmouthing.

And I had a husband who was skidding away from me at crazy angles, leaving me increasingly alone with all these problems. I missed Hunter more than words could say. I believed fiercely that I deserved the luxury of them, and let the tears come.

J.W. had the grace to clear his throat before walking around the side of the store. I blew my nose and rubbed my eyes. "Hey, J.W."

"Hey." He slipped his arm around my waist and sat with me, neither of us saying anything. The sun made clean patterns on the new grass and the weathered steps. The lilacs along the porch railing threw their fragrances about us, and for that moment I could pretend that all was right and good.

Berkley parked the car in back and joined us on the porch. He reeked of garbage and sweat, but he knew that and didn't need to be reminded. "Hunter's in the barn. He said he was going to fix the outer sheep pen. I didn't know whether to leave him or not."

I squeezed his hand. "Thanks. He'll be all right at home, he's better on familiar ground. At least, I have to think that. Berkley, I want to know: Do you believe those fish were poisoned by the landfill? You see what goes in there."

He watched a car speed past, his eyes following it around the turn. "I expect we'll know soon. People from the State were taking water samples this morning. They started outside the landfill fence and worked their way across the road toward the creek."

"They spent a half-hour at the pond," J.W. added. "Found a bunch more fish floating near the bank, hardly moving. Said they were 'distressed.' I told Reba they should call a spade a spade—those fish were near dead."

"What's coming off those trucks?" I asked.

"Garbage. I just deal with the bales as I need to—I don't think much about what's in them."

"It ain't right, Berkley." J.W. spoke softly as he wiped

the dust off his shoes. "To be making money off of your land being destroyed. I can't help saying it, because it's true."

"Don't get into it now, J.W.," I warned. "I'm going to fix you both a sandwich. You can wash up at the spigot out back."

I stepped off the porch, squinted in the bright midday heat. Hunter was walking along the side of the road, shoulders hunched over a cradled bundle. His path was true and straight, and the light shone about his silvery head. J.W. and Berkley forgotten, I stood alone, transfixed. I couldn't bear the sight before me: I didn't want to know what my husband carried; yet I couldn't stand ignorance of it.

Hunter walked up to me and laid Jesse's dead lamb at my feet, her legs tangled like windfall branches in the dirt. My husband's eyes were terrible, dark with anger and fear. "There's another down in the lower field," he said.

I lifted my face to God and screamed. My keening echoed off the mountains and filled the sky like a swarm of angry bees. I could stand it no longer; my tight control had cracked down the center and was spilling my pain on the ground.

We circled the dead lamb like mourners, and her soul spiraled heavenward. Flies buzzed around her eyes and nose, and lit on her swollen, dangling tongue. I saw my dead babies, and Aunt Lucy, and Mama and Daddy, one after the other. I heard the voices of the dead; their last breathing entwined and brushed against my cheek like the tenderest stroke of a lover's hand. What was around me became invisible; all that I knew came from another place. And I wished fervently to stay there, safe from the horror of my life.

A camera clicked, and clicked again. Hunter shielded his face and backed away from the photographer. Reba leaned against a car, watching; her reporter friend sat behind the wheel. "Leave him alone!" I shouted. "Get out of here!"

In two strides Berkley was in front of the photographer. He grabbed the camera and threw it on the gravel. The lens popped off and disappeared into the weeds. Then he went after Reba. I put myself between them, and Reba jumped into the car and locked the doors. Berkley might have killed her if he'd gotten to her.

The photographer picked up his camera. The film dangled out of the back and dragged in the dirt. "You'll get a bill for this," he told Berkley. When he saw Berkley's face, he eased his way around the far side of the car. Reba let him into the backseat.

We wrapped the lamb in an old quilt and laid her in the shade of the pin oak behind the store. Her presence seemed not to bother Berkley; he sat eating his sandwich nearby as if he were used to such in his life. And I guess he was.

JESSE PAXTON

The Chevy's backseat smelled like pee, and the lady drove too fast, but she was good at it. I used my plastic sack for a pillow and leaned against the window, watching the scenery roll by. She turned her rearview mirror to get a look at me.

"Where you going?" she asked.

"Pennsylvania," I said.

"Well, I'm not. I'll take you a ways, though." She lit a cigarette and threw the match on the floor. "Whereabouts in Pennsylvania?"

"Gettysburg." I coughed and opened the window a couple inches.

"I been there. Stayed in the Holiday Inn on my honeymoon. What a dump. The motel *and* the honeymoon." She whipped around a truck, cut back in close; the driver blew his horn at her and she gave him the finger.

"Damn truckers think they own these interstates." She checked me out in the mirror again. "You look sort of young to be going up there all by your lonesome."

"I'm visiting my mother." I closed my eyes and hoped she'd take the hint.

After a while she started going on about West Virginia, the Martinsville Speedway, her husband landing in the hospital after his car spun out at a race. "Really, he was my ex-husband. That's why I wasn't in any hurry to get up there. But I figure if you spend two years of your life with somebody, you have to care a little." The longer she went on about car racing and her husband, the faster she drove, and she dodged traffic like she was in a race herself.

The good thing was that we were putting a lot of miles between us and Collier. The bad thing was that we got stopped by a policeman outside of Harrisonburg. It took the lady a while to pull over, and the trooper looked pretty mad when he walked up to her window. I made myself small and pretended to be asleep.

"I'd think you'd want to take it easier with your boy in the back and all," he said. "It's one thing to take chances with your own life, it's another to fool around with his. You were doing eighty."

"If you spent your time going after the murderers and druggies and worried less about a little speeding, we'd all be a lot better off," she answered.

I opened my eyes a slit and prayed she'd forget about me. The trooper was good and mad now, but she didn't care, she kept on talking, told him she did volunteer work for the rescue squad back home and didn't that count for something? "It's not like I'm a bad person or anything," she said.

"You'd best just take this ticket and pay the fine. You're not doing yourself any favors by arguing."

"I guess I'm not pretty enough for you. If I were ten years younger and a natural blonde, you'd let me go with a warning. Men are just dogs, and their cocks are their leashes. A pretty woman comes along, and she can lead you around wherever she pleases. Shit."

"You want to come along with me in the cruiser to see the magistrate on a breach-of-peace charge?" The trooper's face was truly red, and he fingered the handle of his gun. He opened the Chevy door and waved the lady out.

They stood at the side of the road arguing, and I could see she was getting the best of him. Neither one of them heard me open the back door and jump the guardrail.

I stayed off the highway, cutting through fields, heading north. The ground was rough, and some places I sank into mud over my ankles. It would be dark in an hour, and cold, and I'd need to find a ride.

I wondered if they were out looking for me yet. By now Berkley must have gone up the mountain and found the cabin empty. Maybe he'd called the school from the store, found out I hadn't been there at all. I felt bad to think of him worrying, but not bad enough to turn around and go home.

The cabin was getting too small. Something in me said I had to get out of there for a while. It used to be Berkley and I both had space of our own, but we got in each other's way now. It wasn't like I'd grown a lot. I was still the shortest boy in the seventh grade, and that wasn't fun, especially when Berkley was so much the opposite. His working in the dump wasn't making my life any easier, either.

The only thing I knew different was Sharon. I didn't really think I'd find her—I didn't even know her last name, never heard her use it. And what if I did find her? She probably wouldn't come back to Collier with me; Berkley might not even want her back after so many years. The best I could do for myself was to take a little break, go up North and look at the painting, see if it was as wonderful as she always said.

The sun was about gone, and the wind had picked up. I stuffed my hands in my pockets and wished I'd brought a hat. Up ahead an Exxon sign on stilts pushed into the sky, and I climbed the steep hill behind it to the parking lot. A couple of trucks idled to the side, and all the gas pumps were going. A boarded-up trailer sat at the edge of the lot, with FIREWORKS! HERE! BEST PRICES IN VIRGINIA! painted in big letters along the side.

I went into the E-Z Mart and used the bathroom, then bought a coffee. I put in enough sugars and creams to take away the bitter taste, and stood by the hot dog machine, where it was warm. The good, smoky smell of the hot dogs rolling by the red heat coils made my mouth water, so I quit looking at them.

"You want one?" It was a skinny black guy wearing a gold earring and a bandanna wrapped around his head.

I shook my head and stared at the floor.

"You look hungry enough. Let me buy you one." He helped himself to a hot dog and put it on a bun from the warmer. "I think the catsup and everything is over there."

It tasted better than a hot dog had a right to. The guy watched me put it away and then fixed me another, and I ate that one, too. I felt like I'd seen him before. It happened to me a lot that way, thinking I knew people from somewhere. When you got right down to it, most humans look pretty much alike. And I dreamed a lot every night. The edges between the people I dreamed and those I could actually touch were pretty soft.

"Where you headed?" he asked.

"North." I wiped my sleeve across my mouth.

"Us, too," he said. "We're driving all night, straight through to Massachusetts. You looking for a ride?"

"That'd be good," I said.

He gave me the bunk behind the driver's seat and kept the music real low. Not long after we hit the interstate I was asleep, dreaming about car races and cops.

I woke up in the back room of Sarah Rose's store. She was in her robe, looking down at me like I was a pretty sad piece of work.

"You shouldn't have done that, Jesse. Your daddy and I have enough to worry about right now." She told me I was lucky the trucker had remembered me from being around the store. "There aren't many folks who'll backtrack to return a runaway. Rastin has a good heart."

"He's okay," I said.

"You come on home with me. I'll take you up the mountain in the morning."

We drove around the bend to her house, and every light was on, glowing like Christmas. "Lord. Hunter's up again," she said. "We lost a couple lambs today. He's real upset."

"Mine?" I asked.

She nodded. "I'm sorry."

Inside, she gave me one of Hunter's shirts to sleep in. "Why'd you leave, Jesse? It about killed Berkley to find you gone."

I shut my eyes and pretended not to hear her, and when Hunter called for her she shut the door and left. The sheets were soft, and smelled like something Sharon used to grow in her garden. Outside the window, the moon rose over the mountain in a cold sky.

How could I tell Sarah Rose why I was going north, when I didn't really know myself? Deep down, I knew I'd never make it to Gettysburg, never see that painting face-on, never see Sharon again. I'd have to find another way to get by.

REBA WALKER

Before the SOME meeting started, George asked to sit with me at the front table, and I didn't mind. We watched the church basement fill up; people sat on the floor when the chairs were taken. The air was stuffy, even with the windows open, and George's tobacco-and-wool smell mixed with my own nervous sweat.

"There's the Water Control woman." He pointed to a tall blonde working her way down the center aisle, Richard Kane at her elbow. She carried a leather briefcase that matched her shoes, and I wondered how she got her lipstick the exact same shade as her red suit.

"I figured—she was at the dump this afternoon," I said. "They hire by looks in Richmond?"

"Don't think she's stupid. I've seen her in action." George's eyes stayed on her until she found a seat.

I pushed the hair out of my eyes and sat straighter. "This meeting is starting now," I shouted. "Quiet down!"

The noise kept on, even when I stood and clapped my hands like a schoolteacher. I took off my shoe and slammed it on the tabletop until I could be heard.

"That's better!" I said. "You sound like a bunch of hens laying eggs. We've got a lot to talk about tonight, so let's get right down to business. Most of you know about the water poisoning and the dead fish. Our job is to decide what to do about it. I have my own thoughts, but let's hear your ideas."

"You ought to run this meeting properly. Have the minutes read first," George whispered.

"I'll run this meeting however I damn well please. You just do your reporting job and leave me alone."

I glanced at Kane and the woman from the Water Control Board. She sat leaning toward Kane, her arms crossed and a little smile playing around her mouth. He shot her a sideways glance and adjusted his tie.

J.W. stood up. "If no one's listening to us up there in Richmond, then we have to go and *make* them listen."

Bill McPherson clapped, and J.W. took a bow. The room became noisy again.

"Uh, hold on, let's back up here. We'll take care of a few loose ends before going on to the matter at hand," I said. "Patty, give us a report of what happened last time."

"The minutes," George reminded me.

"The minutes, Patty," I said.

She read, kindly leaving out any mention of the election fighting. Then Bill stood up and talked money as the plate passed from hand to hand. "We're getting into it deep now. These are big problems we're dealing with, and we're going to need a chunk of money. Reba's already rung up some long-distance bills. We have about twenty-eight dollars left. We'll take in more tonight, but we'll have to get busy soon and do some fund-raising."

"Maybe Bobby Halsey will give us a donation," someone called out. "He's making plenty of money these days."

"Let's put J.W. on the street corner with a white cane and a tin cup," someone else said.

J.W. grinned and tipped his hat.

"Speaking of *canes*," Chance Sanders said with a chuckle, "maybe our representative would donate to the cause. How about it, sir?"

Kane flashed his teeth, and someone passed him the plate. "Fill 'er up," J.W. said.

"Perhaps we should defer this matter until after Angela Finnerty gives her report on the water sampling," Kane said. "She may change your minds about the need for funds."

"Like hell," I muttered. George poked me in the side.

After ten minutes of discussion we came up with a plan to sell T-shirts. Karen McPherson volunteered to take charge of designing the shirts, which we agreed would have our group's name and a picture on the front, a catchy slogan on the back.

Miss Finnerty was growing restless, crossing and uncrossing her pretty legs and considering her fingernails. Finally she whispered something to Kane, and he stood up.

"People, this has been an enlightening meeting thus far. But I'm afraid Ms. Finnerty has a long drive back to Richmond tonight. Would it be possible for her to share the results of the water sampling with us so that she can answer your questions and be on her way?"

I moved out from behind the table and made space for her. She spread out her papers, said something to George, and smiled. He blushed and moved to the side of the room with his notebook.

In your dreams, George Candler, I thought.

"It's a pleasure to be here," she began. "As Delegate Kane said, I've learned a great deal sitting here with you tonight, and I want you to know that my agency will do all it can to keep your water pure."

"Amen to that! Lock the landfill gates on your way out of town!" Patty shouted.

"I can't do that," she said. "Closing a business is the attorney general's domain and has to be done with just cause. It's certainly not a simple process."

"All you have to do is turn the key and say good-bye, honey!" It was Chance, shooting off his mouth again.

"Shut up, Chance," I ordered. "Let the woman say her piece."

"Thank you, Ms. . . ."

"Walker, Reba Walker. From up at the shanty?"

"Of course, I remember." I knew she didn't.

"Get on with it," Chance said. "This isn't charm school or anything." Patty elbowed him hard.

Miss Finnerty unrolled a big chart and taped it to the blackboard. On it were dozens of chemical names with the symbols in parentheses after them, followed by three columns of numbers, one headed "Maximum Acceptable Level" and the others "Creek Level" and "Pond Level."

She took a short stick from her briefcase and pulled

it full-length into a pointer. "These are the results of the testing done yesterday for Cedar Creek and Breckinridge's Pond. We analyzed the samples for a number of so-called hazardous chemicals. To make a complicated matter simple, the numbers in the first column, as you can see, are higher than the numbers in the other two. In other words, we found that the water running from the landfill into the creek and the pond had acceptable levels of the tested chemicals. The oxygen level of the pond water was within acceptable range, also."

"Tell that to the fish," I said.

Miss Finnerty turned to face me. "Excuse me?"

"I said, Tell that to the fish sucking for air down in that pond. You know as well as I do it was something coming out of the dump that killed the fish, whatever your numbers show."

"Reba—" George started.

"There are fungi that fish are susceptible to," Miss Finnerty said.

"Those fish didn't have a mark on them," Bill McPherson shouted. "I've been fishing that pond since I was three years old, and I know what a fungus looks like."

"I'll be happy to give you a full copy of the lab results," she said. Her smile was fading fast, and she looked to Kane for help.

"Do sheep get fish fungus, too?" I asked. "Hunter McComb found two lambs dead in his field. There's some real bad stuff coming out of that landfill. Anyone with half her senses can smell it and see it. You don't need to do tests to know that much. Miss Finnerty, you can take your charts and go back to Richmond, because you're a goddamn liar!"

"Stop it, Reba," George said. "You're getting yourself in trouble."

"We're already in trouble here, so what the hell?" I tore the chart off the blackboard and let it drop to the floor. Kane took Angela Finnerty's arm and led her out the back door, carrying her briefcase. Chance went and picked up her pointer, then tossed it into the night.

"This meeting is adjourned," I announced. "Next Tuesday, same time."

George invited himself in for coffee. He moved around my kitchen as if he owned the place. Then we sat on the porch in the dark, listening to the spring peepers. That afternoon I'd planted runner beans along the side of the house, and the honest scent of turned earth mixed with the steam rising from our coffee. George said he couldn't smell the garbage down the road, but I could, and it cut deep into the evening's peace.

Neither of us spoke for a while. George's cigarette glowed orange in the dark, and my chair squeaked as I rocked myself.

"This is nice," George said. "Now I know why all the people around here have chairs on their porches."

"Very smart. Don't you sit on your porch?"

"Don't have one. Two windows and a fire escape are as close as I get to a porch. I'll be moving soon, though. The building's been sold to some artsy group, and this time next year my apartment will be a pottery studio. The painters didn't want it because it was too dark."

"I guess it's hard uprooting yourself," I said.

"Not really. I've moved more times than I can count. It gets easier the more you do it. You learn to travel light."

"I've moved once—from home into this house. I don't plan on doing it again."

I looked sideways at George, wondering what he was up to. Here he was, talking to me like I was somebody, like what I said mattered to him. There were plenty of people he could be talking to. What did he think he'd get from me? I moved my chair away from his.

"Tell me about Lucy McComb," George said.

"There's not much to tell, really. One thing, she never moved. She started and ended her life on the same piece of land. After she died, Sarah Rose and Hunter spent months going through her things, deciding what to keep and what to auction off. I heard she had boxes of notebooks in her attic where she wrote down everything she did, every day of her life. Sarah Rose told Patty Sanders that when she retired she was going to sit down and read them, work her way through Lucy's life."

"Do you think Lucy would mind that?" George asked.

"If she would have, why'd she leave those boxes up in the attic? Lucy was a private woman, but she wasn't a fool. Once you're gone, what difference does it make what people say about you? Besides, I doubt there's much to turn your face red in those things." I peered at him through the darkness. "Why are you so interested in Lucy McComb?"

"I'm just wondering how she would be handling this landfill thing if she were alive." He moved his chair closer to mine.

I crossed my arms over my chest. "Lucy McComb was a mouse. She was an old-maid schoolteacher. Doesn't that tell it all?"

"It tells me she had the gumption to make something of herself," he said softly.

"What's that supposed to mean?" I shot back.

"Just that. She made a choice to use her brain when most women didn't. I've been told she was very well-read, an intelligent woman."

"I suppose she was, for what it's worth."

"What kind of teacher was she?"

I thought for a moment. "Tough. She expected all of us to do our work when we were told to. We gave her a fair share of trouble—I guess we were hoping that if we kept making her ask for things, she'd give up and quit asking. She never did."

"What else?" He leaned close enough that I could feel the heat of his skin, and lit another cigarette.

"I feel like I'm on *Larry King Live* or something. Only

Larry King doesn't smoke anymore. Ever tried to give those up?" I took his cigarette and put it out.

"Don't do that again!" He lit up another.

"Sorry. I didn't know cigarettes were a life-or-death thing with you." I kept the hurt out of my voice.

"I've quit plenty of times, for a day or two. It didn't seem worth the shakes and double vision. I couldn't see straight enough to punch my typewriter keys."

"My father died from cigarettes. I quit the day of his funeral."

George drew deeply on his smoke and ignored me.

"You know, most everyone at that meeting tonight had Lucy for a teacher at one time or another. I remember Bill McPherson in about the fourth grade. One day he showed up at school wearing this old sweater of his mother's. Told Lucy his new coat had been stolen, but we all knew he didn't have any new coat. The next day he came to school wearing a brand-new boy's jacket. I asked him where it came from, and he said his father'd brought it back from Roanoke. But the way he kept his eyes on Lucy all day, I knew the truth."

"People around here take care of their own," George prompted.

"Used to. Not so much now. I see it every night at work, people lying in their beds crying for their children to come and get them and take them home. But the children hardly ever do, and maybe that's all right. I don't know. I do know that my mother kept both her parents when they got too old to live alone. She'd have been ashamed not to."

"My grandmother lived to be ninety-six, and made my mother's life miserable," George said.

"That's what I mean. Maybe nursing homes are a good thing. But I look at those people and think that for all they worked and struggled, they deserve better than to be thrown in some institution to die."

I stood up and looked out into the night. "Don't think

it was all sweetness, growing up here. The other side of caring about everyone so damn much was that we knew each other's business, pretty much all of it. And folks spent lots of time talking about it. Still do.

"But Lucy was different. She stayed to herself most of the time, seemed happy enough to go only to school and church and sometimes to a family dinner. There wasn't much for people to gossip about with her. I can remember just one time I heard someone talking bad about Lucy. It was Patty Sanders—well, her name was Armstrong then. She came to school one day and announced in the girls' room that her mother had seen a man leaving Lucy's house that morning. Now, I was as interested as everybody else in what Patty was saying, but the know-it-all look on her face made me mad. So I told her to shut up, that people had the right to do what they wanted as long as it wasn't hurting anyone else. Patty ran out of there like I'd slapped her, but I didn't care. She always was a talker, and she ruined more than one reputation in town."

"So Lucy had a gentleman friend," George said.

"Who knows? Maybe she did. What people do in their bedrooms is their own business."

George took a last drink of his coffee and poured the rest off the porch into the runner beans. "You know, it sounds to me as if you and Lucy are somewhat alike."

"What do you mean by that?"

"I mean, you take life straight on and do your work. You don't worry a whole lot about what other people think of you. Take the meeting tonight. Everybody in that room knew the Water Control woman was lying. But they sat there and listened, probably intimidated as hell by her expensive clothes and her charts. But you went right ahead and called her on it, ran her out without missing a beat. Mind you, I'm not saying that was the best thing to do, and I don't think Lucy McComb would have acted the same way even if she'd been thinking the same things you were."

"Lucy was scared of her own shadow. She didn't have it in her to stand up to anybody."

"I don't think that's it, Reba. It's a question of thinking before speaking, and looking ahead to see what might happen next. *That* Lucy would have done, and rightly so."

"I don't need you correcting me!"

"Just listen to me. Do you think that Angela Finnerty will ever take a phone call from you? Let's say you find more dead fish, or maybe a whole family gets sick with some mysterious flu thing and can't shake it. You suspect bad well water, so you call Finnerty's office and demand to talk to her. The secretary asks who's calling, and then she puts you on hold. A minute later she's back with the old 'Ms. Finnerty is on the other line' routine. She takes your name and number, and you know from her voice it'll be a cold day in hell before Finnerty returns your call."

"So what? There are other people in Richmond who probably know more than she does."

"So you call someone else. And they don't tell you what you want to hear, so you blow up at them, too. Where do you stop?"

"I get along all right," I said. "You don't need to tell me how to act."

"Maybe not. But you're up against some pretty powerful people. If you're right about what's going on at that landfill, they've got a lot to hide. It's looking more and more as if that place should never have been given an operation permit. You're going to have to catch them with their pants down, so to speak, and you won't do that unless you have entrée into their bedrooms," he said.

" 'Entrée'? Don't come at me with words like 'entrée.' You're telling me I should smile and nod when they tell their lies, pretend I believe them, so I can hear more lies? We don't work that way around here. It's wrong, George. All that garbage being dumped here, it's damned wrong! And I'm going to stop it!"

He slammed his hand on the porch rail. "Not by cursing out the people who can help you do it, you're not. Sometimes you have to play the game and be patient. Kill them with kindness, as Shakespeare put it."

"Shakespeare be damned. I don't have it in me." I stood up and flipped on the porch lamp. We both squinted in the sudden light. "You need to leave now, because I'm working the late shift tonight and I have to get dressed."

My hand was on the screen door handle when he touched my shoulder. "It's your choice, Reba. All I'm saying is that you're not making much progress doing things your way. And you're making it pretty hard to be around you."

His touch took my voice away, surprised me with its warmth and weight. I started as if snakebit. Finally I spoke. "You know, I've never made much progress being sweet and good. What I have here I got by taking what I deserved. Now go on, or I'll be late for work."

He let go of me. "You know what I'm telling you, and you know it's true, even if it doesn't feel right to you now."

From my bedroom window I watched him get in his car and turn on the ignition; it caught and died, and my heart jumped foolishly. He tried again, and this time he gunned the engine and started down the driveway. I pulled the window shade to block out the floodlights from the landfill.

LUCY McCOMB

The ground trembles beneath the weight of the trucks, well over a hundred of them coming each day now. So tiresome, an earthquake that will not stop. The men dig, bury the garbage, and the earth moves and changes, contaminated by unnatural compounds whose firm bonds will never break.

The soil warms beneath the spring sun. The daffodils and tulips and hyacinths wilt, their leaves edged with brown, and the mock-oranges and spicebushes and azaleas burst forth to take their place. I always had fresh flowers in my house, from the earliest snowdrops to the last sheltered chrysanthemums. Dried cockscomb and yarrow kept me through winter.

Yesterday Sarah Rose came, Berkley by her side, and mounded my grave with budding French lilacs that he had cut with his pocketknife from the bush by my cellar door. I marvel at how the flowers persevere amid the stench and traffic, but I believe this will be the last year for them. Sarah Rose does what she feels she must for me, but I wish she'd left the flowers to die where they grew.

Sarah Rose is fragile now, taut with the feelings of guilt she bears over Hunter's mistake. Ought a woman to pay for her husband's sins? I think not. Reba learned that early on, when the Walker boy left her, trailing bad checks and, of all things, overdue library books! She refused to make good on any of the debts and right away closed their bank account. "He isn't my problem anymore," she told people, and she went to work at the nursing home and made her own money, enough to raise two children without help.

People fault Reba for leaving the children alone so much. They ran wild; they were bullies; they made trouble in school because they were never taught otherwise. But no one volunteered to watch them for her while she worked. What was she to do?

About the library books. Reba found them jammed behind some boxes in the toolshed years after Danny left: travel books about the West. Some said the books were clues to his whereabouts, and she replied, "I'm not looking for any clues, thank you!" She lives in limbo still, married, yet not.

But a true marriage depends not a bit on the laws of man. That is something about which I know a great deal.

Mac Avery wore a red apple pin on his lapel. The day I met him, it gleamed like a bead of blood in the warm October sun.

I'd stopped at the store for some aspirin. Sarah Rose was behind the counter, it being a Saturday. The radio was on, and I stayed a minute to listen to the war news.

"I don't know how the Japs are hanging on," Sarah Rose said. "Papa says they're like animals caught in traps, chewing their legs off. The kamikaze pilots, all that—it seems crazy."

"Not so crazy, Sarah Rose. That's the nature of armies, isn't it? Think about Normandy, Tarawa. If you believe in something strongly enough, it's the right thing to do." I fingered a bolt of red velvet, imagining a winter's day cool enough to wear a dress cut from it.

"But then you're dead, and you can't enjoy anything." Even at fourteen, Sarah Rose had a keen and wholly practical turn of mind, inherited, I think, from her father, whose storekeeping success was firmly rooted in his thorough understanding of local reality.

How could I explain to her the moment of exhilaration between such resolve and its consequence, when one is so certain of what's right and so brave that nothing else matters? How, indeed, when I had only imagined it myself?

"Sometimes it's hard to understand the choices others make, especially when our own men are being killed because of them. But it's very important that you try, Sarah Rose. Remember there's often more than one right answer. Don't be afraid to look beyond the obvious." I sounded like a schoolmarm, but Sarah Rose expected no less from me.

She looked at me with serious green eyes, and I saw then that beneath her schoolgirl braids and clothes, she was already a beautiful woman.

"Does that count in class, too? When we answer questions the wrong way?" She laughed and rang up my purchases.

"That depends upon the nature of the question." I reached over and stroked the bolt of red velvet. "This is beautiful, isn't it?"

She nodded. "We're getting more next month, some green, I think."

"But the red, it's such a rich color. Look how it changes." I unrolled a length of the fabric and moved toward the window. Dark and light played over the cloth like clouds scudding over rounded mountains.

"It's a right nice color." A man stood behind us; my eye fell straight to the bright red pin on his chest. "McIntosh Avery, but call me Mac." He stuck out his hand. "I'm looking for"—he pulled a square of paper from his inside jacket pocket—"John Paxton."

"I'm his daughter," Sarah Rose said. "What're you selling, Mr. Avery?"

"Vacuum cleaners, young lady." He leaned against the counter and looked around the store. "You find your daddy and I'll demonstrate my machines. You'll have a brand-new store when I'm through!"

"Papa's up at the house. I'm in charge. And we're happy with our store as it is."

He smiled at me. "And you're the young lady's mother?"

"No," I said, blushing. He had the whitest teeth I'd ever seen. "Her customer—and teacher."

He noticed my staring at his apple pin. "I bought it in New York," he said. "The red's real rubies, tiny chips bonded to gold. Here, look right up close." He moved so that the sunlight fell directly on it. I closed my eyes against its brilliance; I smelled faraway perfume, tobacco, and dust on his jacket.

"A lot of folks don't believe me when I tell them that John Chapman was my great-great-granddaddy." He polished the pin with his sleeve.

"Johnny Appleseed," I said.

"I figured you'd know the name. Now, let's get down to business. If you'll show me an electrical outlet, I'll give you a free demonstration." He unwound the sweeper cord. Reluctantly Sarah Rose switched off the radio and pushed aside a bin of potatoes. Mac Avery plugged in his machine and moved about the store, talking above the din. When John Paxton came in the back entrance and stood beside his daughter, I slipped out the front and walked home.

I wasn't really surprised to find Mac Avery at my door an hour later, upright in hand. "This machine is now selling at Paxton's store, but you can buy it direct for five dollars less. Let me show you what it does on carpets—you have carpets in here, I'm sure." He peered over my shoulder into the hall. "Ah, there's an outlet, and there's some dirt. Connect the two with my machine and you have a marriage made in heaven—at least for the lucky housewife." I looked him in the eye and he looked right back at me. If his glance had wavered even a bit, I'd not have let him in.

He stepped into the parlor. "You've got some fine things here."

"A number of them are good imitations. It's hard to tell the difference sometimes."

"Maybe for you. Not for me." He picked up a cup, translucent and fragile. "I bet you don't sip tea out of this one," he said, smiling.

"I don't drink tea at all. I prefer coffee, which isn't

easy to come by these days." I was growing uneasy, and I wished I hadn't let him in so readily.

"You do your wash on Saturdays, that's unusual." He pointed out the window at my undergarments hanging limp from the clothesline in the warm sun. Suddenly I wanted him out of my house; he knew much more than a traveling salesman—any stranger—had a right to know about me.

"Please leave," I said. "I can't afford your vacuum cleaner, and I don't need it anyway."

He plugged it in. "That's all right, I'll clean this carpet for you and then be on my way. I apologize for sticking my nose in your private business. I forget myself sometimes. It feels so good to be inside a home, being on the road as much as I am."

He started the vacuum and pushed it about the parlor, taking care around the floor lamp and sofa legs. I pulled the plug and handed him the cord. "You may go now," I told him in my sternest classroom voice. "Now." The heat rose in my cheeks.

"I understand," he said quietly. "Living here alone and all. To be honest, I was surprised you let me in."

"I know you mean well," I said. "But it's not necessary for me to take up your time, when I have no intention of buying what you're selling."

"And it's not right for me to be so personal. I don't think sometimes, how it'd be to live by yourself and have a strange man in the house. I'm traveling alone most of the time, and I get hungry for company."

He carried the machine out to his car and came up the steps with a parcel, which he put on the rosewood table. "This is for you. An apology. And because you're pretty, even if you don't think so." He left without another word.

Inside the package was a length of the red velvet from Paxton's store, with a postcard of Natural Bridge. *You in this velvet: you would be the eighth wonder of the world,* he'd scrawled across the back.

*

In December, Mac Avery returned. By the most extraordinary coincidence, I was wearing the dress I'd made from his velvet when I answered the door. The hem was pinned up, and the lace trim was basted to the collar and sleeves.

"Thought so. The color's right on you." He handed me a sack of coffee. "Happy New Year. You going somewhere?"

"Tomorrow. If I finish the dress." I stood in the doorway, holding my collar shut against the cold and his eyes.

"You going to let me in? It's mighty breezy out here." Pellets of sleet struck the tin porch roof like tossed gravel, and the dried leaves clinging to the red oaks rustled in the hard north wind.

I forced my eyes away from his stare. "I don't think so. I have a great deal to do. Thank you for the coffee."

"Fix me a cup?" Shoulders hunched against the cold and head tucked deep in his overcoat collar, Mac Avery looked miserable and harmless. But there was no sense in letting a virtual stranger into my house so near dark.

"Mr. Avery, if you would like to call tomorrow, I will fix you some coffee. It was good of you to think of me." I shut the door and locked it, then stood with my back pressed tight against it until I heard his car start up.

As I hemmed my dress, I listened to the record Sarah Rose had given me for Christmas, selections by the Glenn Miller Orchestra. What did Mac Avery want with me, I wondered. Somewhere he must have a home, a wife, children. Why had he singled me out, watching my every move with his curious tawny eyes? Was it pity? Did my voice sound plaintive and lonely to those around me, or did my appearance label me so, like a sign around my neck? I cringed at the thought.

Still, I preferred to think he felt sorry for me than to believe he saw me as prey, my defenses so weak they'd be easily removed, my heart left vulnerable to his feigned affections. In my mind's eye the red apple pin glittered on his lapel.

I tapped my foot to the music and ran the velvet between my fingers. When I finished the hemming, I took off my robe and put on the dress. I stood before the mirror, and the red velvet glowed in the soft light as if emitting its own heat. The rosy reflection smoothed out the lines at the corners of my eyes, gave my hair a reddish cast, touched my cheeks with a schoolgirl blush. Hugging myself, I swayed to the rhythm of the music, slid my stockinged feet across the carpet. I was all to myself and heartily loved it, loved myself. I felt I had been given back twenty years of my youth, a gift few of us receive.

That night, as the sleet rattled against the windows and the wind howled about the corners of the house, I dreamed outlandish things. I ran like a crazy person through town, my hair loose. I sang from the tops of trees and set fire to my bedroom and drove Mac Avery's fancy car all the way to Lexington and back. All of it in my red velvet dress.

The following spring he planted three apple trees in the far corner of my yard.

"Why do you come back here?" I asked. "You can't be selling too many vacuum cleaners, with John Paxton carrying them in his store."

He tamped the dirt around the slender trunk of the last tree and leaned on his shovel. "It's on my route," he said, wiping his hands on his overalls. "And it's pretty here. And I like to see you."

"Maybe I'm on your route, too." I was too old to believe I was the only woman receiving gifts from Mac Avery.

"Uh-huh, you are." He sat down close to me.

"Where do you live?" I asked.

He shrugged. "Used to have a place in Richmond. Wasn't worth keeping, as little as I was there. So I have a post office box there and stop through every few weeks, stay with a friend. The rest of the time I'm on the road."

The sweet smell of rich dirt rose from his hands as he rubbed them together. "You must get tired of that, and lonely," I said.

"Sometimes. I guess it's in my blood, wandering like I do. But I've put down some roots here now, haven't I?" He smiled and put his arm around my waist.

The warmth of his touch made everything around me disappear. All I knew was Mac Avery: the spicy fragrance of his skin; the certain rightness of his presence; the perfect clarity of his intent.

"Let's walk. Up there, along the ridge." He pointed to the mountain, which rose steeply beyond my garden.

There, inside the cabin where Berkley Paxton now lives, Mac Avery pierced my blouse with his red apple pin and loved me with strong arms and a straight gaze throughout that afternoon and evening.

He returned to me often. He would park his car in town, walk the mile to my house, enter through the kitchen door, bring me presents from here and there and stories of the world as he knew it. It was a marriage that suited us both for fifteen years, though no preacher ever sanctified it. That there were other women I never doubted, but he left them behind when he came to me. He was mine, and I was his, and it was he who made me understand the fullness of love lying beyond rings and vows.

McIntosh Avery died in my bed just before midnight, Thanksgiving 1960. A young Catholic named John Kennedy had been elected president, and things were changing in Collier.

That night we'd loved each other well. We lay side by side; sleepily, Mac told me about the new road being built between Richmond and Lexington. "They're cutting right through the mountains," he said. "It'll seem funny bypassing the little towns when it's all finished. Won't help their business at all."

I pushed my head up against his chest and felt his heart beating. "Like Paxton's," I said. "I don't think they're doing much anymore, with the new A&P in town. But Hunter and Sarah Rose are smart. They're offering things people don't get at the big stores—home-baked bread and pies, a place to sit down and visit."

Mac nodded. "They'll survive. They're far enough out that people will always need to stop for bread, milk, things like that. Just as they'll always need vacuum cleaners." He kissed me and rolled over to sleep.

I woke after midnight. The moon shone brightly through the bare trees, casting long shadows on the foot of our bed. I rose and went to the window. Below, the yard and garden lay in the deep shadow of the mountain. Brown pumpkin vines curled among the dry cornstalks. A few wizened apples clung to the trees Mac had planted fifteen years earlier. The trees needed pruning, and I meant to ask him to do it before he left in the morning.

When I climbed back into bed, the absence of his large heat struck me like a hammer. He lay faceup, his arm flung across my pillow. And I realized I knew nothing at all about him other than that I loved him and he, me.

I called Edith Halsey, because I could not bear to be alone in the house with Mac's body. I knew I could rely upon her silence, as she had often relied upon mine, our front-porch confidences safe with one another.

Edith came right away, stood at the foot of the bed and looked. Then she folded me in her thin arms and held me until I had no more tears left. "We'll get Berkley Paxton," she said. "We'll need help with the burying."

We went up the mountain in silence, relying on moonlight to make our way. The shadows fell as heavy and twisted as my heart; I followed Edith without fear, glad that she had taken charge. Berkley showed no surprise at seeing two old women at his door in the dead of night, and he came down the mountain willingly, honoring our silence. I was certain he'd known of Mac Avery—from his high perch, he learned much about the lives spread out in the valley below. He held worlds of secrets within.

Berkley carried Mac's body into the garden and gently laid him on the quilt I'd spread out. We dug and dug, the ground blessedly soft after a warm and moist autumn. I dug and cried and dug some more; Edith and Berkley left me alone in my grief. When the time came, I could not bear to cover up my lover, so I fastened the red apple pin to his nightshirt and let Berkley finish.

Of course they searched for Mac Avery, you say. Someone must have called the town hall and asked about the car taking up valuable parking space in Halsey's lot for a week. Or his sales supervisor traced him to town and told everyone that Mac owed the company money, or at least his demonstrator vacuum cleaner.

Indeed, all of this happened. But Mac's supervisor, a burly man named Hammond, seemed content to have his vacuum cleaner and inventoried supply samples returned. He removed Paxton's store from the company route, mentioning low sales volume and slow turnover. Before leaving town, he arranged to have Mac's company car towed back to Richmond. So the physical evidence was removed, Mr. Hammond received his due, and after several weeks of gossip, Mac Avery's disappearance was nobody's business but mine.

Six months later a Mrs. Clarence Detweiler of Welch, West Virginia, came looking for her husband, a vacuum cleaner salesman. With her was a boy of about twelve, who seemed embarrassed by his mother and bore no resemblance to Mac Avery. She wore neither a wedding ring nor a red apple pin; she had nothing to do with Mac and me.

People talked to her and listened to her story, then went on with their lives, while McIntosh Avery lay rotting in my garden, making my corn grow taller and greener than anyone else's in Ambrose County.

REBA WALKER

Patty and I took fifty T-shirts and the anti-landfill petition Chance had written, and set up a table outside the Kroger store, leaving J.W. and Karen at the shanty to log trucks. The manager made us locate on the far side of the Coke machines so we wouldn't get in the way of his customers. He looked at the petition but wouldn't sign. "I'm not about to put my name to anything criticizing Richard Kane. He's done a whole lot for this area. This garbage deal isn't his fault."

"Maybe we should take that out, about Kane not helping shut down the landfill," Patty said. "He *did* get the Water Control lady down here and all."

"How much good did that do? She lied to us." I handed Patty a blue shirt. "Put this on. We've got to advertise our merchandise."

"You don't know for sure that she lied to us." Her voice was muffled beneath the shirt. "Help me with this thing, it's too small."

"Your hair's too big. When you going to get rid of it?"

She popped her head through the neck of the T-shirt, her face red. "I guess when you start dressing like a human being. You own anything but jeans and sweats?" She took a mirror from her purse and pushed her hair around.

"Sure. I have three uniforms for work and a navy blue dress for funerals."

"Seriously, Reba. You should look after yourself a little better. Now that you're out in public and in the paper."

"How the hell do you find the time to worry about me with all the attention you pay to yourself?" She shot me a dirty look as she put on her lipstick. I couldn't tell whether she was kidding or not, and it didn't much matter.

After two hours on the folding chairs and just one sale, we moved closer to the entrance and caught people going in, before they spent their money on groceries. "Buy a shirt and close the dump!" Patty chanted.

"What are you ladies doing out here?" Douglas Patterson, the librarian, stood in front of our table holding a sack of groceries and staring at my shirt. " 'Don't dump on us! Save Our Mountain Environment!' I like that. Turn around—anything on the back? Yeah, that's good, too. 'Ambrose County: Trash-free zone.' "

"Go on and sign our petition," I told him. "Hey, Patty, look at his shirt. 'Love a librarian—we're never overdue.' Explain that one to us."

His round cheeks turned pink. "Uh, you know. I got it at the state convention. It's library humor."

"Oh, I get it," Patty said. "It's like, 'Love a plumber—we never leak.' "

Douglas turned red.

"Quit, Patty, you're embarrassing the boy to death." I waved a T-shirt in his face. "How about paying us for one of these, and helping shut down the dump? We're trying to raise enough to charter a protest bus to Richmond."

"I can't sign the petition. Richard Kane's wife is on the library board, and I'd lose my job. But give me a shirt." He handed me the money and stuck the shirt on top of his groceries. "Come by the library sometime in the next couple weeks. Memorial Day would be good—we're closed, but I'll be in my office, and we can talk privately. I need time to check on a few things, but I think I can help you out."

I pushed the petition toward him. "It'd help us out a whole lot if you put your John Henry on this."

"You mean 'John Hancock.' Trust me, and come by for a visit."

"What's he talking about?" Patty took five more shirts from the box and arranged them neatly on the table.

"Hard to tell with Douglas, he's got a wild imagination." He'd grown up alongside my boy, and the two of them had been tight friends. Not that they were so much alike—Tim had never cared about reading, and had taken to the woods for the freedom he found there; Douglas's asthma and weight had slowed him down a lot—but neither of them had fit in at school, and they found some kind of comfort in each other's company. After Tim left Collier, I didn't see Douglas around much. The library wasn't a place I went too often.

Patty counted the shirt money. "We've made eighty dollars—more if we pay for ours."

"They're free. We're due that much," I said.

The rest of the morning passed slowly. People stopped and read the petition, and a good number of them signed. Most who refused balked at the Richard Andrew Kane part and said it wasn't right to blame the landfill on him. I bit my tongue to keep from telling them what I thought about that, and by the time Karen and J.W. showed up to relieve us I had a terrible headache.

They'd been busy at the dump: more than fifty trucks had gone through the gates in four hours. It was hot for May, the sun hazy and the air still and damp; there'd be rain before dark.

"I need to get some laundry done," Patty said. "Chance is grumbling about me never being home."

"Why should he care? He's not around during baseball season to know one way or the other," I said. "He can run the washing machine same as you."

"I know. I told him that yesterday and he said, 'You don't talk to me that way,' and stalked out the back door like I'd called his mother bad names or something."

"Tell him to get his ass down here, then, so you can stay home and wash his socks. Patty, you stand up for yourself, now, because no man is going to do it for you!" I took my notebook out into the road, ready for business.

"Relax. It's just a little marital spat—we're not getting

divorced over this or anything." She walked into the road so she could see the license plate numbers of the three trucks lined up at the gates. One of the drivers leaned out his window and whistled at her. "You can check out my number anytime, sweetheart!" he said.

"What, your police file number? Shut up!" I shouted. "You can dump your filth on our land, but we don't have to listen to it, too."

"Nobody's talking to *you,* lady!" The driver jumped out of his truck and walked across the road.

"Be careful, Reba," Patty warned.

"Careful of what? He's nothing."

"Go on and talk to me like that *now!*" He shoved his face close to mine. "You're no better than we are!"

My notebook fell to the ground as he backed me up against the shanty. "Like hell we're not," I said.

He grabbed hold of my T-shirt, his eyes full of hate.

"Leave her alone!" Patty screamed.

"Get off me!" I raised my knee toward his crotch, and he jumped clear, stumbling over my notebook.

Before the driver could come at me again, his partner hopped down from the cab of their truck and grabbed him by the arm. It was Rastin, the young man with the bandanna, the one I'd argued with at the store.

"So you're two for two. I have to give you credit—you're tough," he told me. "I heard out at the truck stop you've got a petition going. Give it to me, I'll sign." The driver who had started the trouble climbed back into the truck and slammed the door.

"Why would you want to sign a petition to close this dump?" I asked. "You'd most likely be out of a job."

He laughed. "Hardly. We'd just haul it somewhere else. There's a little town over in West Virginia that's begging for a landfill like this one, they need jobs so much."

"They can have it," Patty said. "How about buying a shirt to help us out?"

"Give me two, I'll give one to my partner."

"I'm sure he'll appreciate that," I said. Patty giggled.

Rastin handed me a twenty-dollar bill and signed the petition. "Let me tell you ladies something. Talk at the truck stop isn't running in your favor right now. The drivers are wondering what you're writing down in those notebooks and what you're planning to do with them."

"That's none of their damned business," I snapped.

"Let him finish," Patty said.

"That guy who grabbed you wasn't real serious about it. He's just got a chip on his shoulder in general. But some of the others, well, they aren't talking like they're playing around. You need to watch yourselves, you especially, Reba. I know how you feel about what's going on here. But something bad is going to happen."

"Is that some kind of threat?"

"I'm not threatening you—I'm just telling you the truth." He walked back to his truck.

"What's wrong with you, Reba? He's trying to help," Patty said.

"We don't need help from them." I crossed the road to the landfill and leaned against the fence. Berkley stood in the torn-up dirt that used to be Lucy's front lawn. "Hey," I called to him. "Tell Halsey I want to talk to him, will you?"

"What about?" Berkley walked over to me, pulling off his heavy leather gloves.

"One of his drivers just assaulted me. I need to use his portable phone."

"Assaulted you? What'd you say to him, Reba?"

"None of your damned business. Just get me Halsey."

Berkley shook his head and walked to the house. Halsey was on the porch, talking on his phone, and he took his time coming down to the fence.

"I've got a little problem and I need to borrow your phone, if you wouldn't mind," I told him.

"Reba, I'm flattered you'd think of me." Sugar coated his voice. "Really. I'll let you use the phone if you'll talk to me for a minute. Berkley told me you had an incident just now with one of the drivers. I'm sorry about that. But I warned you somebody was going to get hurt standing out in the road and shouting at these men the way you do. You need to be more careful."

"See, Bobby, there's this feeling I have, and it's real strong, that being careful isn't going to do us a damn bit of good here, while someone else's trash is pouring down on us."

He stared at me for some time. "The phone," I said. "I listened to you, so how about handing over the phone?"

"You know, I think you just don't understand what we're doing in here. How about coming for a landfill tour sometime soon? Bring Larry Hopkins and the old guy from the Richmond paper who's been hanging around, and invite any of your group you see fit."

I laughed. "You want us to take a tour of garbage? Do we have to pay?"

"Now, see, that's the problem right there. You think we're all about garbage, when what we're really doing is scientifically and ecologically disposing of waste. You wait until you see what's inside this fence."

"Bobby Halsey, now I've heard it all. I don't need to go inside this fence to see what you've got—I see it and smell it and hear it every day. Now give me the phone."

"The offer stands. Spread the word, and I'll be here for anyone who wants the tour." He passed the phone over the fence.

I called the sheriff's office and reported the attack.

"Give me that! You didn't tell me you were getting the law up here on my own phone!" Bobby stretched his arms over the top of the fence and grabbed air.

Then I called the local paper. "Let me talk to Larry Hopkins," I said. Bobby had given up trying to reach the phone over the fence and was half running for the gates. "Come on down to the landfill," I said when Larry answered. I strolled across the road to the shanty. "There's been an assault. The sheriff's on his way. . . . What? . . . No, nobody's hurt." And just as Bobby reached the shanty, I added, "I'm using Halsey's phone. Isn't that something?"

Patty was laughing herself silly. "Bobby, slow down," she gasped. "It's just a *phone,* for Lord's sake."

"You ladies enjoy yourselves today, because pretty soon you'll be out of here! I've called the State Highway Department to come survey your little playhouse, which I estimate is approximately four inches too close to the road."

"I'm glad they're coming," I said. "I've been wondering about White's Bridge, with a ten-ton weight limit and all. What do you think they're going to do about all those eighteen-wheelers using it?"

"Have you checked that limit lately? I think you're a little off," he said.

I looked at Patty; she shook her head, as puzzled as I was.

"It's posted for thirty-eight tons now. I took care of the sign myself." Bobby's jaw was squared off, shadowed by a day's growth of beard. I stared at him: he'd changed from a boy to a hard-edged man.

I guess we'd all changed in the past few months.

A couple of hours later, Bobby Halsey posted a worker with a Day-Glo orange vest and a pistol on his hip to stand guard at the gates.

"That's Chuck Mitchell. Since when does he work for Halsey?" Patty checked her watch and wrote down the time as a truck pulled out of the gates.

"I guess since the railroad laid him off three weeks ago," I answered. "Hey, Chuck. What you doing over there?"

He acted like he didn't know me, so I crossed the road to talk. He was busy hammering a hand-painted sign to Lucy's walnut tree. "Buena Vista Landfill—No Trespassing," it read. "Hours: Mon. thru Friday 9:00–5:00. NO ILLEGAL DUMPING." And in small letters, "Mr. Bobby Halsey, Supervisor."

"Now, that's so official," I said. "Like this place is a

real business. You've got to laugh at the last part, though, huh?"

"You'd best stay on that side of the fence. You're pushing it being this close to the gates."

"Come on, Chuck. You mean to tell me this is the only job you could find?"

"He's paying me nine an hour, twice what I'd get anywhere else around here." His voice took on a whiny edge.

"The nursing home is hiring male aides. You can work your way up to seven dollars an hour there and be doing something decent."

"I ain't going to lift old ladies in and out of bed for a living!" he said. "Now, move—here comes a truck."

I stood next to the fence and waited. The driver—the same one who'd grabbed me earlier in the afternoon—waved at me with his middle finger stuck straight up.

I ran across the road to the shanty and checked Patty's notes. It was the same cab, but with a different trailer. "They must be dropping off the trailers at the truck stop and running a few cabs back and forth to bring them here," I told Patty.

"But why would they want to do that?"

"I'm guessing it's to save them time. It keeps the drivers from sitting on their hands when things are backed up. This way they can just unhook the trailers in the lot and use three or four cabs to do the short hauls, while the other drivers head back north for more trash."

"I don't see how it'd make all that much difference. They still have to haul them here one at a time," Patty said.

"It's the waiting. J.W. told me they're backed up overnight sometimes, and that's a lot of miles these drivers aren't making." I flipped through the notebook to the previous week's records. "See? They've been doing it for a while. The same cab number, different trailer license. It's all getting real efficient and neat, isn't it? Just real neat."

Up on Lucy's porch, Wesley Ferris stood like a statue.

I didn't need to see his eyes to know they followed every move I made. Next to Ferris, Bobby Halsey mattered not a bit.

George stopped by my house on his way to the motel and asked to use my phone. He'd been down in Grayson County and had driven back through the mountains. "It looked a hell of a lot shorter on my map than taking the interstate. I should have known better." He swallowed a couple of aspirin and collapsed in the recliner.

"You look pretty bad, George. Catch your breath while I change for work," I said from the bedroom. Buttoning my uniform, I noticed it didn't pull as tightly across my hips. "What were you doing down there?"

"Checking on Wesley Ferris. Bobby's found himself quite a backer. Seems the man runs a string of coal operations, most of them shallow strip mines. He also had drug charges brought against him a few years ago, but they were dropped."

"Dropped?" I stood in the doorway brushing my hair.

"He was getting into marijuana farming, using the played-out mines and grow lights. He had the locals doing the dangerous stuff—checking the plants, fertilizing them, harvesting. They got caught, and nobody had anything on Ferris. He must have paid his people mighty well to take the rap for him. He's an interesting character, all in all. A real go-for-broke type."

"What do you mean?"

"I mean, he doesn't lack for guts. Apparently he was the kind of kid who'd do anything on a dare. He was expelled from high school three times for fighting, once with the guidance counselor at the junior prom, for God's sake."

"Well, some folks just aren't made for school rules and all that," I said. "Come on, leave your car here and I'll drive you to the motel on my way to work. You still look a little green around the mouth."

The sun shone against the mountain and made it glow

red, like a good fire when you knock around in the ashes. I walked into the garden to check the peas, which were coming on fat. I picked a handful for George and me, then cut across the yard to my truck. Black dirt clogged the ridges of my shoes, and I knew I'd track up the shiny floors at work. "So what, it's good clean dirt," I muttered to myself.

George liked Bobby's idea of a landfill tour. "How else are you going to get inside the gates, especially now that they've got the no-trespassing sign up?"

"If I want to go on Lucy's land, their sign isn't going to stop me," I said. "Not that I'd want to ruin a pair of my shoes in that filth."

"Have you thought about what's in that holding area they've got behind the first ridge of dirt?" George wiped a pea pod on his sleeve and ate it whole.

"It's a gigantic swamp back there. J.W. and I climbed the mountain last week and took pictures."

George raised his eyebrows. "You have them back yet?"

"Unh-unh, they couldn't find them at the drugstore when I went to pick them up. They put a tracer on it."

"Halsey's Drugstore?"

"It's the *only* drugstore, except for Revco, out on the other side of— What, you think Halsey's stole the film?"

He shrugged. "Who knows? What other pictures were on the roll?"

"Oh, some of the shanty, J.W. clowning around, a few of Lucy's front porch with Bobby and his buddies."

"I'd think about sending film by mail to be developed from now on, Reba." George crunched the last pea pod between his front teeth. "If you take me up on the mountain tomorrow, I'll shoot some more pictures. Henry left a camera with me, said he wasn't coming back here. We'll use the telephoto lens and see what we come up with."

We drove through downtown, past Halsey's and the hardware store and the boarded-up movie theater. George liked the window at King's, where two moth-eaten beavers and a young bear guarded the hunting and fishing gear. Mary Cantrell was locking the door of the Dollar General, her deposit pouch lying on the sidewalk as she worked the key.

"If she let go of her money like that in Richmond, it'd be gone in a second," George commented. "She'd have at least one man closing up with her, pulling down a wire gate across those windows. Must be kind of nice living like this."

"It's all what you're used to, I guess. Suits me well enough," I said.

I dropped George off at the motel and took the back road to Stoneleigh. Big black clouds rolled in from the west, hiding the pink sunset. We were due another thunderstorm; this time of year we'd get two or three a week, late in the day. The wet spring had been good for the gardens, but not for people prone to sadness in bad weather.

The storm broke just after we'd served dinner. The lights dimmed and flickered, and the only residents who slept were the stone-deaf ones.

I went into Edith Halsey's room and stood at the foot of her bed. Watching the lightning flash across her sheet, I recalled the day Russell and Bobby brought her to Stoneleigh.

What I remembered was her pride: how hard she worked to stay ahead of her son and grandson, with her shoulders square and her weight off her cane, her mouth set in a straight line. Russell and Bobby trailed behind, talking a mile a minute, pointing out the pictures on the wall like they were in some museum, stopping to lift the lids off the dinner plates and say how good the food smelled. She ignored them the way you'd ignore a stray mutt at your heels.

"Mother, this is the ambulatory wing. It's like a motel, really," Russell said. He brushed past me as if he didn't know who I was. "The Lees are here, and Virginia Baker."

Edith stopped in the middle of the hall and banged

her cane hard on the floor. Black marks to scour off, I remember thinking. "The Lee twins are crazy as loons, and Virginia Baker died a month ago!" she said.

Shirley Carter had come along and taken charge, and Bobby and his daddy had cleared out of there as fast as their feet could carry them. Later, when I went into Edith's room, I'd found her sitting in the plastic-covered recliner by the window. I checked her bathroom and pulled down the bedspread for her.

"What's that statue out there?" Edith asked.

"It's a fountain, with an angel in the center."

"Can you turn it on?"

"Sorry. I'm not allowed."

"It's a good sound, water," she said. "Lucy McComb and I used to sit on her porch of an evening and listen to the creek run. That was a long time ago." Edith got quiet then, as though she'd used up all her words. The silence set like concrete.

After dark, I'd gone back to her room and found her still sitting in the chair, fully dressed. I touched her shoulder and she looked up, her eyes hard and bright as diamonds. "I don't belong here. Damn Russell to hell."

"Everybody feels that way at first," I said. "It'll get better."

"Don't treat me like I'm stupid. It's not going to get any better. This place is like a tomb."

There was no use denying her words. The best I could do was try to make being there a little easier on her. "I'll be right back," I told her. I opened her window, then went out the fire door into the courtyard.

The sky that night was dark with storm clouds that slid across the moonlit sky like black oil on water. You could smell more rain coming, and the air was prickly with electricity. I felt along the side of the fountain until I found the handle, and then pulled it up. The water spilled around the angel statue like streaming light. Edith stood at the window, her ear pressed to the screen. "Thank you," she shouted.

It was the last I'd heard her speak. That night seemed a century ago now. We'd all changed, all of us but Edith, who was suspended in time, wrapped like a mummy in her silence. I shut her drapes and left.

Helen Sanders started with her buzzer and rang it for ten solid minutes before I got around to her room.

"Well, there you are! I dropped my tray. I'm hoping my legs aren't scalded from having coffee soaked into my dress for so long. Of course, the coffee's never that hot, now that I think about it," she complained.

"Helen, what would I do without you here to keep me on my toes?" I scooped up the food the best I could, and mopped the floor with a towel.

She chuckled, looking me over from top to bottom. "Reba, I do believe you're losing some weight. You're still a sight, though."

"Like I said, Helen, what would I do without you?" How Chance and Patty stomached her I'd never know. The woman acted like she was the Queen of Sheba, and I wasn't sure whether she was worse when she was thinking crazy or straight.

"It's the hair." She pushed her chair toward me and squinted. "A good coloring would brighten up your whole face."

"That's what Patty told me this morning," I said. "You two must be in cahoots."

"Ha! Patty's out of hand. Did you know she's having an affair?"

"Helen, a while back you told me that Chance was seeing someone else—now it's Patty?" I wheeled her down the hall to the lounge. Every evening she played gin rummy with Grover and Cleveland Lee, and cheated like sin.

"She's a whore, Patty is," Helen said. "I warned Chance, but he wouldn't listen. Since when does a son ever listen to his mother?"

"You've got that much right." Tonight Helen was just lucid enough to be frightening. You never knew what you'd hear from her. A lot depended on whether she'd been given her medicine early or late in the day. I meant to talk to Patty about all the drugs her mother-in-law was getting. To my mind, most of the people at Stoneleigh would be better off without them. I parked Helen at the game table and turned to go.

"Hey," she said. "I hear you and Patty and some others are fighting the government. Good for you—they're all crooked as a dog's hind leg, and every bit as pissy."

I patted her on the shoulder. "It's not quite like that."

"Give 'em hell. Right, Cleveland?" He grinned and nodded; he didn't hear a thing.

Helen had given me an idea. At eight o'clock, after the assistant administrator had left, I went out to my truck and picked up a box of extra-large T-shirts. As I helped people into bed, I gave them their choice of color. Everybody but Helen was happy as a clam to have a new nightshirt. "I want pink," she said. "I don't look good in yellow."

"No pink, only yellow, red, or blue," I said. "Take it or leave it."

"All right, give me the blue. No, red."

"This isn't the House of Fashion, Helen. If I put this red one on you, it's on until morning."

"Maybe, unless I wet the bed tonight. Do you think I will?" she asked anxiously.

"As long as it's after my shift," I muttered.

Tamyra came into the lounge during my break. "Boy, are you going to catch it for dressing everybody in those shirts."

I shrugged. "Why? They all gave their permission."

"For what that's worth." She was painting her nails a new shade of red. "I mean, do they really know what they're saying?"

"Some do. The ones who don't would be on our side if they did understand."

Tamyra looked up from her nails. "How come you're so sure that everything you do is right, Reba?"

"I don't have a whole lot of time to worry about what's exactly 'right,' to weigh all the pros and cons in life. You have to go and act on what you believe, or else your life turns into a fat bundle of maybes and maybe-nots."

"Well, it bugs me. Everything is either black or white to you. Don't you ever kick back and enjoy yourself?"

"Sure I do. In a couple of minutes I'm going to make my rounds and check on everybody. I'm going to look at all my people lying in bed wearing those T-shirts. And I'm going to enjoy that a whole lot, because they'd be out at that dump protesting with us if they could be."

LUCY McCOMB

The fire of 1959 burned long and hot in downtown Collier. It took the Baptist church and parsonage, the produce stand and the hardware store, the Majestic Theatre, and Halsey's Drugstore. Two people died in that fire: Russell Halsey's first wife, Dorothy, and their two-year-old daughter.

It was the Sunday before Christmas; we were all hoping for snow. The night was crystalline, gripped by bitter cold, and the moon and stars shone brighter than I'd ever seen them. Hunter and Sarah Rose walked me to the car, one at each elbow, afraid I'd stumble in the dark and hurt myself.

They wanted me to come for Christmas dinner. I wouldn't say yes or no, waiting as I was to hear from Mac. As we passed under a streetlight, I looked at Sarah Rose and saw how beautiful she was, lovelier at twenty-nine than she'd been at seventeen. She was expecting again, about four months along, and her cheeks were flushed with that life and the cold.

"I'm setting a place for you, Aunt Lucy. It doesn't make any sense for you to spend Christmas alone in that big house."

"If I feel lonely, I'll certainly come," I said.

We stopped to look at the Christmas display in Halsey's window: trains winding around cotton-covered mountains, elves hanging from the striped railroad-crossing arms, and suspended from the ceiling, a Santa Claus, waving and dropping presents from his sleigh onto the town below. It was set up to look like Collier, with the churches and stores and railroad tracks in the correct places. Right in front of the miniature drugstore was a woman holding a baby.

"That's Sarah Rose, next Christmas," Hunter said.

"Quit pushing!" It was Reba, her two children in tow. Tim and Angie wore the sullen look that Reba had had as a girl; clearly, they wanted to be somewhere other than standing with their mother in front of Halsey's.

"Hello, Reba," I said. "It's hard to believe your children are so big already."

"Yeah, it is." She glanced at Hunter and then stared at the ground.

"If it weren't Sunday, I'd think you were out Christmas shopping," I said.

"Well, I'm not. I'm on my way to work and I'm taking these two with me. Last night I left them alone and they broke my best lamp fighting."

The boy had the decency to look ashamed; the girl glared at her mother as if she'd just as soon kill her. "Let's *go,* Mother," she sneered.

"I'm about ready to haul off and hit you," Reba said. "I thought you wanted to see the window."

Hunter and Sarah Rose turned away, embarrassed for Reba.

"*He* did, not me. It's dumb." Angie pushed her brother and laughed when he fell.

Reba grabbed a child in each hand and set off down the sidewalk without a good-bye.

In the window the train went 'round and 'round, and Santa Claus stayed in the same piece of sky. "Reba has her hands full," Hunter said.

"She always has," I replied.

That night I fell asleep sitting straight up, fully dressed, waiting for Mac to call. At the ringing of fire bells I jerked awake and, thinking it was my phone, ran to answer it. I stood half asleep at the illuminated west window. Why was the phone still ringing when I held the receiver in my hand, I wondered.

As soon as I realized what was happening, I tried Sarah Rose's number, but no one answered. Karen McPherson's phone was busy; Bill was the head of the volunteer firemen, and everyone in town knew to call his house for news. There was nothing for me to do but sit and wait for morning.

"Dear God," I prayed, "please spare the school. And don't let anyone die."

The sky became brighter, as if the sun were coming up at two a.m. I walked out on the porch. The moon had set, and the stars were erased by the fire's brilliance. All of Collier might have been ablaze. The sharp smoke burned my nose and brought tears to my eyes. I watched for a long time, until the cold pushed through my slippers and crept up my dress, until I could stand it no longer. I went to bed and dozed in fits and starts, dreaming that my house was burning and no one was there to save me.

Sarah Rose called just after dawn. The deep cold had made fighting the fire difficult, she said. The hoses had frozen, and the men could only watch helplessly as flames spread from building to building. She saved the worst for last, the news about Dorothy Halsey and her daughter. I knew she was thinking of her own dead baby, and about the one she now carried.

"Russell was out for the evening," she told me. "He came home after midnight and found the store on fire.

Chance said the smoke killed Dorothy and the baby early on, that it went up through the heat vents and suffocated them before the firemen ever got there. They think it was the Christmas display that did it—bad wiring."

That afternoon Edith Halsey came and sat with me on the porch, both of us wrapped in comforters. I held her hand as she rocked and wept cold tears, wordlessly sharing the awful knowledge she carried within: that her only son was a murderer.

Three days later Sarah Rose lost her baby. It was a girl this time, whom she named Deborah. After the funeral she seldom spoke of her, bearing the pain silently and alone.

JESSE PAXTON

Hunter gave me some old two-by-fours and I dragged them through the field to the deer blind at the edge of the woods. I fixed the broken rungs on the orchard ladder and climbed up into the Castle, which was going to be the new home of the Cyclorama.

I stretched out on the rough wood floor and warmed my belly in the sun. Berkley hadn't said much about my running away, and didn't keep after me to tell him where I'd planned to go. He told me I had to think about other people, not just myself, that Sarah Rose couldn't take any more worry.

"She mentioned the same thing about you," I said, and he went out on the porch. I wanted to tell him I was sorry, because I was, but I couldn't make myself go out there and do it. I picked up a book and pretended to read.

"The school said if you have another unexcused absence, you might have to repeat the year," he said from the doorway.

I turned a page. Berkley had gone back to the dump without another word.

Now I wished I'd put everything behind us, just told him the truth of things. But it was too late. Sometimes you could hurt people more by what you didn't say than by what you did. And here I was, cutting school again, making trouble. It was like I didn't really have a choice about how I acted anymore. I just did things, and felt bad about them later.

From so high up, I could see Amber McPherson's house and fields. Her pony, Sunny, stood all by himself beneath a tree and looked pretty lonely. I thought about writing Amber a note and telling her to buy Sunny a friend, but that was her business. Maybe she was friend enough for him.

I whistled the way I'd heard Amber do, but Sunny went on eating grass, too smart to be fooled. The sun shone through the leaves onto his back and turned it coppery red, like a new penny, and when I closed my eyes and thought hard about it, I smelled the heat coming off his hide, a good scent touched with enough danger for me to want more.

Was that what brought Amber to the field every day, looping Sunny around in countless figure eights until the grass wore away? Did she think each time that this would be the day she would either ride her pony perfectly and rise into the sky, like Berkley had in the dream she'd told me about, or fall off and crack her backbone in two?

There was always that with horses, I thought, as there was with drawing. Each time you picked up a pencil, you had the chance to lift that picture off the paper or grind it into nothing.

I used a rope to haul up the plywood and got busy putting up the walls. My hammering echoed off the mountain like gunshots, and Sunny's ears twitched. It was good, being in the tree fixing something. I thought maybe I'd quit school and become a carpenter. I'd draw and paint at night, my hands strong from the day's work.

I left one side open for light and stretched clear plastic across it to keep out rain. I put up a shelf for my paints and pencils and laid them out neatly. Someday I'd have the right things—oilsticks and tubes of oil paint, special chalks and good watercolors—like they had in the art room at school. Like what the Frenchman had when he did the Cyclorama.

I took out the pamphlet Douglas had given me from the library and read it out loud: " 'The Cyclorama at Gettysburg National Park is a huge panoramic painting of Pickett's Charge, the "high water mark" of the Confederacy. Standing twenty-six feet high and three hundred and fifty-six feet around, the painting gives viewers a chance to feel what it was like to stand in the midst of battle.' "

I studied parts of the painting on the next page. Scenes of horses rearing, men falling to their knees with blood staining their uniforms, cannons black and shiny in the hot July sun. A tree sheared in half, a wagon tipped on its side, flags limp and torn, everything smudged and confused by smoke. I smelled the fear, and the stink of death. One soldier had his back arched in agony. I wondered what his last thought had been, wondered if he had ever given in to the sureness of death, and how it came to him, finally.

In the painting two women watched the battle from a high ridge. One of them covered her mouth, her eyes big; the other laid her hands over her broad belly. Her baby would be born with rifle shots ringing in its ears. The battle was no place for an unborn baby to be, or any person. Life wasn't supposed to be like that, I thought, but it seemed as if that's what things usually boiled down to.

I turned the page and read on. " 'The cyclorama was a popular art form and source of entertainment in the late nineteenth and early twentieth centuries. The viewer, standing within the center of these giant paintings, was made to feel a part of the scene depicted. Three-dimensional foregrounds or landscapes, including figures, blended with the painting to complete the "illusion of reality."

" 'The painting was usually a team effort. The master artists usually had assistant artists, sometimes as many as sixteen. Each artist had a particular responsibility or area of expertise, such as animals, landscapes, or uniforms and military equipment. Giant studios were constructed for the painting of cycloramas. Tall scaffolds that could be moved on tracks enabled the artists to work on the giant canvas.' "

Amber's whistle traveled across the field and straight inside me. "Sunny, here, Sunny," she called, and he trotted toward the gate as if he'd been waiting for her all day. She looped a rope around his neck and rode him bareback, her long legs clamped against his sides. Sunny trotted and cantered, and Amber sat tight and followed his rhythms like they were her own idea. And when the two of them came closer to me, Sunny's ears went straight forward—he knew I was there, but Amber didn't—and she talked to him, "Good boy, Sunny, good," like he was her baby, more tender than a woman talking to a man, in a way I remembered from a long time back, before Sharon left.

I looked at the bare walls around me. I wouldn't be working with assistants and special equipment. I'd be drawing with pencil on plywood and coloring with dime-store paints; my painting would be flat against the wall, not curving all around me, and maybe the illusion part of what I made would be bigger than the reality part. But I'd go at the work the best I could by myself, and it would be mine, the closest I could come to having something of my mother, separate from everything else messing up my life.

LUCY McCOMB

Real love obligates us to live a brave and daring life. It is a fire that at its hottest burns away all fear and inhibition and leaves us open to do what in our hearts we most desire.

I knew that kind of love with McIntosh Avery, although I took longer than most to own up to it. Our first nights together were brief; I made him leave well before first light, and he never argued, understanding my position. But each time we loved one another, the length of his lingering mattered less; in the final year of Mac's life it ceased to matter at all.

I remember especially Memorial Day 1960, when I let him lie in my bed until the early light turned the room gray. Then it was he who jumped up, saying he was looking out for my reputation.

I pulled at his arm, coaxed him back to me, and loved him slowly and fully again. The sun made a lacy pattern on our quilt by the time we finished; again he tried to rise, but I held him tight and told him it didn't matter to me if someone saw him walk out of my house.

"You say that now. But when I'm gone selling and you're here with everyone talking about you, this may not seem worth it." He kissed my cheek and rubbed my leg with his foot.

"I'll take that chance," I murmured.

"We could get married," he said.

"There's no need for that. You'd not be here any more than you are now. We're married enough." He let the subject drop, and I was glad, because I was happy with my life as it was, and believed he felt the same about his.

He pulled on his pants before he opened the curtains, letting in the sun. "Must be close to seven-thirty." He looked out the window. "Someone's already over in the cemetery with flowers. Now what'll we do?"

"Have breakfast. And then you'll leave through the front door."

While we ate, I told him true stories about lovers, about Martha and Edward Jordan, she a schoolteacher and he a farmer. How in 1804 her school, used as a church on Sundays, was attacked by three Delaware Indians. She and the eight pupils inside were destined to be murdered and scalped, when in burst Edward with a gun in each hand and a knife between his teeth.

"Between his teeth?" Mac asked.

"Absolutely. He handed a gun to Martha—she shot one of the Indians, which so startled the other two that they ran for the door, carrying the two youngest schoolchildren with them. Martha threw down her gun and blocked their exit, giving Edward time to club one Indian. The other dropped the boy he was holding and dove through the window. Edward fell to his knees right there in the schoolhouse and asked for Martha's hand."

"And of course she said yes," Mac said.

"Of course. And it's a good thing she did, or I wouldn't be here to tell this story. They were my great-great-grandparents."

"I'm not surprised, Lucy." He peeked through the kitchen curtains. "I'd better go now. Things are getting busy over at the cemetery."

I wrapped my arms around his neck. "One more story, and then you go. This one isn't so predictable, and it doesn't have such a happy ending." I poured him more coffee and began.

"I was a girl when this happened, about six, I believe, of an age when the facts matter less than what you believe to be true. We had a neighbor, Mabel Pendleton, who fell in love young with a boy named Stuart Gay. Mabel had the biggest, darkest eyes you'd ever want to see, but the way they slanted down at the corners gave her face a touch of sadness, even when she smiled. She was a bright girl, and her mother had hopes of sending her to college.

"Why she fell in love with Stuart Gay no one seems to know, or at least they wouldn't talk about it later. He was a weak-chinned boy, skinny and jug-eared, who didn't stand out in any way but his very ordinariness. The best that people said of him was that he was kind and reliable."

"That's not so bad, is it?" Mac said.

"I suppose not, but it doesn't seem enough to leave home for. Mabel and Stuart arranged to meet in the cemetery one night in the middle of June, and they took his father's driving horse and buggy north to Staunton to catch the early train to Washington. They left the horse and buggy with her cousin—all this had been carefully worked out. And when the train pulled into the station and the two of them were about to board, who should be standing there but a police officer and a woman custodian. They say Stuart began to cry when he saw them, but Mabel looked the woman dead in the eye and said, 'Please retrieve our belongings from the baggage car if we'll not be going on to Washington.' It was Mabel's carpetbag that finished the two of them."

"Lucy. Someone's coming up the steps," Mac warned.

It was Sarah Rose, who wanted to borrow my trimmers. "Go on and help yourself, out back in the shed," I told her. "I'm slow this morning. I'll be over to the cemetery soon."

Sarah Rose rubbed her hands together, hoping I'd ask her in. "I'll bring coffee over with me, it's not ready yet," I lied. She looked over my shoulder into the hallway. I smiled and shut the door, tempted to turn the lock.

"She knows something is happening," Mac said.

"Let her wonder. After this many years she's due that luxury. For heaven's sake, Mac, sit still and let me finish the story." He moved his chair farther from the window, and I continued.

"The sheriff and his matron took Mabel and Stuart home on the afternoon southbound train. I have always imagined that the woman sat very close to Mabel and whispered to her, 'Are you in trouble?' as if she had the right to know that of her ward. Mabel wouldn't have answered her, I'm sure. Stuart and the sheriff probably didn't say more than two or three words the entire trip. The sheriff had done his job by finding the two runaways and didn't care to know the details afterward.

"I've never figured out why the sheriff let them head home by themselves after they got off the train. Perhaps he didn't want to miss the return train to Staunton. Certainly he didn't want to be nearby when the parents got hold of Stuart and Mabel. They were children, really, and what can children who have run away and gotten caught do but give up and go home?

"So Mabel and Stuart set off, and not in any great hurry. When they came to the swinging bridge that spanned the river, Mabel went first. She took her carpetbag from Stuart and gave him a kiss as they stepped on the bridge."

"Lucy, how do you know she did that?"

"What else would she do before she killed herself, but say good-bye to her lover? It's what I would do for you."

"Yes, I believe that." Mac squeezed my hand.

"She walked halfway across that bridge and jumped, just jumped," I said.

"Might she have fallen?"

"Mabel jumped. She knew that bridge better than she knew herself, after crossing it every day of her life. And she knew full well what was waiting for her on the other side."

"And Stuart?"

"He followed. I think he wanted to save her, but he should have known better. They found her body the next morning, his a day later. Stuart and Mabel made the Richmond paper. The headline claimed she had a smile on her face, looked as natural as life. That was a baldfaced lie: after a day in the river, her body couldn't have been that beautiful a sight."

"I suppose they're buried across the road, too," Mac said.

"Mabel is. Stuart's family put him in their plot in town."

Mac stood and stretched. "And are the two of them remembered by their loved ones on Memorial Day?"

"I like to think so. I suppose my telling their story to you was a fitting memorial." I kissed him hard on the mouth and let him out the back door, then watched him slip into the woods between my place and the McPhersons'.

From the way people looked at me that day, I was certain they'd seen my lover. Helen Sanders seemed fascinated by the red apple pin on my collar. But I went about my business, lining up the children for the cemetery decoration. The flowers were never lovelier than on that Memorial Day.

Now here is Berkley, coming up the driveway. It is dark, and the trucks are gone, having left behind their own memorials. His huge boots leave deep prints in the churned-up clay, and if the sun rises tomorrow it will turn the boot marks into fossils to be crushed beneath hard double tires.

Berkley walks to my garden, buried deep in garbage and dirt, and now a parking lot for the workers. In the corner where we buried Mac Avery so many years ago, he gently places a handful of peonies in the mud. He switches on his flashlight, stands for a time above Mac's bones, as if waiting for my lover to rise and walk with him up the mountain. He stoops and picks something out of the dirt, wipes it on his sleeve, and stares.

The red apple pin gleams in Berkley's huge hand like the eye of a trapped animal.

SARAH ROSE McCOMB

I left the house just after sunrise on Memorial Day to ready the church for worship. Berkley met me at the gate, carrying a scythe, clippers, and a small saw; we set to work without talk.

He stayed along the road, cutting back the tangle of vines on the bank, and left me alone in the family section. When I saw the ragged weeds growing wild among the stones, I realized how I'd let things go the past months. The lambs on Benjamin's and Deborah's stones were choked with Virginia creeper. I pulled at the vines with my bare hands, tore my skin against the rough stone as I scraped at the lichens, as if by doing so I could give my babies air and light.

Benjamin had come to Hunter and me after nine years of marriage, born on my twenty-seventh birthday. We'd waited and prayed for a child, worrying that something was wrong with one of us but having no idea how to find out. My cycle had always been erratic, and we did the best we could, our lovemaking driven by burning instinct and, always, by our deep and true love for one another.

Benjamin was born perfect, bloodlessly, his tiny fingers and toes immediately shell pink. I insisted on holding him right away; he looked as if he'd been on earth forever, as if he'd never had to struggle for that first breath. The doctor said he could hear Benjamin crying inside my birth canal. "Push hard now, Sarah Rose," he told me, "this baby is already one of us!"

Three months later I found Benjamin dead in his crib. After he'd been buried and after the food and flowers and callers had stopped coming, I sat in his room and thought on and on about him. I wondered if each of us was given a carefully measured allotment of breaths, and if Benjamin had used up his small number long before, breathing inside me. The doctor said no, of course not. Benjamin's death was unexplained, crib death, not my fault or anyone else's (but maybe God's, I whispered in the dark). The doctor told me that I wasn't to worry myself sick over how it could have been different. But what else was there for me to do?

Deborah had been stillborn, two years after Benjamin; I'd carried her four months knowing she would never be one of us. I didn't say a word to anyone about it. The doctor kept telling me everything was fine, but I knew all along it wasn't. Everyone claimed that I was in shock, because I didn't cry and wail for my dead baby. I'd done all my mourning before the birth; there was no need to make a show of my sadness after.

The sound of Berkley's scythe broke my remembering. He glanced at me as he moved among the graves, his long arms swinging back and forth in rhythm. I waved to let him know I was all right, as all right as I could be. Berkley had built Benjamin's coffin, lining it with a piece of our mama's best quilt. Hunter wanted to buy a box from the showroom at Stanley's, but I said no, Berkley was hurting, too; we should let him do this for Benjamin. He did the same for Deborah. There's nothing sadder than the sound of a hammer against a coffin nail, except maybe the hollow sound of dirt on the lid afterward.

I moved on to Mama's grave, then Papa's, pulling away the wild onions so that the wood violets showed better. On my hands and knees, I clipped and pulled and remembered, and by the time Berkley walked over to get the church key, the sweat was dripping off my forehead and mixing with the tears.

Together we entered the church, Berkley bending to clear the door frame. The stale air closed up my throat. "Lord, what a stink," I said.

Berkley raised his head and sniffed. "It's the garbage," he said quietly. "It's worked its way in here, too."

"How are we going to have a service here today?" I

ran my fingers along the top of a pew and rubbed the dust on my pants. "We could clean from now till sunset and still not get rid of that smell."

He looked down at me with hollow eyes. "We'll do the best we can."

We worked our way around the sanctuary, me wiping off the pews and window ledges with lemon oil, Berkley washing the tall, narrow windows with vinegar and newspaper and then opening them. "Lucy used to do all this by herself—she must have started days ahead." I laid a fresh cloth on the altar and straightened the candles on either side of the cross, and arranged the flowers. "Remember what she'd do with the flowers after we were finished? I never did understand it. She'd carry them across the road and stick them in the vase she kept in the corner of her garden. The last year she was alive, I believe we had to wait the picnic blessing on her, she stood so long over those flowers."

"I guess that was her private business," Berkley said.

I touched my brother's arm. "I thank God that Lucy's not alive to see what's happening to her land. How'd we get in the middle of all this?"

He shook his head, took up the mop to do the floors. "We're not to blame. Why do you keep asking yourself that question?"

"You've got to quit that job over there, Berkley. Come work at the store—I'll pay you what I can. Or give Hunter a hand with the farm. God knows, he needs it."

"You can't pay me near what they do. And what makes the store any different from the landfill?" he said tiredly. "The only way you're making any money there is from the truckers and us workers."

I wiped away cobwebs from the underside of the pews. "Our store's been there for more than seventy years. And it'll be there long after that dump's full and Bobby Halsey's crew is gone, your job with them!"

We didn't say much after that. By ten o'clock we'd cleaned the place as well as we could. Karen McPherson was in the churchyard, trimming the grass from her brother's grave. She'd stuck white lilacs in a mason jar and pushed it up against his headstone. He'd died young in a car going too fast; Karen had named her first son after him. She waved at us as we climbed the stairs to the parking area.

I rested in the car for a few minutes. Watching Berkley climb the mountain, I wished heartily I'd not started in with him about the dump. But I couldn't help it. Like the stench that filtered up through the floorboards of the church, the landfill had pushed its way into all of our minds and lives. It wouldn't leave us alone anytime soon.

Reverend Miller came out from Collier Presbyterian to do the service at Cedar Creek Church, as he had every Memorial Day since our old church had had to close for weekly worship because it wasn't wired to code. He was a good man, and had buried more than a few of the folks in the cemetery.

The noon whistle blew in the railroad yards as Jesse and Berkley, Hunter and I walked down the aisle to the family pew. Reba was sitting next to her newspaperman, holding a handkerchief over her nose. I stared at her until she looked at me.

"This is our pew," I whispered. "You know that."

"You don't own it," she said. "George needs to be close to hear the preacher right. He's reporting."

I wasn't about to sit with her, but I also wasn't interested in making a scene in church. So I moved back and looked around for another seat. Then Hunter pushed in front of me. "Get up, Reba," he said. Anna Layton had started the piano music, but it wasn't loud enough to cover Hunter's words.

George stood and pointed to a spot two rows back, near the window. "We'll move," he said. Reba glared at me as she pushed past us with her handkerchief still pressed to her nose.

Reverend Miller waited until everything was quiet to

start the service. Then he read from Genesis. " 'God said to them, "Be fruitful and multiply, and fill the earth and subdue it; and have dominion over the fish of the sea and over the birds of the air and over every living thing that moves upon the earth." ' "

He looked out into the congregation. No one moved. I fixed my eyes just past his right shoulder, where the tall gold cross stood on the altar, flanked by vases of peonies and irises.

What did God mean by giving us dominion over the earth, I wondered. Did subduing the earth mean defiling it? Who, or what, had dominion over Hunter now? I took his hand and tried to listen to Reverend Miller.

"The landfill across the road from us is wrong. We all agree on that. We live with its smell and pollution daily. What we might not agree on is what makes it wrong. Is it wrong that it's someone else's garbage dumped there? Or that some people are making money while we suffer the consequences of their action? Is it wrong that the South is once again being aggressed upon by the North? Wrong that some among us have chosen to work for the landfill, drawing a paycheck from the devastation?"

"Amen," Reba said. The congregation stirred and nodded.

"We feel like victims, powerless against the odor of the garbage that chokes us as we gather to remember our departed loved ones—husbands and wives, parents and children, soldiers and teachers and farmers. We ask ourselves, 'What can we do?' "

I knew better than to think that a preacher could give us a real answer to that question. We needed more than words about God, patience, and faith. I looked to either side of me, and the worn faces of my friends and neighbors made me want to cry.

"We must understand that the enemy in our struggle is more complex than we think. Yes, it's wrong that this landfill was brought upon us secretly. As guilefully as the serpent tempted Eve, some of us were deceived into thinking that the land would be brought to honest use." He looked right at Hunter and me. "They are not to blame—and we must forgive those who suffered this deceit." He paused, stared over my head at Reba. My cheeks burned.

"Yes, it's wrong that others live wastefully and thoughtlessly send their waste to us. But well beyond the facts of this garbage nightmare lies a hard truth: that God has called *all* of us to be stewards of His creation, and that we *all* have failed Him in doing that. Not to care for the earth as He would is a sin, just as it is a sin to take God's name in vain, or steal, or lie. Friends, in the words of one of my favorite comic characters, 'We have met the enemy and he is us!' "

The congregation was buzzing, shocked at Reverend Miller's words. "Which side are you on?" Reba called out.

He raised his hands to ask for quiet. "Our guilt is not carved in stone. As we fight against the ruination of our land, we must ask God for forgiveness of our own sins, our failure to care for our earth and others with gentleness and understanding and love. Only then can we go forward, united, and stop the ruination of our land and our lives.

"Let us present a united front rather than point fingers. The Buena Vista Landfill will be closed, of that I am certain. I pray that the victory comes soon, and with a minimum of pain."

Hunter leaned his head on my shoulder and I squeezed his hand hard. If anyone in the church could talk about pain, it was my husband.

We were halfway through the second verse of "This Is My Father's World" when the trucks started across the road again. I checked my watch. Bobby Halsey had promised an hour of quiet for the service, and time was up.

REBA WALKER

The library was dark when I got there at three o'clock. I banged on the door until Douglas let me in.

"I was just packing up to leave. I thought you'd forgotten about coming by. Where were you?" he said.

"Take a guess. The trucks didn't stop just because it was Memorial Day, you know." I looked out the window and started to cry.

"What is it, Reba?"

I shook my head, as surprised by my tears as he was. He shuffled papers on his desk to cover my noise.

"I guess it's the holiday," I said, finally. "Being in the church again, like we've been every Memorial Day since I can remember. Seeing everybody tending the graves, trying to pretend there was nothing different or wrong, as if the dump wasn't even there. I kept thinking about my grandfather and my parents, how they'd feel today if they knew what was happening at Lucy's place."

"What do you think they'd do about the dump?"

"I know what my grandfather would have done. He'd have shot every last one of them without thinking twice about it. The dump would never have grown this big if he were here."

"That was a long time ago," he said. "What you're doing out there at the shanty, gathering information and calling people—that's just what you should be doing. This is going to come to a head, and when it does, you'll have all the information you need to close it down."

"I'm scared. Whatever is running out of the dump and into the water is killing things. Who's to say this stuff isn't seeping into our wells?"

"It may be." He handed me his handkerchief. "Crying won't determine that. But science can."

"Ha! Look what happened when we had the State test the water!"

"Reba, listen. I've been talking to a friend from college who works in a government lab in Richmond. He can run some tests on the water for you. We'll see what the State comes up with this time, and see who's telling the truth."

"Catching Angela Finnerty in a lie would be fine with me," I said.

"What you have to do is take water samples from inside the holding ponds, the same places where the government people take theirs. But don't let them know the water's going to a lab. Tell them you're using it on your plants, or looking at it yourself with a toy microscope."

"That won't be too hard. The people who came down last month didn't pay much attention to any of us."

"Good. Now, the other thing I want to tell you is this. You need to be careful around Bobby Halsey."

"That fool? He doesn't scare me one bit!"

"It's not just Halsey we're talking about. His silent partner in all this—"

"I know about Wesley Ferris. About his mines and all. George told me."

"Did he tell you Ferris was charged with rape twice when he was in the army? That he received a dishonorable discharge, even though the charges didn't stick? And that he's planning to open two more dumps, one in Highland County and one in Southside?"

"How do you know all this?"

Douglas smiled. "Librarians' network. We do more than mail out overdue notices, you know. This computer gives me access to plenty."

"You should come to our meetings," I said. "And to Richmond."

"I can do you more good inside this library. You know, people tell me things they don't tell their hairdresser. They stand here flipping through the card catalogue, and I'll come up and ask if they need some help. Most folks say yes. They'll want to know a good mystery writer, or maybe they're into romances—mostly book talk. But the really lonely ones will tell you everything. About their sick husbands or wives, or about their kids, how they don't help out enough. I've seen men meeting women who weren't their wives among the shelves—they'll slip out the back door when they think I'm busy in my office. And over at the courthouse I learn an awful lot. I turn in my budget figures and stay awhile. Ninety percent of what I hear is idle gossip. The rest I file away mentally.

"For instance, how much do you think Bobby Halsey makes every time one of those semis dumps its load?" he asked.

"I don't know, Douglas, I'm not his bookkeeper." I was getting tired of all his talk.

"I've done some figuring. Each truck brings in about a thousand dollars for Halsey and Ferris."

I leaned across the desk and grabbed Douglas's shirt. "A thousand a load? My God, that's easily seventy thousand dollars a day!"

"That's about right. With that kind of money at stake, Halsey and Ferris aren't taking any chances. I'm telling you to walk very carefully. You're dealing with major-league players here. You've done a good job so far. Don't cross these people more than you have to, and you'll find out what you need to know."

"You sound like George."

"I've been told worse." He looked at his watch. "Bring me water samples as soon as you can, and we'll get to work on them. In the meantime, buy bottled water."

"No joke."

The trees were throwing long shadows across the road as I drove to work. Bill McPherson's fields were a soft green in the afternoon light; the first cutting of hay would be ready soon. Chicory and clover bloomed along the sides of the road, and I rolled my window down to enjoy the rich summery smells.

On this side of town, it would be easy to forget about

the stink and filth of the dump; to stretch out on clean earth and feel the heat of the day's sun warm your back; to breathe in sweet air, drink clean water, and feel good about living in the mountains. This was where the right people lived, the lawyers and doctors, the ones who would never have let a dump be thought of for their neighborhood. Right now, they were sitting down to nice dinners served on pretty tablecloths. And I was on my way to the nursing home to take care of their relatives.

Shirley Carter was waiting for me when I walked in, her "Supervisor" badge riding high on her huge bosom and her silly starched hat perched on her head. "We need to talk about the T-shirts," she said.

"I have one for you, too, Shirley. Extra-large." I smiled.

"If you dress the residents up like that again, you'll be fired."

"Some of them said they wanted them on."

"Most of them didn't. You keep your leisure activities to yourself. This is a state-regulated nursing home, not a circus sideshow. Understand?" I nodded, thinking about what Douglas and George had said about smarting off to people. *Kill them with kindness,* I thought. *Go ahead and die, Shirley.*

I walked into Edith Halsey's room, filled the wash-basin, and set it on the bedside stand for her sponge bath. "What's new, Edith? We missed you at the service today. The preacher asked about you." The last was a lie, but so what? "No picnic this year, because of the dump. Got to give credit where it's due, though. Your grandson stopped the trucks from coming during the sermon. Wasn't that nice?"

"Damn him," she said.

"What, Edith? What did you say?" Water splashed down the front of my uniform.

She didn't speak again. I lifted her nightgown. She lay still as a stone while I washed her arms and belly. "You can't fool me. I heard you talk. It's all there bottled up inside you, isn't it, Edith? I guess you're not the only one who does that." I dried her with a soft towel and rubbed lotion into her papery skin. Then I covered her with a sheet and left to check on Helen Sanders.

I found Helen in a wheelchair, peering down the hall. "Patty said to say hello," I told her. She stared at me blankly, and I knew she'd already been given her nighttime dose of Haldol.

She smiled uncertainly and shuffled her feet. "I need to pee. Quick."

I helped her to the bathroom, chattering on about the Memorial Day service to pass the time. She nodded and told me about long-gone celebrations as if they'd happened yesterday.

"And Lucy McComb, keeping her lover a secret like she did. Last week, the day of the picnic, I saw him leaving her house in the morning, sneaking out the side door," she said.

"Lucy's been dead eight years." I tucked her blankets in tight and hoped she'd stay in bed.

"Then who was it I saw sneak out her door? Jesus?" She was getting agitated; it was time to leave her be, so she'd drop off to sleep.

"No, Helen, it wasn't Jesus," I said softly. "If Jesus was living at Lucy's place, there sure as hell wouldn't be a dump there now."

3

STANDING THEIR GROUND

REBA WALKER

"You're going to have to stay calm," George told me. "Let them show their cards, and we'll find out what we need to know."

I set a full pot of coffee in front of him. "That's what you keep saying." It set my teeth on edge to think about being so passive, turning the other cheek, but I'd promised George I would try. I had to admit that my way of doing things hadn't gotten us very far yet.

"We have a full bus to Richmond on Friday," I said.

"Good. At least one television crew will be at the hearing, and numbers count." He lit a cigarette and made a face.

"Television? We're going to be on television?" I reached over to take the cigarette, but he grabbed my wrist before I could.

"It's just the stuff the media people are looking for. The common people get exploited, and then they get angry. It's environmental, too."

"Wait till Patty hears. She'll spend hours trying on dresses, and working on her hair."

"That'd be the worst thing she could do. They'll point the cameras at people like you, who dress plainly and act mad as hell. In fact, the best thing you all could do would be to wear your shirts. Make them your uniforms, the way the coal miners did with camouflage. It's an image you're after. That's what'll get you on television."

"So you want us to look like hicks." I set my coffee cup down hard and crossed my arms.

"Not hicks," George said gently. "But there's no sense in gilding the lily. No one in Richmond is interested in looking at people like themselves. You play the game and win the prize, or you don't play the game and you watch the cameras pack up and go home. The stories I'm doing are fine, but fewer people are taking the time to read the newspaper these days. Get yourselves on television, and things will break wide open for you."

Chuck Mitchell stopped me as I walked through the landfill gates. "What the hell you coming in here for?"

"I'm with them." I pointed to Chance and J.W. and Patty standing on Lucy's porch. "We're taking the tour—the price was right."

"You're not allowed. Mr. Halsey told me to let in only the folks on the list," Chuck said.

"Let me look at that list," I demanded.

"You see if there's anybody named Crazy Bitch on this piece of paper." He held it out and smirked.

"Fool," I muttered, and pushed past him.

J.W. was drinking a Coke from the machine, probably his breakfast. I checked his tie: emerald green, with four Chinese ladies twirling umbrellas in front of their private parts. From what I could see, all they wore were sandals and a lot of hair. "That's an X-rated tie you got there, J.W. Don't plan on wearing that one to Richmond."

"I'm already packed. I'm taking extras in case I make a mess of myself."

"Yeah, there's nothing worse than a tie with a spot on it." I looked at his wrinkled pants and stained shirt.

"Lay off, Reba." Chance yawned and stretched. "Where's Halsey? I've got to be back at school in an hour—I only took a half-day."

"He's probably cleaning up for us. Dusting and such." J.W. laughed at his own joke.

"*Covering* up, more likely," I said. "You can't see it from the road because of the piles they've built close to the fence, but they're leaving garbage exposed overnight at the foot of the mountain. It's against the law to do that."

"How do you know?" Chance asked.

"I've got my sources."

"Him?" Chance looked meaningfully at George, who was walking up the driveway loading his camera.

"And others," I said.

George took pictures of us on the porch, the dump laid out behind us.

"Can I be in it, too?" Bobby came out of Lucy's house with his phone hanging from his belt.

"As long as they make it clear in the caption that you're not one of us," I said.

Bobby pretended to be hurt. "You know, Reba, that's the problem. You forget I was born and raised here, just like you folks. I *am* one of you."

"No, I don't forget, I just can't believe it when I look at this hellhole you're making. Come on, let's get started."

Bobby kept George at his side and pointed out some scenic views: piles of fill dirt, the fence and lights, one weirdly clean-looking mound of trash, brightly colored flat-fold cloth on top.

"And you ladies will be happy to see that we're taking care of the wisteria along the porch. It's my grandmother's favorite flower. I couldn't stand to see it die."

I burst out laughing. "Next thing you know, you'll be president of the garden club!"

He ignored me. "Now, come over here and see how we cover the garbage. This is all according to state code, six inches of dirt per foot of garbage, layered like a chocolate cake. It seals in the trash."

"So it won't break down and leak into the water system?" George asked.

"Well, eventually it will decompose. But we're building a whole network of drainage pipes to route the leachate into our holding ponds. We'll see the largest one in just a minute."

"So all the garbage water goes into these ponds?" I asked.

"We believe we're containing it, yes," Bobby said evenly. "This is all state-of-the-art engineering work and materials we're using."

"What about the dead lambs? The water in Cedar Creek stinks so much the kids won't wade in it."

"Let's not get started with that again, Reba. The State is monitoring the runoff quality—take it up with them. Watch your step up here, the ground's a little soft. Try to stay on the boardwalks."

"As if we'd want to walk anywhere else in this cesspool," Patty said.

"This is the holding pond. It'll handle over a million gallons of water," Bobby announced. "When it's completely full, we'll bring in tankers and pump it out."

Chance spoke up. "What do you do with the leachate once it leaves here?"

"That's being taken care of." Bobby grinned. "We're negotiating a contract with a nearby sewage-processing plant to purify the water for us."

"And then?" Chance pressed.

"Then the purified water will go into the river."

I looked at George and bit my lip to keep from saying anything that would set Bobby off. "Show us what you're doing over by the mountain, how you're keeping it from falling down." Then, while his back was turned, I scooped two samples of the water into Tupperware containers and capped them tight. As I stuck them in my bag, I saw Berkley leaning on his shovel, watching me. I hurried to catch up with Patty, who'd followed Chance and J.W. to the second holding pond, where Bobby was showing them the heavy black plastic liner.

"Doesn't this go to prove what power does to people?" I asked Patty. "Bobby Halsey is puffed up like a peacock over this damned dump. Either he's really stupid, or somebody's got a good hold on him."

"I don't think Bobby's a bit stupid," she answered. "He has plenty to gain from this dump, and he'll find a way to take it as far as he can."

"And from the looks of things, he's doing it as *fast* as he can," I said.

Patty stared at the gates. "What's going on down there?"

A police cruiser with New Jersey plates was blocking the entrance. Behind it, trucks stretched around the bend.

"Go see what you can find out," I told Patty.

Bobby stood hemming and hawing about the cutaway mountainside that was eroding with every hard rain. ". . . And we send one of our men up the mountain every afternoon to gather any bits of trash that've blown up there during the day. We're working hard to make this landfill the best of its kind. Any questions?"

Chance asked about the underground springs we all knew dotted Lucy's place. "Seems to me I remember some caves around here, too. You filling those with trash?"

"We haven't come across anything like that," Bobby said smoothly. "But I'm glad you mentioned it."

"I've got a question," I said. "What're two New Jersey cops doing at this landfill?"

Bobby turned to look, and his jaw tightened. "Tour's over, folks. Chuck will show you out. Hope you enjoyed it as much as I did." He half ran along the boards toward the gates.

"It was real informative," J.W. called after him. "Can we come back?"

"Anytime," Bobby answered over his shoulder. "I'm always available for questions."

"Good—it looks like you'll be getting lots of them about now," I said.

*

I waited at the shanty until close to noon, even though no trucks were coming or going. Bobby had sent them away still loaded. Then J.W. and I drove up to Sarah Rose's store.

I parked in the shade to wait for the landfill workers' lunch break. "They're hunting for something. But what's important enough to get two cops down from New Jersey to muck around in garbage?"

"Maybe somebody lost a diamond ring, or a lot of money," J.W. suggested. "One time I threw away my pay envelope with three hundred dollars in it, and I crawled into the dumpster behind my building. Tore it apart looking for that money—it was a full month's pay."

"It's something more than money, J.W."

Sarah Rose walked onto the porch and shook out a rug. I slid down behind the steering wheel, but she didn't even look our way.

"Uh-huh, and then somebody came along and dumped their garbage on me while I was in that thing. Diapers, of all things. I sure did stink when I got out of there!"

I looked at him. "J.W., you have a story for every occasion. Is every one of them true?"

"True enough. Besides, who'd know if they weren't? That's why it's good to keep moving. You never repeat yourself to people and you can gather new stories from all over. I'm thinking of going north for a while, maybe Baltimore. I've got a cousin there."

"Why would you want to leave now, with all this excitement going on?" I didn't let on how much I'd miss him if he left; that wasn't my way.

J.W. shrugged. "They say Baltimore is something to see. My cousin lives on a houseboat. I've never lived on water before. There are jobs, too, if you want one."

"You've been thinking about this for a while, haven't you?"

He nodded. "The landfill thing, it's real bad. I like a

good battle as much as the next person, but this one isn't going right."

"You can't just turn your back on us, J.W. We need your help."

"Collier's not my home. I decided a long time ago that I'd move on when I was ready. You've been real good to me. But I didn't ever say I wanted to die here."

"Just don't leave without telling us, in the middle of the night or something."

He laughed. "I'm in no hurry. Long as I'm there for the Fourth of July, I'll be happy. They do big fireworks, right over the water. My cousin says—"

"There they are. The cops, and Bobby's with them. You go on in the store, make sure you get in before they do. Order two or three sandwiches from Sarah Rose, and listen real hard to what the cops are saying while they're waiting around for their lunches. Go on, fast!"

After the policemen disappeared into the store, I walked around back. Through the window I saw Hunter asleep in the big recliner, the television tuned to a golf match. Carefully I let myself in and edged over to the curtain covering the doorway into the store. I heard J.W. ask for extra onions on his ham sandwich and then change his request to horseradish, and then change it again. "Just on half, I guess. Leave the onions on the other half."

Through the gap in the curtains I could see the cops paw over Sarah Rose's merchandise. "My boy would like this," one of them said, waving the Stars and Bars. "He's studying the Civil War in history class now."

"How about this?" The other policeman picked up a cap and stuck it on his shiny bald head. The patch on the cap read: "Don't like my driving? Dial 1-800-EAT-SHIT."

"That'd go over great on the Jersey Turnpike," his companion said. "Go on, buy it."

Bobby Halsey looked jittery. "You boys get what you

want, and put it on my tab. I'm going out to make a phone call. Be right back."

"Oh, and one more." J.W. was still at the counter. "A roast-beef with all the fat cut off, and a slice of cheese on that, on a hard roll—and some lettuce, but only if it's fresh." I stuck my hand between the curtains and motioned for him to quit.

"I'm about done here, fellas," he told the policemen. "We get mighty hungry down at the landfill."

"Suppose you do." The bald one came over to the counter and watched Sarah Rose work. I moved away from the curtain and flattened against the wall. "You boys are getting a real workout today, huh?"

J.W. coughed. "Yeah, sure are. Just hope we find what we're looking for."

The cop rubbed his shiny head as if he was smoothing back hair. "It's a sick world we're living in, it really is."

"What do you mean?" J.W. bit into his sandwich.

"I mean, who'd toss a baby in the garbage? Christ almighty, what do you think I mean?" the cop said.

"Well, yeah, of course. We've been wondering, I mean, what makes you think it's buried here?" J.W.'s hands shook.

"The baby's been missing for over a week. Some route driver in Queens calls and says he might have seen her go into the truck from a dumpster over there. Says he thought it was a doll at the time." He turned to Sarah Rose. "I'll take a salami and onions on the wheat bread, with mayo and mustard. Make that two. It's going to be a long day."

Come on, J.W., don't let him stop talking, I thought.

"You all right, Sarah Rose?" J.W. asked. I peeked between the curtains in time to see her fall to the floor.

"Lay her out flat," one of the cops said. "She's fainted."

Wasn't that just typical of Sarah Rose! Though I wasn't feeling any too wonderful myself thinking about that baby. Hunter snorted and sat up in his chair, and stared at me like he'd never seen me before in his life. I left before he figured out who I was.

I ran around to the front of the store and met Bobby Halsey on the steps. "Sarah Rose is hurt. Call the rescue squad!" I told him.

J.W. sat with her while the bald policeman wiped her forehead with ice wrapped in a cloth. "She's okay," he said. "I don't see any cuts."

Bobby knelt and helped Sarah Rose sit up. Her face was dead-white, and when she took his hand her fingers were blue. "What happened?" he asked.

The bald cop stood. "We were telling your man here about the baby, and the lady fainted."

"Who—J.W.? You told him about the baby? He has no business knowing anything about that!"

"Sure he does," I said. "You couldn't keep it a secret past this afternoon, anyway. You know this place better than that, Bobby Halsey. Now you've got a mess on your hands. A dead baby up there."

He glanced at Sarah Rose, who was beginning to get a little color. "Enough of that talk. You want Sarah Rose to black out again?"

"She'll have to toughen up if she's going to hang out with the landfill crew. Now that it's a graveyard and all."

"Shut up, Reba! Not now." J.W. helped Bobby lead Sarah Rose to the back room. Then he returned to make the policemen their sandwiches, and said he'd stay the afternoon at the store.

The paper came out the next morning with a big picture of the New Jersey policemen and Bobby Halsey standing over Berkley digging in the garbage. The police left late in the day, empty-handed as far as we knew, the Dixie flag flying from the rear antenna of their cruiser.

JESSE PAXTON

Berkley walked in the back door and seemed not to notice me at all.

"Hey," I said. "I got us some spaghetti for supper."

He sat down at the table and looked at his hands.

"Sarah Rose gave it to me." I set the jar of sauce in front of him, and he turned away as if it made him sick.

"I'm not hungry just now. We'll eat later."

I saw that his eyes were full of tears. His sadness was as big as he was, and took up all the air in the cabin.

I touched his shoulder and sat with him. After a while he started talking, told me about digging all day for the baby. "We didn't find her." He stared straight ahead with his eyes like glass.

"Did you expect to?"

He thought for a little bit. "No, but it's a hellish thing not to know about something like that. It would have been hard on us to hit that child's body with a shovel and bring it up. But at least her parents could rest." Tears ran down his cheeks—I'd never seen that before, though I'd heard his sad sounds late at night.

"Quit that job," I told him.

"You don't know anything about it."

"I know I get picked on at school because of it."

"And because of me," he said. "I know what goes on in school."

There was no use denying the truth. The silence got so bad I couldn't stand it, and when he hid his face on the table I left and went down the mountain.

I thought about those tears, about how they'd fall and fall until the water leaked into Berkley's boots and how they'd leave wet prints on the rough wood floor when he got up from the table. That was how much sadness I felt in my father then. And it scared me more than anything else in my life.

*

It took me fifteen minutes to get to the Castle, cutting through the McPhersons' field. I'd picked up two apples at the store for Sunny; he ate them in big, slobbery bites and nosed my pockets for more. He followed me across the field as if I was his best friend. I wished it could be that easy with Amber.

Inside the Castle I looked over the Cyclorama. I'd gotten the sky right, the smoky yellowish-gray that Sharon had described. I'd used the grain lines in the wood as trees, blurring the leaves among them, the way you'd see them through smoke. The rim of hills was at eye level. Sharon had told me that the mountains up there in Gettysburg were different, gentler, she said, and smoother than they were here. I thought I'd gotten them right, too, arching in the background like hogs' backs.

I opened my tin of markers and started on a group of Confederate soldiers camped along Seminary Ridge. Some of them were lying down with their heads propped on their knapsacks. I made one of them get up and dance to the harmonica being played beneath the oak tree. "You all dance now," I said. "Some of you'll most likely be dead this time tomorrow."

Then I put a woman in a wagon alongside the road, but I had trouble with the horses in their harnesses, so I let the wagon sit there, broken down. It made me feel better not to work on the shooting part just then, as if I was making a little spot of peace and quiet for myself and the soldiers.

I drew pots of stew and loaves of bread. I drew a dog wearing a Yankee cap, its paws crossed, lying in front of a tent. I drew a soldier not much older than I was, reading a book; I guessed it was the Bible. Stars were coming out in the darkening sky, and in the corner the sun was just a slash of red above the hills. As I worked, I heard metal clanking and smelled the stink of too many men together in the heat. I smelled gunpowder and bad meat and fear—all that Sharon had told me was there in the Frenchman's painting. And I wished there was something I could do to keep those soldiers from the next day's harm. Right then I wished I'd never started the picture at all.

To make it better, I drew a couple of angels floating in the smoke above the fire, and one in the big tree the sentry leaned against. And I put in a hospital tent, but without the saws I'd read about, the ones they used to cut off legs and arms. Then I drew some daisies growing in the field, like the ones getting ready to bloom in the pasture, and put a chain of them around the sentry's neck.

Below me, Amber climbed through the pasture fence and put her arms around Sunny's neck. They stood that way for a long time, and it looked as if they'd been carved whole from one piece of wood. How would it feel to be so joined with something, I wondered, to care about it so much you'd leave your friends without a second thought? Amber's mother came to the fence and called her, then called her again, louder, until Amber finally let go of Sunny and went into her house. I closed up the Castle and went home.

Berkley was at the stove stirring the spaghetti. "Get your plate, son," was all he said.

At dinner we talked some about school. I didn't tell him about Ford punching me after gym class, and he never asked more than I wanted to say. Sometimes I wished he would, wished he'd ask where I'd been and who with, like I heard kids at school say their parents did. It seemed to me not such a terrible thing that a father would put himself in the center of his son's life to keep him safe.

He looked almost happy when I showed him the yearbook with my sketch on the cover and inside. "That's real nice," he said. "You're getting good."

"As good as Sharon?"

"I can't say. She drew things different than you do."

He carried his plate to the sink. "I have to go back down for a couple hours. We're getting time and a half for working nights."

"Talk about her, why don't you, Berkley? Tell me about my mother."

He turned to me, and in the dim light of the single bulb above the table, his face was washed out and terrible.

"I want to know," I whispered.

"She doesn't matter anymore," he said.

But I knew better. When he hugged me, I smelled his remembering, like damp cardboard in summer heat. Berkley hadn't thrown my mother away; he'd just stored her someplace I couldn't get to.

I stood on the porch and watched him work his way down the mountain, his flashlight like a firefly in the darkness. Fireflies—I needed them in my picture. Fireflies were everywhere in July, even on a battlefield, even in Amber's room, even where there was no one to see them.

The landfill glowed orange in the lights; a bulldozer beeped and ground its gears working the garbage. The wind had shifted, and the stink pushed up the side of the mountain, sharp as the edge on Berkley's pocketknife. Close below, the men were working to cover a load that looked like a whole house had been bulldozed: a kitchen table, chairs missing legs or seats, a rocking horse without its tail, splintered boards, paper everywhere—was it letters, or homework, or pages from a book? Red fabric strung across the dirt like a royal carpet, like a river of blood, like the creek running red with the soldiers' blood in my mural, when I had the stomach to paint it.

Then I saw Berkley, throwing a long shadow across it all, take up his shovel and begin to dig, the metal ringing sharp against the rocks.

I couldn't stand to watch anymore. I walked into the cabin and lay on Berkley's bed, tried to read a book, but the words didn't make sense. I walked around inside the cabin and knew how a caged tiger felt. I slid Sharon's chest from under Berkley's bed and tried the lock. Then I took a hammer and broke it open.

I lifted out the clothes, putting them up to my face and breathing in the smell of dark and my mother. But that wasn't what I wanted.

Then her shoes and books, even the tortoiseshell combs she'd used to hold her hair away from her face and the skin oil she'd left behind. Patchouli, the label said, and when I unscrewed the cap the smell of faraway places stung my nose. Impossible places, where maybe she was now. I tucked the bottle in my shirt pocket to keep.

Down deeper in the chest I found what I was looking for. I spread the sketchbooks on the floor and flipped the pages. One whole book of Berkley, without the sadness. My father in a tree, the dead chestnut that had fallen the year before and taken the clothesline with it. Sitting with Sarah Rose and Lucy beneath the wisteria vine in bloom, the flowers such a real purple you smelled the spice in the air. Standing on the cabin porch, a ponytail hanging down his back. Naked, half lying down, one huge hand over his private parts. And I wondered if she had done these from memory, or if Berkley had lain there for her as she drew and looked and drew some more.

One of the pads was mostly empty, and the clean cream-colored paper begged to be filled. Once more I went into the chest and pushed deep in it until I found her supplies. Charcoals and pencils and pastels, watercolors and tubes of oil paint, some of them unused. I took some pencils and the pad of paper outside and began to draw. It was all fast, right there before me; there was no need to stop and remember or make up a life for what I saw, because the dump had a life of its own and all I had to do was let it charge through my hand onto the paper.

When I finished, I hid the pictures under my bed; they burned and glowed all through the night. I pretended to be asleep when Berkley came in. Long after he fell across his bed fully dressed, I lay awake and felt my bones stretching and my joints popping and aching, and I hoped I wasn't growing into a giant like my father.

REBA WALKER

We boarded the bus in the Kroger parking lot at six o'clock Friday morning. In the east the sky showed red through fish-scale clouds; we'd be driving home in rain.

I'd set up our meeting with Miss Finnerty and her people for eleven. George was driving back to Richmond and wanted me to ride with him, but I told him no, I wanted to be right there on the bus with the others.

Karen and Bill were first on, took the rear seat and snuggled up together under an afghan. Patty followed, her hair still in rollers, carrying a little suitcase.

"It's her beauty stuff," Chance explained. "She never goes anywhere without it."

"I want to be ready for the cameras," Patty said. "After Reba looked so sloppy on television last night, people need to see we're not all so careless with our appearance up here."

How I looked wasn't what bothered me about my television appearance. It was what they'd done to me—or hadn't done. A fresh-faced reporter named Rick and a cameraman had come the day George's story about the dead baby hit the Richmond paper. We'd sat in the shanty, J.W. and I, and talked to them for more than an hour. I forgot about the camera and microphone in front of my face and told Rick everything. About the big wind that blew the trash into the churchyard, about the dead fish, about the traffic, about the mud all over the road, and about the bridge weight limit being changed. I told him that nobody would listen to me in Richmond, and how I'd gotten through to the governor and been hung up on. I talked up our committee and made sure he knew what SOME stood for. And I used Bobby Halsey's name in as many bad ways as I could, mentioning Wesley Ferris now and then for good measure.

Afterward I'd walked them over to the church and told them about the Memorial Day service, how the preacher had had to spend his time talking about garbage and sin instead of remembering the dead. When we crossed the road to take pictures of the dump, Rick's face turned a little green with the stink, and I thought to myself, Hell, we'll get the whole thirty minutes tonight.

I'd saved up my breaks at work so I could watch the late news. Tamyra sat with me, doing her nails. "So *that's* what you have to do to get on TV. You have to cause trouble." I moved my chair closer to the set and turned up the volume.

We got forty-five seconds right before the sports announcer did his thing on Little League. They showed me in the shanty, J.W. sitting behind me nodding, and I said, "It stinks to high heaven." As if you wouldn't know already that a dump would stink. A whole four seconds of me talking. The rest of the time they showed the garbage and the road, broken up and filthy. And Rick's golden voice taking what I'd told him and making it all sound so smooth and matter-of-fact, like everything was under control.

"He's real cute," Tamyra said.

"Real cute. He's just real cute." I went back to work and tried not to think about it all.

George told me that's what they do, take plenty of film and then go back and chop it into pieces to fit a slot. "As much as you talk, you must have been a dream to film and a nightmare to edit. You came across fine. Remember, this isn't about you. It's about the garbage, and that report helped plenty."

"That's all well and good. But next time I'll do it different," I replied. "I'll play politician, I'll know ahead exactly what I want to tell people, and whatever question they ask me I'll turn it around so my comment fits."

The bus rolled onto the interstate, and the wheels thumped across the concrete in a steady rhythm. I closed my eyes and leaned against the window. Nobody was talking much; Bill was snoring in the back, and I heard Patty rummaging around in her case. "Lock that damned thing up," Chance told her. "You've got three hours to get yourself pretty!" J.W. put on a Patsy Cline tape, and I dozed off, a sack of truck logs on my lap.

In my dream I was back at the Jackson School again, in Lucy's class. She was young, prettier than she'd been in real life, her cheeks pink and her hair a chestnut brown that gleamed in the sunlight. The funny thing was that I wasn't a schoolgirl: I was middle-aged and dressed in sweatpants and sneakers. Lucy didn't seem to notice and went right on with her lesson.

Sarah Rose sat in the front row, directly in front of Lucy; her head nodded in time with Lucy's voice, and she raised her hand like a shot when Lucy asked for a volunteer to read. "Figures," I said to myself. When Sarah Rose stood up and faced the class, I saw that she was young, too, and the hate I'd always held for her flooded my dream.

A car horn cut into the quiet and woke me up. Below the bus window, George's Honda kept pace; he smiled and waved at me. I looked, and looked again. He was reading a book! It was perched on the steering column and George moved his eyes between it and the road. I pointed at the book and shook my head. He showed me the cover: Louis L'Amour. The man was going to get himself killed over some damned western. "Put it down," I mouthed. He laughed and sped up, settling in front of the bus, as if he thought our driver would maneuver his car for him.

"He must be some kind of smart, reading while he's driving," J.W. said from the seat in front of me.

"Huh. It's pretty stupid, if you ask me. He's going to run himself into a ditch." I settled back in my seat and listened to Patsy sing "I Fall to Pieces," and thought about George wrecking his car and going up in smoke the way Patsy did in those Tennessee mountains. I tried to shut the picture out of my mind.

You could hear it in Patsy's voice—she knew she was going to die young, and she couldn't keep the sadness out of her songs. That's what made her so good with the words. She knew firsthand about love and pain and being left behind; she didn't have to pretend.

"Let's sing something," J.W. said. "This ride is getting long."

"Later. Keep quiet for a while and give us some peace." I wanted to find my dream again, Sarah Rose and all.

I closed my eyes, and pretty soon there was Hunter, sitting in front of me, his back straight and his hair black as jet. He wore the red flannel shirt Sarah Rose had made for his sixteenth birthday. I tapped his shoulder, and when he turned around he'd become George, with a cigarette between his fingers and a notebook in his shirt pocket. He winked at me and whispered, "It's your turn next. Do you know your lines?"

I didn't. I stood up and opened my mouth, but nothing came out. And then Hunter, or George, began to whisper the words I needed. I read perfectly, the rhythm all mine. When I finished, Lucy smiled and told me I'd done the best in the class.

And oh, the victory I felt when the bell rang and I stood up to leave with my man on my arm.

*

We stopped for breakfast at a Shoney's. George was in the parking lot asleep when we pulled in. I banged on his window and he sat bolt upright with the worst look on his face. "Dammit, Reba, don't ever wake me up like that. You'll give a man heart failure." He lit a cigarette and got out of his car.

"It's smoking, not me, that will do that to you, George." I took the cigarette from between his fingers and threw it to the ground.

"I've warned you about doing that!" he snapped.

"I'm just trying to help you. Don't get all riled." He'd hurt my feelings, but I'd never let him know.

"I have an ex-wife who used to try to help me out. She called it saving me from myself."

"Fine. Lord knows I don't want to be like your ex." I caught up with the others and let the restaurant door swing shut in his face.

"Is this a bus?" the hostess asked.

"Chartered," I said.

"We ask buses to call ahead." She stood there with her menus pressed to her chest and her feet planted on the tile floor.

"Well, some of us came by car," I said.

She scanned the dining room, which was half empty by my calculation. "I'm afraid we can't accommodate you all at once."

"Well, I'm afraid you're going to have to, honey. We're on our way to Richmond to meet with the governor, and we have to be there by eleven o'clock."

She looked me up and down, and then J.W., whose pink tie was five inches wide and had tiny green crocodiles on it. She didn't need to find words for what she thought of us; her face said it all.

George stepped up front of the group. "How would it be if we split up and took two tables in each section? That way we wouldn't be so much trouble for one or two waitresses. They really are meeting with the governor. And I'm covering it for the Richmond paper."

"All right," she said finally, as if it was going to break her back to seat us. "I'll take you eight at a time."

I looked at George. "Thank you so much, Mr. Big Shot. I guess we can't even get seats in restaurants without your two cents' worth."

"Cool off, Reba. Let's just do the job here and get back on the bus." He followed the hostess and left me standing there.

I made sure he was seated far away from me, and I hoped he burned his mouth on the bad coffee.

Patty skipped eating to fix herself up, and she did look good when she came sashaying by the breakfast bar trailing Elizabeth Taylor's fancy perfume. "I've got you a couple muffins in my pocket," Chance said. "Grab a coffee to go—we're leaving."

She sat down next to George and took a piece of toast off his plate. He looked at her and smiled, and I knew he was smelling that perfume and loving it. Her breast was about an inch from his arm, and I watched that arm to see if he'd move it, but he didn't. He thought about it, though.

I stood up and whistled. "The landfill bus is leaving in five minutes. Hit the johns and load up." The hostess hurried over and shushed me. I thoroughly enjoyed the look on her face when I asked for separate checks. I was sure she went in the back and washed her hands real well after we left her restaurant.

We crossed the Blue Ridge and skirted Charlottesville. I pointed out Monticello to J.W. and told him about the dumbwaiter there, how Thomas Jefferson had used it to bring wine up from the kitchen, and about all the nooks and crannies in his house, how he had it fixed up so it suited him perfectly. "I read they were digging in his garbage dump now. They're finding all kinds of things in there. That's how they discovered he was probably having an affair with one of his slaves."

"Maybe someday they'll dig in our dump like that," J.W. said.

"Yeah. There'll be plenty to find. That baby, for one thing."

We stopped talking and looked out the window at the mountains flattening out, the trees thinning, the dirt turning to red clay and then sand as the outline of Richmond rose in front of the bus.

I stood in the aisle. "Listen up, people. We're going to be in some heavy traffic pretty soon, so let's get a few things clear while we're moving along smooth. We'll be at Miss Finnerty's office in less than an hour. She said she'd meet with all of us at once, as long as we keep things orderly. We have to agree right now that there'll be no shouting or smarting off."

Karen raised her hand. "That hold for you, too, Reba?" Everybody laughed.

"Sure it does. We have them all to ourselves, but just for a few minutes, so we'll have to work fast. The schedule is this: Finnerty and her people will let us speak our piece. I'm guessing they'll follow that by reading the results of their latest water tests. Then we'll give them the results of *our* water tests. We have fifteen minutes with the attorney general—Kane promised me that—and maybe with the governor. Kane's making sure he gets credit for arranging everything, and he'll be there with us through it all."

"Sure he will," Chance muttered. "He'll get himself on television, too."

"We're not in Richmond to worry about Richard Kane," I said. "Or the television cameras. We're going to have to watch ourselves and be good, plain and simple. If everything goes as planned, they'll be found out as liars soon enough."

"Get down, lady." The driver frowned at me in his rearview mirror. "I can't see a thing with you standing there."

I sat, feeling the crush of traffic on the beltway. Richmond was a thousand times the size of Collier, and it looked to me as if every single citizen's car was out on the road. When we crossed the James River, muddy and dark, I thought about Cedar Creek, carrying the filth of the dump into the Jackson River and then into the James, Richmond's water source, George said. And I resolved right then not to drink a drop of tap water the entire day.

Kane met us at the front door of the Capitol Office Building. "It's always special to have Ambrose County folks visit," he said, grabbing at everybody's hand. "I get lonely for home when we're in session." George had done his job: his photographer friend was shooting pictures, and two television crews filmed us walking up the stairs to Angela Finnerty's office, Kane's hand on my shoulder as we walked.

Miss Finnerty had three of her people around the table, half buried behind stacks of paper. When she saw our T-shirts she tried hard to keep smiling for the television people. "So many of you—wonderful!" she lied through her pretty white teeth.

"Isn't it? Fifty-seven in all. We raised the money by selling these shirts. This one is for you, compliments of the Ambrose County Save Our Mountain Environment group." I held it up in front of her and the cameras rolled. She kept right on smiling, and when the cameras cut off she handed the shirt to her secretary.

"I appreciate your being here today," she said, "so that I can hear your concerns and share with you our latest findings. You're to be commended for your actions."

Patty stood as close to Miss Finnerty as she could, smiling at the cameras. George moved in so he could take notes. "Stay cool," he mouthed to me.

Finnerty and her people went into action. She gave charts to everyone, which she claimed showed safe levels of seven chemicals in the water samples taken after Memorial Day. The lambs had died of natural causes, she said, handing out the autopsy reports from the Fish and Wildlife people. It was just what I'd expected. She went on for more than twenty minutes, tossing around numbers and words and paper.

When Miss Finnerty asked for questions, I raised my hand. "I don't think you're telling the truth, like you didn't last month. But this time I can prove it." I reported on what Douglas had found out from his scientist friend. "I took my own water samples at the dump a while back. We had them analyzed by someone outside your office. The water sitting in the landfill holding ponds is full of PCBs, nitrates, lead, and toluene."

"That water is contained and hauled away for treatment. We're talking about the water in"—Finnerty checked her notes—"Cedar Creek, which you claim is poisonous and is killing fish and animals."

I cut in. "Water from the landfill is running straight into Cedar Creek. You can see it plain as day."

"In order for the results to be scientifically comparable, water samples have to be taken at the same time, the same place."

"That's hard to do, seeing as how your people are never out at the landfill!" My face was hot, and I worked hard to keep my voice civil. George cleared his throat.

Chance pushed forward. "That's right. The only time we saw you at the landfill was back in April, before you showed up at the meeting. Why should we believe your results any more than you believe ours?"

Kane moved next to Miss Finnerty. "Let's keep this peaceful."

"Let's tell the truth!" I said. "Mr. Kane, you live in Ambrose County, too. How can you stand there and listen to this?"

"Of course I'm concerned about our water, Ms. Walker. If I'd had my way, the facility never would have opened on that piece of land. But it did, and it's my job, working with these people, to assure it's run safely. Which Ms. Finnerty tells us it is."

I'd had enough. "That's a goddamn lie, Richard Kane. You had the weight limit changed for White's Bridge so those garbage trucks could use it. You're good friends with Bobby Halsey and Wesley Ferris. Most likely you were the one who steered them to that piece of land!"

"Accusations don't belong in this meeting," he said.

"They're true." The television cameras were turned on me, and I knew this was my chance to set the record straight. "You're making money on the poisoning of your own district, aren't you?"

"This meeting is over," he said.

"We were promised some time with the attorney general and the governor."

"I'm sorry, friends, but Mr. Lanier was called out of town last night on government business, and Governor Andrews had some unexpected business come up," Kane announced.

"You could have let us know!" Bill shouted.

"Calm down. The governor left word he'd be happy to meet with you all first thing Monday morning."

"We can't stay over the weekend. We've got jobs and families waiting back home," Chance said.

"I'm sure the governor will reschedule at your convenience," Kane responded. "I'm sorry about this. Really, we did try for you folks."

Chance kept after him. "Where the hell do you think we're going to get the money to charter another bus? Is the State going to pay?"

Miss Finnerty had disappeared, leaving an assistant to hand out copies of her charts to the reporters. Kane tried to attract the cameras, but both crews followed us down the stairs. There was Rick again, sticking his microphone in my face. I made certain that both cameras were on me. "The State of Virginia is allowing its waterways and wildlife to be poisoned by northern garbage. And the people of Richmond are drinking that poison out of the James River every day, sure as I'm standing here with this folder full of evidence."

George pulled me aside and hugged me when I finished talking. "You did great. Your statement will tie up Angela Finnerty's phone lines for hours. You need to be here to follow this up. Can you stay the weekend? I can drive you home Monday afternoon. My editor wants a full-page overview of the landfill story for next Thursday, so I need to go back then anyway."

"I can't. I have to work the weekend."

"Reba, you can't back away from this. You just accused the State of Virginia of poisoning its citizens. If you go away now, you're nothing but a crazy woman. If you follow through, see the governor Monday, you're a citizen hero. This is what you've been working for. Don't lose it all."

Patty came up behind us. "Come on, Reba, we're eating in the cafeteria downstairs, as Mr. Kane's guests. Then he's giving us a tour of the Capitol." She pulled on George's jacket. "C'mon, he'll feed you, too."

George grinned. "I doubt that—I don't vote in his district." He looked at me and waited for an answer.

"I can't afford a motel for three nights."

"I have two bedrooms. And I'll be working most of the weekend, so you'll have the place to yourself."

"If you think it's that important, I'll stay," I said.

Patty stared at me. "Reba—"

"Just shut your mouth and go eat, or go eat and then shut your mouth, Patty. You and Chance make sure everybody is at the bus by three o'clock. And I don't want any of your gossip flying around town while I'm gone. This is strictly business."

She stood up tall and saluted. "Right. No questions, sir." Then she went back to the group and took Chance's arm. When she passed me, she winked.

*

George's apartment came as no surprise to me. It was cluttered with newspapers and magazines, and the floor-to-ceiling shelves were loaded with books. The stale air stank of cigarettes and rotten bananas, so I opened the windows.

"Keep those shut, I'll turn on the air-conditioning," George said.

"Bad air is bad air, even if it's cool. If I'm sleeping here, I'm going to need to breathe."

He loosened his tie and tossed his notebook on the kitchen table. "Suit yourself. Once the sun moves around this side, you may change your mind."

While he called his office, I checked his refrigerator for something cold to drink. Three beers, some dried-up cheese, a box with two half-eaten slices of pizza. A wrinkled apple and three spotty carrots, a jar of spaghetti sauce black around the lid, a quart of milk I knew was bad without smelling it. I popped open a can of beer and wiped off the top with my sleeve. I didn't much care for Budweiser, my taste for it ruined by having heard stories about it being flavored with piss from those big Clydesdale horses that pull the wagons. But I'd rather drink horse piss than Richmond water.

"Make yourself at home," George said. "My editor wants me in the office this afternoon—he says he's forgotten what I look like. So watch some television or something. I'll show you the city after we have dinner."

"I need to call Shirley and let her know I won't be working this weekend. Then maybe I'll take a walk, buy myself a toothbrush. Are there any stores near here?"

"You shouldn't go out by yourself." He stuffed papers into a briefcase. "You don't know this area at all."

"Hell, George, I'm not an idiot! I've been in a city before, and I read maps just fine."

He tossed me a key. "Do what you want, then. Just lock up when you leave, and don't lose this key. It's the only one I have—my ex kept hers."

From the front window I watched him walk to his car. Why was he letting me stay here? Did he do that for all his stories? Maybe that's why his wife left him, that or his never being home. One thing I was certain of: She didn't leave because he beat her up. He just wasn't the type. But then, I guessed smart people, the ones who lived by their brains the way George did, found other ways of hurting the ones they loved. Maybe hitting wasn't the worst of it.

I walked down the hall and checked out his bedroom and the bathroom, which smelled like the underside of a mushroom. In the closet of the second bedroom I found a woman's robe and slippers behind some boxes, and I wondered who they belonged to. Probably his ex-wife, but maybe George was a real ladies' man, a city swinger. You never could tell with men. I finished my beer, put the key in my pocket, and headed outside.

Before I'd gone a block, my dress was stuck to my legs, and my panty hose had rubbed my thighs raw. I pushed my hair off my forehead, and when I looked at my hand it was orange with the makeup I'd put on before facing Miss Finnerty. I was melting like a tar baby.

All around me walked men and women who seemed not a bit troubled by the heat. The men hung their jackets over their shoulders and showed off their starched shirts. Their pants had creases sharp as skinning knives. And the women were all pretty, and their clothes expensive-looking. Some of them wore sneakers and socks and walked fast for exercise. I was wearing shoes I'd grabbed from the back of my closet. They were too tight, and my feet were swollen from the long bus ride and the heat.

Being surrounded by so many pretty people made me think about the difference between Patty and me. She put a lot of effort into her appearance, and it showed. I didn't, and that showed, too. Mostly I didn't care; I just went about my business and forgot how I looked, figuring people were going to talk about me one way or the other. But here I felt like a mutt at a fancy dog show.

The drugstore I found was cool, and I took my time wandering the aisles with a plastic shopping basket hanging from my arm. I stopped at the perfume counter and tried on a few scents; the girl behind the counter watched me with her eyes slitted. She acted like she owned Richmond, or at least the store. My hand itched to slap her smooth cheek. Hard.

I picked out a twenty-eight-dollar bottle of cologne, thinking about the stunned look on George's face as he sat in the restaurant breathing in Patty's movie-star fragrance. I added some fancy bath oil and a seven-dollar lipstick and headed to the register, tossing a toothbrush into my basket on the way.

I didn't have enough cash with me, so I started to write out a check.

"Sorry, we don't take out-of-town checks." The clerk crunched on ice from a McDonald's cup. "Collier—where's that?"

"West of here, Ambrose County. Look, my money's good." I worked hard to keep my voice down.

She pointed to a sign on the side of the register. "It says right here, 'No out-of-town checks.' "

"I can read," I said. "I'm just telling you my check is good."

"If you need cash, there's a money machine down the street. Let the guy behind you pay for his things while you decide what you're going to do."

"I don't use money machines. We don't have them where I live," I said through my teeth. "Do you want to sell me this stuff or not?"

She shrugged. "If you pay cash, sure. If you don't, no way." She crunched on her ice some more.

I turned to the man behind me. "What the hell kind of place is this? This store would be out of business in a month in Ambrose County. All I want to do is pay for a few things."

He stared at me. "Say, you were on the news the other night, weren't you? With Rick what's-his-name, Channel Nine. You're that garbage-dump lady."

"I guess I am." I smirked at the girl.

"Hey, you people are doing good things down there. That's a disgrace, all that garbage from up North being dumped in Virginia." He tapped the counter with his bottle of antacid. "You go on and take her check—she's all right."

The clerk looked at him uncertainly. "I can't. I'll lose my job."

"You sure were good. Stood right there in front of all that garbage and told it like it was," the man went on. "Look, I'll tell you what. You write me a check for what you owe, and I'll pay for everything."

The clerk seemed satisfied with that and totaled the sale. "There you go." She handed me my bag. "On TV, huh?"

"Watch the news tonight. We'll be on again." I was enjoying the attention plenty. I thanked the man, and he pumped my hand as if I was a famous politician.

"And little girl, let me tell you something about that ice you're crunching on," I said.

She looked at me, then at her cup.

"That ice, it was made from city water, right? And your city water comes from the river flowing by our dump. Lord knows what's in it these days. You'd best start drinking bottled water." I turned and walked out of the store.

The humid air hit my face like a steaming towel. The sidewalks were less crowded, most folks back at work after their lunch hour. Those who were still out seemed to look at me differently now, as if I was somebody, shining bright in the city sun.

LUCY McCOMB

Reba takes her victories where they lie. A man in a drugstore says to her, Push on, fight to the bitter end, and she walks proudly down the street, fire burning in her eyes, her shoulders thrown back like a conquering soldier's. There is nothing she cannot do, she thinks, and she feels it is a good thing to be in Richmond after all.

It is good she has this confidence. For this war is like every other: not to be won easily, and not without the waste of spilled blood. The garbage buried on my land will poison much more than simple water and earth.

You ask, Doesn't it pain you to see what they've done to your house and land? Everything you did—keep the yard and garden weedless, starch the curtains each fall, throw open the windows and wash down the walls just before Easter, dust the baseboards every Saturday and climb on the porch roof to do the upstairs windows four times a year, hang handmade garlands on the porch at Christmas—was for nothing. They've torn down the curtains and used them as towels for their filthy hands. Bored and angry, Chuck Mitchell shot out all the upstairs windows the day they closed the gates to look for the baby. And that baby, that tiny girl, is she lying buried somewhere on your land?

The house and the yard don't matter. They were mine for as long as I needed them; I kept them clean and neat because it suited me to do that. Now I am gone, and they are gone, also.

The baby bothers me. They will never find her, although they will search again. Her mother will live in sorrow the rest of her life.

It is for this mother that I grieve: for the pain and struggles endured by the living. For Sarah Rose and Hunter, eaten alive by the guilt of selling my land. Reba, banging her head against the wall trying to make herself heard. Berkley, doing the best he can for Jesse, all he has in the world. And Jesse, who will bear the burden longer than any of them.

The night wears on. Sarah Rose lies with Hunter in my bed, the bed in which Mac Avery died. Hunter's eyes are clear—it has been one of his good days—and he holds his wife, looks out into the moonless night and sees the future.

She rubs the fur on his belly and slides her hand lower, feels his hardness and shivers, remembering the past. She knew both times when his seed had taken, from the way her body had arched toward him so eagerly and held him so long. During fertile times hers was an absolute hunger that demanded his attention throughout the night. And in the morning she would rise and let her breasts hang free beneath her dress, as if the joined cells were already crying out for sustenance.

Sarah Rose lies in Hunter's arms and looks out the window into the night, drapes her leg over his groin and waits for him to move. Although she is well past menopause, from somewhere deep down the urgency comes and she wants only to love her husband as a young woman, as if he were a young man again. She wishes that the future still stretched before them like a fragrant tunnel, lit by the belief that their lives would be whatever their dreams willed.

Hunter takes Sarah Rose in his arms and runs his hands over her body, delighting in her heat and soft curves. He shuts his eyes and loves his wife frantically, his hands seizing the fire that burns brightly beside him.

Reba lies in George's bed, and yes, George is beside her. The streetlights shine through the slats of the blinds, and that doesn't suit Reba well.

"How the hell do you ever get to sleep here?" she says. He looks at her and shrugs, touches her cheek gently and kisses her. Reba stiffens and sits up, the sheet pulled tight beneath her armpits.

George rolls over and reaches for a cigarette. She says, "Is this a goddamn romance movie or something, you smoking in bed with a woman?" He smiles and says, "This isn't any romance movie, it's a horror film!" She glances at him with a scared look in her eyes, and when she sees he's teasing, she laughs and leans her head on his chest. They stay there until the ringing phone takes George away. Reba fans herself with a magazine and thinks maybe she will ask George to turn on the air-conditioning after all. She is grateful that at home it cools off at night.

He comes back grim-faced. He sits on the edge of the bed and takes Reba's hand. The hot air moves between them in waves. "They've burned down the shanty," he says.

JESSE PAXTON

They said Berkley was the one to light the fire. The sheriff came up the mountain with a welfare lady and told us we'd both have to go with them. "Somebody called and claimed they saw you carrying something into the shanty last night, Berkley. A man burned to death in that fire," he said.

"I worked my shift and came on home. It wasn't me." Berkley buckled his belt and ran his hand through his hair.

"There aren't too many folks around here your size, Berkley. We got a witness saying it was a real big man, big as you," the sheriff said.

"I told you, it wasn't me."

"You're the only one it could have been. There's nobody else around here to mistake you for."

Berkley bent to tie his boots and didn't answer.

"You going down with them?" I asked. "You didn't do anything. Don't—"

"Pack some things, and we'll run you over to Sarah Rose's place, son," the sheriff interrupted.

I moved behind the table. "I'm not going."

The welfare lady moved toward me. "We can't leave you here, Jesse. You come on to your aunt's, or we'll have to put you in a foster home until this gets straightened out."

"I'm not going—you don't go with them either, Berkley. They can't make us go." I looked at him, and he looked back at me with his eyes empty. "You say something!" I shouted.

The sheriff put his arm around me. "Come on, your aunt's waiting on you. Otherwise you'll have to be with strangers. You don't want that."

"It's Hunter's fault," I said. "I won't live with them."

"Go on, Jesse. Get your things," Berkley said quietly.

The sheriff and the welfare lady went out on the porch and left Berkley and me alone for a minute. "We could run," I whispered. "Go out the back, hide. I've got a place—"

Berkley shook his head. "No use doing that. We'll get clear of this. Don't make it worse than it is."

Nobody talked going down the mountain. It was hot for so early in the morning, and the garbage smell was powerful. The welfare lady held a handkerchief over her nose and kept saying, "Phew! What an odor!"

What an odor! I mimicked her in my head. An odor. No, a stink. A black, bad dream. Like the hole where the shanty had been, still smoking. Men wearing big gloves bent over what was left of the shanty, picking up pieces of burned wood and looking at them like they were some kind of treasure. People stood around and watched, and when we drove past in the sheriff's car, most of them turned and stared.

When we got to the bridge, the sheriff slowed the car and let two trucks come across. The drivers waved and he waved back. "Phew," the welfare lady said again, putting that handkerchief over her nose and mouth. "My Lord, that's bad. How do you tolerate that odor on the job, Mr. Paxton?"

As bad as things were, a smile tickled the corners of Berkley's mouth. I knew the things he was thinking and hoped he'd go ahead and say some of them. But all he said was, "You get used to it. The smell doesn't matter."

The sheriff was looking at Berkley in his rearview mirror and didn't notice the old green car coming toward him right down the center of the bridge. "Watch it!" the welfare lady shouted, and grabbed the sheriff's arm. He hit the horn and slammed on his brakes, and luckily the driver of the other car did, too.

It was Reba with the newspaperman. She rolled down her window and called for the sheriff. He walked over and leaned against the car, his holster at a funny angle. I couldn't hear Reba, but I knew from her expression she wasn't happy. The sheriff put his face right up close and shook his finger at her, and Reba jumped out of the car, hitting him in the stomach with the door. The two of them stood in the middle of the bridge yelling at each other until the newspaperman got between them.

"That woman better be careful. She's going to land herself in jail," the sheriff said when he came back. "I know Reba's upset and all, but you don't yell at an officer of the law, you just don't do that."

Sarah Rose was on her porch watering plants when we got to her house. She kept on, even when the sheriff and the welfare lady led me up the steps with my things. Hunter sat at the open window with his chin on the sill. The sun shining through the lace curtains speckled his face.

"It'll be temporary, just until your brother posts bail," the sheriff told Sarah Rose.

She turned to the welfare lady. "Jesse's welcome here as long as need be. I'll make sure he gets to school. Take your things inside, Jesse." I smelled her anger burning deep within her, like scorched milk. But her face was smooth and pale, beautiful to look at. I went in the house and listened at the window with Hunter.

"You know Berkley didn't do this," she said to the sheriff.

"I don't know that, not yet. We've got fire experts here now, looking for evidence. I hope as much as you do that it points somewhere other than at Berkley."

"The last thing Jesse needs is to be taken away from his father," Sarah Rose told the welfare lady.

"I don't think it's going to hurt the boy to be down off that mountain for a while," she answered.

"He belongs with his father," Sarah Rose shot back.

"He belongs with other people," the lady said.

"He's with other people all day at school—whatever good that does him."

"Give her hell!" Hunter shouted. I bit the side of my mouth to keep from laughing.

The sheriff took the welfare lady's arm. "We'd best be on our way. She'll be by to check on things," he told Sarah Rose. "Don't take it personal."

Sarah Rose ignored him. She walked to the car, hugged Berkley's neck, and whispered in his ear. She made me wish I had a sister who might someday do that for me. The last I saw of my father was the back of his head hitting the roof of the sheriff's cruiser as it bounced down the rough driveway.

The parking lot was full when we got to the store, a half-hour late. I sat in the back room with Hunter while Sarah Rose took care of customers, explaining over and over why she had opened late, and being polite when they asked questions about Berkley. Hunter flipped channels on the television every three seconds. "Where's Geraldo? He's on mornings. He's good."

"It's Saturday, about all that's on is cartoons. I'll try to find you something." I turned to TNT, and after a bunch of commercials, a movie came on. Hunter heard the music, and his eyes lit up. "I remember this one, it's got everybody in it. Gregory Peck, Jimmy Stewart, John Wayne, Henry Fonda, Walter Brennan. *How the West Was Won,* 1962. I drove Sarah Rose all the way to Richmond to see it on some special screen that made it like you were part of the movie."

He went on about feeling the buffaloes' feet crushing your bones, and how the steamboat whistle cut right through to your heart, and how the gunfights went back and forth across the screen with you in the middle of the flying bullets. It made me want to see that movie on the big screen, too, instead of on a little black-and-white set in the back room of the store.

"And Debbie Reynolds, she's real feisty. She looks good in those long dresses because they cover up her short legs. She has the prettiest red hair. I think Sarah Rose named Deborah after Debbie Reynolds. She always admired Debbie's spunk, and how she played in clean movies and was still a star." He settled back in his chair with a happy look on his face.

It was funny how Hunter could remember everything about a movie he saw almost thirty years before, and forget my name as often as not. But that was how it was with his mind these days.

I heard Amber's mother out front, and sure enough, Amber was there too, holding a carton of milk and a bag of Sarah Rose's rolls and looking at the candy bars. She chose a Snickers and put it on the counter with the milk. She was probably hoping her mother wouldn't notice it among the other groceries. Mrs. McPherson was at the counter with Sarah Rose, talking about the shanty. Sarah Rose had a terrible look on her face. Amber moved up front to the tapes, and I listened the best I could to what Mrs. McPherson was saying.

"They're thinking it was J.W. killed in the fire, but they won't know for sure until the fire investigators finish up. The thing is, nobody's seen J.W. since we got off the bus yesterday and went our separate ways. And when Bill and I went to his place this morning, it didn't look as if he'd been home at all."

There were tears in Sarah Rose's voice. "I knew it was J.W. I knew it when you called and told me about the fire. They don't need to waste their time sifting through the ashes for clues. Lord, Karen, a man's dead, and he lost his life over a garbage dump. And my brother's in jail."

"Sarah Rose, we don't think Berkley did it. I can't say I like his working there, but he's not a killer. Bill and I . . . we plan to raise the bond for him."

"No need for that. I'll put up the farm."

Amber walked over and took her mother's arm. "You promised you wouldn't be more than five minutes. I want to ride Sunny before it gets too hot."

"Let her go, Amber, let her finish," I whispered. She glanced around with a funny look on her face.

"Jesse, come take Amber's money," Sarah Rose called.

I came out to the register, and Amber handed me a five-dollar bill. "I'm sorry about your daddy," she said.

I shrugged. "He'll be home soon—maybe tonight."

I knew that wasn't true, and so did Amber, but she didn't say anything, just pushed the candy bar toward me and asked if she had enough money left over to pay for it. She didn't, but I said, "Sure." When I handed her the bag, I was surprised that my eyes were level with hers. I was definitely growing.

"I found your fort yesterday," she said. "It's pretty weird, you drawing those pictures all over the walls."

"Maybe it is." I smelled her curiosity strong as the honeysuckle that wrapped around the legs of the Castle.

"Where'd you get that idea, about those soldiers and all?" She peeled back the wrapper of her Snickers and took a big bite. She had a dreamy look on her face, like the angels floating up to heaven in Sarah Rose's Bible storybook. Chocolate stuck to her upper lip, and her cheeks were pink.

"I could explain it to you if you want—the picture, I mean. Sometime."

"Do you watch me ride when you're there?" she asked.

"Mostly I go to draw," I lied. I rattled the pennies in the register, wishing she'd stop asking questions.

Hunter poked his head out between the curtains. "Come in here and watch this movie with me, boy. They don't make them this good anymore."

Sarah Rose led Hunter back to his chair. She'd been crying, but she tried to act like nothing was wrong. When Amber and her mother left, she went into the back room and cried some more.

Amber was in the Castle when I pushed up the door and lifted myself inside. "Your horses are terrible," she said, without turning around. "I'm working on them."

I sat and watched her, breathing in her good scent. A little part of me wanted to tell her to leave; she was in my place, putting herself in my mother's and my own picture. And I wanted to touch her, but I didn't, couldn't. This was good, I thought, this was enough, the way the sun heated up the air and added an edge of her sweat that cut somewhere deep in me.

"So how come you're doing this?" she asked.

"It's the Battle of Gettysburg," I explained. "There's a huge round building up there, and inside is a famous painting by a Frenchman, called the Cyclorama. They turn out the overhead lights and spotlight the painting, talk about the fighting and all. It's like you're right there."

"But how come you're drawing this? It's sort of strange, but it's really good, except for the horses." She pushed her hair away from her eyes. Her shirt had damp half-moons under the arms. Looking at her made my muscles go tight.

"It's something to do, you know?"

"There are lots of things you can do besides paint war

pictures on old deer blinds. And how come you know so much about that Cyclorama thing?"

"I've seen it."

"You've been up there, to Gettysburg?"

"I didn't say that. I just said I'd seen the painting. In a book."

"You can remember all this from seeing it in a book?" She tapped her pencil against her knee and then tossed it to me. "Keep on. Pretend I'm not here. Just leave me the rest of the horses."

I saw she'd drawn the horses just right. She knew how their necks would turn when they were scared and how they would stand tied up at night, with one side of their hind ends higher than the other, their heads low to the ground. She drew horses from the inside out, the same way I did the soldiers lying on the ground, part of the Army of the Confederate States but really pretty much alone.

She sat and watched me while I worked on the angels I'd left from last time. Why they were in my picture I wasn't sure; the Frenchman hadn't done angels, at least not that I could see. I drew them perched in trees, like big white birds, their eyes turned toward heaven. Their sweetness was everywhere around me. "My mother used to tell me about this painting before she went away," I said. "She's why I'm drawing it here, I guess. I don't know, it's just the right thing to be doing now."

Even before Amber touched me, I felt her hands: those good hands that knew so many things, that could unwrap a candy bar as if it was a present from God and that someday would take a horse into thin air and disappear. Her touch made me put down my pencil and forget the Frenchman and the guns, the smoky air and the pain that hung in it. Laying her hands on my back, Amber walked into the center of my life. There was no reason to ask why; all that mattered then was the light and arc of it in the small wood box that was my Castle.

REBA WALKER

No one had to tell me it was J.W.'s ashes in the shanty. I knew all along, and he did, too, that he'd never go to Baltimore. He had everything he needed in Ambrose County and nothing to gain up North.

George and I left Richmond before dawn. George called his editor and told him he'd be gone again, then hung up before the man had a chance to yell. We drove through the city and ran the red lights; that was all right, George said, because nobody else was fool enough to be out in a car this time of the morning, and if we got stopped he'd just tell the officer he was going to a fire.

"And he's going to believe you?" I said.

"It's the truth, isn't it?" He looked at me, and I turned away so he wouldn't see my tears in the brief flashes of the streetlights.

"Who do you think did it?" he asked after a while.

"Halsey and Ferris, Chuck Mitchell, maybe. Or a trucker. It could have been any of them, tired of seeing us there. Hell, we didn't deserve that."

"Of course you didn't, Reba. You've got to give up the idea that things happen for a reason, for something you've done. That shanty burning had nothing to do with you. It was a warning to everybody there."

"Just shut up for now," I said.

I thought about George's hands on my body. At first I'd pulled away, afraid that he was using me, that he'd tricked me into staying the weekend so he could have a woman to sleep with. Then it didn't much matter, because I realized I could use him as much as he could me, now that I was beyond worrying about getting pregnant. It had been a long time since I'd been with a man. And George was as good a man as any, better than most.

I played the whole thing back in my mind. He'd not

been in any hurry, and he seemed truly interested in knowing my body, what made me feel good. Why was it that all the time I was married I never once understood what pleasure was? You can read about that kind of thing, listen to other women talk, and think on it till the cows come home. But until you feel it, you'll never really know.

I cracked my eyes open and peered at George, half visible in the exit-ramp lights. There he was, big belly and thin hair and all. Here I was, gone soft and country-dumb. And together we were better than Richard Burton and Liz Taylor.

George lit a cigarette and the match flared, and I remembered why it was we were in the car, driving west at five-thirty in the morning. Behind us, the sun worked its way between the land and the night sky, a sliver of red that soon grew broad and pink. George took my hand, and neither of us said anything until we crossed the Ambrose County line.

Four trucks idled in Sarah Rose's lot, the drivers lounging on the porch steps. "The fire has everybody limping," I said. "I can't remember Sarah Rose ever being closed this late."

We started across the bridge. "Now, take it easy up here at the shanty, Reba. It's going to hit you hard," George told me.

I crossed my arms and stared out the window at the trainyards below without answering. He took my arm and squeezed. "Come on. I'm as tired as you are. I'm just trying to help."

I saw John Anstett's cruiser just as George hit the brakes to avoid it. I caught my breath, then rolled down the window. "Come here, Sheriff."

"Careful, Reba." George got out of the car.

"John, you always drive with your eyes closed? You could have killed us all!" I said.

"Watch your mouth, Reba." He hooked his thumbs in his belt loops.

I opened my door and hit John in the gut. He grunted and moved back enough for me to get out of the car.

George stepped between us. "Sorry, sir. My mistake. Didn't get much sleep last night, and we've been driving since before dawn."

"What's your excuse, John? You were over the line, too." I looked into his cruiser and saw Berkley in the backseat. "Taking somebody in?"

"That's none of your business, Reba. You're on thin ice here. Just get in your car and we'll all go on our way." He was a little man, barely five and a half feet, and it was good he wore a gun, because it was about the only thing that made people listen to him.

George pulled John aside to talk. Two trucks idled behind us on the bridge and made it shake. I imagined the bridge collapsing and us falling, pieces of us scattered along the railroad tracks. "George! Get this car off the bridge, dammit!"

He motioned to me to be quiet and kept writing in his notebook as if he had all the time in the world.

It took an ambulance with lights flashing to get the sheriff and George in their cars and off the bridge. "They're moving the remains to Richmond," George told me.

"What's their hurry?" I got no answer.

We passed the shanty site, where two county workers wearing paper masks were shoveling the mess into a dump truck. "They're dressed like they're working around the plague," I said.

George parked next to Chance's pickup. Bill was in the back unloading lumber. "It's a little narrower here," he said, "but the new shanty ought to fit if we scale it down some."

"Well, there'll be one less person taking up space," I said loudly. "We could hang J.W.'s picture on the wall, I guess." Chance looked at Bill, and they both stared at me, but I didn't care. I'd push through this the way I'd always pushed through hard times.

"Come on, Reba, I'll drop you off at your house. I want to make a few calls."

I ignored George and took up a shovel. "Where do you want me to dig?" I asked Chance.

He pointed at two blocks of wood a few feet off the road. "There's where the front end will sit. The back posts will go along the edge of the cemetery."

George left, and I walked down the hill, using the shovel for support. Bill tossed a ball of string to me. "Pull it tight," he said. "And start just where the knots lie. Go about three feet down. We've got a post-hole digger when you're ready."

I set to work with a vengeance, bearing down hard on the shovel. On the bank above me, Bill and Chance measured and sawed the lumber. The garbage stink was all around me. It clung to my skin, and as soon as my sweat washed it off it was back again. I worked until the holes were almost a foot deep, then stopped for a rest, my breath coming fast.

I walked among the graves, picking off the dead flowers left from Memorial Day. I was surprised to see that Sarah Rose hadn't been back to care for her babies' graves, or Lucy's. I sat next to Lucy's headstone and let my mind wander.

Who'd have imagined it would come to all this, Lucy McComb? That your home would be on television, that I would, too? That pretty Sarah Rose would have a crazy husband on her hands, that she'd be feeding the very people who pushed him to craziness? And now, an innocent man dead. All the poems and commas you taught us don't mean a damn thing in the face of this kind of trouble.

And yes, me, too. Who'd have thought I'd be taking care of your friends at the home: Helen Sanders, wetting her pants; Grover and Cleveland Lee, deaf as you are now, going on about The War; Edith Halsey, staring silently at the ceiling. Here I am, with a newspaperman lover, up against the governor. Reba Allert, the worst student in your class every year you had me. You didn't need to say what you thought of me, what everybody thought of me. I was the one headed for trouble from the very start.

But you cared about me, even though I treated you the way I treated everybody else, angry all the time. Even after I quit school and married Danny, had two kids one after the other and stopped thinking about things for ten years while he was beating me senseless—you still talked to me when you saw me on the street.

It was you who left the basket of food outside my door that first Christmas after Tim was born. I know it was you, knew it then, but I couldn't say thank you, and I don't think you expected me to. Is this fight—the shanty and the meetings and the long days eating truck dust—is *it* my thanks to you?

I stood and brushed myself off, took up the post-hole digger and stabbed the hard earth. Lucy's face remained before me, stern but clear of judgment. By the road Chance and Bill measured and sawed, while Patty sat on the tailgate of Chance's pickup and logged trucks; other people came to kick around in the ashes and stare. I worked until the shadows were short and my stomach growled for lunch, then walked up the hill and handed Chance his tools. "I did what I could with those holes," I told him.

"They look fine. Go on home and get some sleep."

"Yeah, maybe I will."

Bobby Halsey and Wesley Ferris watched us from Lucy's porch, the two of them sitting on lawn chairs like passengers on a cruise ship. I knew beyond doubt that Bobby was responsible for the fire. He may not have put the match to the wood himself, but he might as well have.

Bobby came down the driveway and called me to the gates, an orange soda in his hand. "Here's a cold one. I'm real sorry about the shanty."

I took the can and waited for him to say more.

"Who do you think was inside there?" Bobby took my arm and moved me out of the way of a truck entering the gates. "It's awful what happened. I hate it. You folks ought to lie low while they find who did it. Nobody wants any more violence."

"You'll have to kill me next," I said.

"You're getting in deep, Reba."

"Not as deep as J.W. will be once his ashes come back from Richmond, you goddamn murderer!" I slapped his face.

"I'm not going to report this, because you're upset." Bobby rubbed the red blotch on his cheek.

"You're damn right I'm upset, Bobby. Tell me who burned down the shanty. Was it one of your men, or one of Ferris's? Where's he hiding now—down in the coal-fields someplace? In Richmond?"

"Watch what you're saying. This isn't a game we're playing here, with club T-shirts and stakeouts in a playhouse!"

I started for home, and gave him a one-finger salute without turning around. Chance and Bill clapped and whistled as if I'd won a gold medal. But to my mind I hadn't won much of anything except the right to take a nap before work.

"Did you have last night off?" Helen Sanders asked when I came to get her for dinner.

"I was out of town. Come on, Helen, lift your feet. You know how it works."

"Wait a minute, come around here in the light," she ordered.

"You're going to be late, and Cleveland's going to get all the rolls." I tried to work her wheelchair through the door, but she stuck out her arms and held on to the frame.

"There aren't rolls—this is pancake night. Come here and let me see you!"

I gave up and stood in front of her chair.

"Look at your eyes! You've been with a man!" she shouted. "I thought I smelled it on you!"

"You don't smell anything but my soap and the pancakes down the hall—which are probably stone-cold by now. Come on, I've got other folks to take care of." The last thing I needed was Helen spreading gossip around Stoneleigh about my sex life.

"Don't lie to me, Reba. It's all right. God made us as he did for a reason, don't be ashamed of yourself. Why, when Arthur was still alive, we had a very satisfying carnal relationship." She went on about this the full length of the hall, me pushing faster and faster, until Shirley Carter caught up with us and planted herself in front of the wheelchair.

"Helen," she said, "we don't talk about those things in public." She glared at me, as if I'd put the idea in Helen's head.

"What?" Helen looked up at Shirley and cupped her hand to her ear. "I didn't hear you."

"We don't talk publicly about men and women being together," Shirley repeated.

By now Cleveland Lee and two of his buddies from the west wing had wheeled themselves to the doorway and sat watching Helen and Shirley. From their expressions it seemed they knew just what was happening.

"I don't know what you're talking about," Helen whined.

"Sex—we don't talk about sex in public!" Shirley yelled. "That's enough!" She turned to me. "You know better than to let her ramble like that. Now, get her in there. Dinner's half over. You've got a phone message at the desk—which you can return during break."

My shoulders ached as I changed beds, and I thought about J.W. If I hadn't believed in heaven, I'd have quit right then, walked away from my job and the landfill mess, maybe gone to Baltimore myself, or somewhere far away from Ambrose County. The weight of J.W.'s death was heavy on me, but I knew he was in heaven, wearing those wild ties and winking at the angels.

I took my break early and hoped no one would be in the lunchroom. I read my phone message: Someone named Kelly Holt had called long-distance. I slipped the paper in my pocket, stretched out on the vinyl sofa, and tried to sleep. Buzzers rang. Someone was crying. I could hear Ruthie Sims restrained in her bed chanting, "I don't know, just tell me," over and over.

In my mixed-up mind, J.W. came to me, smiling his toothless smile. "Did you make that phone call?" he asked.

"No, I'm just plain tired, J.W. Maybe I'll get around to it tomorrow."

"Did you make that phone call, Reba?" he repeated, and shook me until I opened my eyes, and there was Tamyra, her long red fingernails digging into my shoulder.

"Get those claws out of my arm!" I looked around for J.W., but he wasn't there.

"That phone message I took—the lady said to call before six, that it was important." Tamyra sat down next to me on the couch, hiked up her skirt, and worked out the wrinkles in her panty hose.

"You should be a stripper, girl," I said.

"My boyfriend thinks so, too." She smirked. "Who's calling you from New York City? That's the area code. I know because I have a cousin there who sings and dances in shows."

"So it runs in the family, the stripper act," I said.

"Ver-ry fun-ny. So, who is it?"

"I don't know who the hell is calling me from New York City, and the way I'm feeling, I don't care. I have to get back to work."

I splashed water on my face and took the long way to the nurses' station, catching some fresh air in the courtyard. I turned on the fountain; the water made a smooth sound in the shadows, wore the prickly edges off my nerves.

Stoneleigh was a little town unto itself, I thought, with people coming and going and minding each other's business enough to keep busy. Some of them got along and others didn't, and some were crazy and some weren't, the same as in all towns. They had church services and played cards and had their private corners to go to.

But then it wasn't really a little town, in that not many of the people living at Stoneleigh wanted to be there. That made it more like a jail, with Shirley Carter as the warden and me as guard. When I stopped thinking straight and couldn't do for myself, I'd just as soon meet my maker all at once, fast, instead of bouncing between heaven and earth like a yo-yo.

When I went inside, George was at the desk chatting with Shirley, who made over him like he was famous. She handed me some charts and told me Edith Halsey needed a bath.

George followed me down the hall. "Did you return that call?"

I laid the charts on the nurses' stand outside Edith's door. "How do you know about it?"

"She called your house first. I gave her your number here. I figured you should hear the news from her."

"I've been busy, and I'm dog-tired." I started into Edith's room.

"Wait a minute, Reba. The woman who called you is a producer for CBS. They want to do a segment about the landfill for their *Faces of America* series. This is big, Reba. National coverage. It's the best thing that could happen." He was beaming like a five-year-old on Christmas morning. "She wants you to be the spokesperson. They'll be here Tuesday."

"Good. They can film J.W.'s funeral."

George looked away.

"It was J.W., wasn't it? You heard."

He nodded. "The lab called Anstett an hour ago. It looks like he was shot first, then his body was put in the shanty and burned."

"Damn, George—" I couldn't say anything more. I cried hard, my face pressed into the front of his shirt. "Let the newspeople come on," I said finally. "We'll give them an earful."

LUCY McCOMB

Do not ever let anyone tell you there comes a time when you are ready to die. That is something the living imagine to make themselves feel better. They say, "She lived a long time, she was in pain, she wanted to leave this earth." I might have uttered such platitudes myself, empty thoughts over which I now cringe. No one ever wants to let go of life. In the deepest curves of the heart, hope and desire linger.

That is not to say you don't prepare yourself, once you know Death is due to come knocking. (And you always know that, somehow.) It's just common courtesy, in which I believe strongly. You don't invite guests into a messy house; neither ought you receive Death in one.

Here is how it was with me. The day I died, I woke well before dawn. Not gradually, but all at once. My room was still and black, the air brittle with night chill. I stared into the darkness, and it came to me like a train whistle that splits time down its center: I was starting my last day on earth.

"All right," I said to the day, "let's get on with things, then."

I dressed in the dark, putting on my violet dress, Mac

Avery's favorite. I felt my way downstairs and made breakfast. Then I gave it to the cat; feeding myself was no longer necessary. After washing the dishes, I went out on the porch to watch the sun come up. And it did, edging the horizon with a fine line of blood.

We'd buried Mac where he'd have the benefit of the early sun, and that morning I chose to share it with him. I dragged my Adirondack chair across the grass into the garden and set myself near his grave, lifting my skirt so the sun would warm my legs. Wrinkled and sagging as I was at eighty-seven, my legs were still good, my one vanity.

"Well, Mac, here I am." The pumpkin vine curled around my feet, and my chair quivered. On top of the mountain, hounds bayed—Berkley was up.

"I must clean house today. I'm starting out here with the garden. You mind?"

"Go on," he answered. "No reason for me to keep pushing up these plants for somebody else, Lucy."

"I thought as much. This garden gets tiresome. There's nothing worse-looking than a garden gone to seed." And as the sun rose above the mountain and began its climb noonward, I pulled up the pole beans, tomatoes, and peppers and threw them in a heap at the edge of the garden. The turnips and potatoes I left, so the deer might paw them out of the ground the next winter. And the pumpkins, for Jesse's Halloween.

I tucked the hem of my dress beneath my belt to keep it clean as I worked. My back hurt terribly, and I felt a headache coming on, but I continued pulling and tossing. "There go the tomatoes. Lord, look at those roots!" The ground moved and rolled as I tore at the soil, and Mac talked to me. I did not dare speak to him of the hereafter, of my absolute faith we would be together again very soon. For if he had been silent at my mention of it, I'd have known it was all for nothing: that I would never see him again.

"Ears are getting fat on the corn. I suppose I'll leave

it for the coons. They'll expect their usual share." I wiped my forehead and looked at the sun, which stood past nine o'clock.

Mac's laughter came right through my shoes. "Let them work for their food like everyone else. God knew what he was doing when he painted masks on coons' faces, didn't he?"

I unbuttoned my dress to the waist and went on working, humming a tune without a name. Mac fell quiet; he'd always known when to be still.

"Aunt Lucy. You come on in the house with me." It was Sarah Rose, standing right on top of Mac.

"I'll be in when I'm finished here," I said.

"You're ruining your garden! You come inside and get out of this sun." She thought I was crazy; that was plain. She talked to me the way one talks to a wayward schoolboy.

"Sarah Rose, will you please mind your own business. I know exactly what I'm doing!"

The earth shifted beneath her feet and she fell backward into the tall grass. She sat there with a puzzled look on her face.

I stretched out a hand to help her. "You go open the store. I'm just fine. In a minute I'll be going inside."

"I'm not leaving until I get you settled," she said.

"I'm settled—have been since long before you were born. Just leave me be, honey."

She brushed the grass from her dress. "I'll call in an hour. If you don't answer, I'm sending Hunter over to find out why."

When the phone rang, I was in the middle of cleaning the kitchen cupboards and ignored the clanging intrusion. On the last day of your life, there is no reason to answer the phone when you know who it is and you have nothing to say.

When Hunter came, I had all the doors locked; I talked to him through the screen. He sat on the porch for a while, then fixed a loose spindle on the railing and went away.

I worked well into the afternoon, following the sun from room to room as I straightened and cleaned. I looked at my house with an outsider's eye, packing away my clothes and books and carrying them to the attic. The photograph albums and family Bible I left on the parlor table for Sarah Rose. When I finished, anyone might have lived there, or no one.

From under my bed, I took the shoebox full of postcards Mac had sent, and spread them out on the floor. More than a hundred of them, from Virginia, West Virginia, North Carolina: a carpet of glossy color. My mind was keen, and I remembered the day I received each of the cards, which had come tightly sealed in brown envelopes for privacy. On all of them Mac had written the same thing: *Someday we'll honeymoon here.* On a few he'd drawn little people in the pictures and labeled them *You* and *Me*. Sometimes he'd carried one with him when he slipped into my house late at night. "Hand-delivered," he'd say proudly, and I'd prop it against the lamp to look at until the next one arrived, a month or two later.

What I had spread out in front of me was a geography of love, as true as anything I'd ever taught at the Jackson School, as big as the world, as big as the human heart. I laid the postcards in their box, which I put at the back of the closet, where the slanted ceiling met the floor.

Late in the afternoon Sarah Rose came with some food for my supper. I opened the door for her, and she walked into my kitchen looking around as if she'd never seen it before, looking at me as if I were someone to fear, and maybe I was, standing so close to Death. She struggled with words, uncertain of what to say to me, and I wanted to hug her, tell her it didn't matter, all the little day-to-day worries that clutter our minds. But as with so much in life, you must know this firsthand before you can hear the words spoken to you. I sat at the kitchen table and drank well water from a jelly jar; the cold absence of taste was delicious.

"Are you listening to me?" She shook my shoulder gently.

"No," I said. "I'm not."

"I said I went to the Stoneleigh home today to see about a room for you. I'm worried about your being alone. I can't be out here as often as I should be."

"I'm not asking that of you, Sarah Rose."

She made me tired, with her nervousness and held-back thoughts. She went on about selling the house, a pained look on her face.

"I'm leaving the house to you and Hunter. The cabin is Berkley's, it always has been. Go on home and make dinner for your husband," I said.

"Think about Stoneleigh. You'd have friends there, someone else to take care of things." She hugged me and left.

I walked out on the porch and settled in my chair. The sun was low now; its slanted light hit the side of the mountain full-face, and the trees blazed orange as if autumn had come out of turn. "You will not see the mountain in fall color again," I told myself, and my heart clamped down tight.

The gentle rocking of my chair soothed my fear, and I thought about what I had done in my life, and what I had left undone. I smelled the chalk dust and children of the Jackson School, felt their initials carved deep in the maple-top desks. I heard their shoes shuffling down hallways, their words moving together into a breeze, then a strong wind that swept the world clean. Decades of gardens grew fragrant with fresh, perfect vegetables, and leaves as green as the eyes of my youth. Books turned to dust beneath my fingers, and only the true words remained. The most important were mine: *I love the world and all that is in it, beneath it. Mac Avery.*

SARAH ROSE McCOMB

Berkley refused my offer to put up the farm to get him out of jail. They'd set the bail high and wouldn't post a hearing date. "The judge does what he wants," John Anstett told me. "You know if Berkley was somebody else, he'd have his trial over with by now. Best get your brother a lawyer."

I sold the sheep and took Richard Kane to the jail. Berkley turned his back on us and wouldn't talk except to say, "Get him out of here. Now." I knew better than to press.

It was as if he wanted to stay there, alone. Mr. Kane told me to let Berkley be; he'd work on things and see what he could do for us. I believed him, because there was no one else in my life to believe in right then.

The church was full and then some for J.W.'s funeral, people standing in back and spilling out into the cemetery. His ashes were on the altar, in an urn bought with everyone's donations.

Reba spoke at the service. "You look around in this church, and you won't see anybody here you don't know," she said. "J.W. didn't leave behind any clues about his family, all those wives he claimed were his. I don't know anything about his cousin in Baltimore, either. What I'm saying is, we were J.W.'s family. And I think he liked that pretty well.

"There's plenty you could say about J.W. He lived right, without worrying about money or things. We could take a lesson from him on that. You look across the road at the landfill and see what people waste. If we were all like J.W., a good share of that garbage wouldn't be there, because we'd buy only what we needed and wouldn't have a lot of extra stuff cluttering up our lives.

"I hate that J.W. won't be with us to see the landfill closed down. Because he worked harder than just about any of us at the shanty. Most of us, we had other things that we put first: jobs, our families, beauty shop appointments. But J.W. gave it all he had. We owe it to him to fight as hard as he fought and make sure the people responsible for the dump and for his death are brought to justice. Soon."

Chance and Bill each took a handle and carried the urn outside to the far corner of the cemetery, by Thomas Isaacs's statue. The minister reached his gloved hand into the urn and brought up a handful of ashes. He scattered them around, speaking words from the Bible, and most of the remains fell into the grass. But the wind was strong—a storm was coming out of the northwest—and it picked up the lightest bits of J.W. and carried him high into the air.

Behind the fence, the landfill workers stood and watched us. Most of them had their hats off. Bobby Halsey had stopped the trucks during J.W.'s service, and he stood on Lucy's porch talking on his phone.

"He's probably setting something up with his hit man," Reba said for everyone to hear.

"Maybe he's got a direct line to God. Maybe he *is* God," Patty said. Her eye makeup had run down her cheeks, and she looked as if she hadn't been sleeping much.

"He's closer to the devil than to God, Patty," Reba commented. "Speaking of which, how about you run over there and *scare* the dump shut." Patty gave her a dirty look and took out a mirror.

"Reba—you did a nice job for J.W.," I told her.

"It wasn't hard." She started up the hill to the shanty.

The wind blew the first fat drops of rain into my face. "I'll miss him, too," I called after her, but she didn't hear me above the noise of the trucks and the wind.

I ran for my car and sat inside crying, knowing my tears were as much for myself as for J.W. The rain came hard, in sheets driven by the wind. The florist's truck pulled off the road behind me, and the delivery boy ran to my window with a wreath of pink carnations that had seen better days.

He banged his elbow against the glass. "Who gets these?"

I rolled down the window. "The service is over. Who are they from?"

He shrugged and handed me the flowers, then hurried back to his truck. I read the card. *Please know that we are thinking of you in your time of sorrow. Bobby Halsey and staff.*

I got out of the car with the wreath in my arms, a funeral stink rising up from it. Then I walked to the landfill gates and threw the wreath into the driveway. "Damn you all to hell," I shouted.

The carnations disappeared beneath muddy truck tires as the rain fell harder and thunder rolled off the side of the mountain. When I got back into my car to leave, I saw Reba standing like a statue, watching the trucks come and go at the dump.

A television crew arrived at the store early in the morning a few days later. When they got out of their rental car they looked as if they'd been lost in the woods for a couple of days. The woman in charge was named Kelly Holt, and it seemed everyone else was there to do her bidding.

She was all business, explaining to me what they'd be doing. "We'll be filming for two days. I want to talk to everyone you can think of, Mrs. McComb. We'll shoot at the landfill quite a bit, and also get the area as a whole."

I fixed coffee and a plate of rolls, and the TV crew settled on the porch. The sun shone bright and clean, the wind blowing from the east, clear of the landfill. The cameraman ate as if he'd run out of food back in New York; Kelly stuck with coffee, black.

"I'd like to start with you, Mrs. McComb," she said. "Can you tell me a little about yourself, anything that might help me understand your perspective on the landfill?"

"I'm not very good at talking about myself. Maybe it would help if you called me Sarah Rose."

"Fair enough. But only if I'm Kelly to you."

Just then Reba pulled up in her truck and came to join us. She stuck her hand in Kelly's face and introduced herself. "Sorry I'm late."

"Not at all," Kelly said. "I was just getting a little background information from Sarah Rose. I understand you went to school together. Maybe you can add a different perspective."

Reba smirked at me. "Sure. Well, Sarah Rose was what you might call a good student—always had her homework done on time, paid attention to the teacher, had her finger in everything. It got tiresome, really."

"Now, wait a minute, Reba," I interrupted. "I'll talk for myself!"

"What do you mean?" Kelly asked.

"I mean," Reba went on, "you have to wonder why somebody would spend all her time trying to be perfect."

"Oh." Kelly smoothed her hair. "Now, the store. Sarah Rose, how long have you been running it?"

"This store's been in the Paxton family for three generations. It's not much now, with the big chain stores taking over."

"And the land—had it been in your husband's family that long?"

"Longer. McCombs owned that land right off, since the eighteen-twenties. They donated the site for the church and cemetery from the original parcel, and the mountain behind the landfill was theirs before it became National Forest."

The camera whirred, and we talked about the dump, about what we noticed and when, how we felt about things. Reba put in her two cents' worth whenever she could, even though Kelly asked me the questions. Finally she had one for Reba.

"Tell me why you think the McCombs sold the land." All three of us sat very still, and the quiet grew bigger the longer it lasted.

Reba looked up the road. "Same reason I'd sell you something, or you me, I guess. They needed the money, plain and simple. Sometimes you can't afford to hold on to things, you know?"

Kelly turned to me. "Sarah Rose?"

I nodded, not trusting my voice to say anything. The camera stayed on my face until I got up and went inside without a word.

"They gone?" Hunter asked. He'd wet himself, and the store smelled of urine.

"No," I said. "But Reba will do the rest just fine."

REBA WALKER

I gave Kelly my coveralls and said I'd take her up the mountain for a bird's-eye view of the dump. We drove my truck to the shanty, and the cameraman filmed Patty logging the dump traffic. She kept turning to glance at the camera, and Kelly told her to just do the job and forget they were there. "My profile's bad," Patty said. "I look better face-on."

The sun beat down on the garbage, and Kelly covered her nose with her hand. "You get used to it—not that you don't smell it, you just learn to live with it," I told her. The cameraman vomited in the ditch.

In Berkley's absence, the path to his cabin was already

starting to narrow. Thorny vines pulled at my pantlegs, and in the shade the rocks were slick with moss. We stopped for pictures at the overlook. Below us, the bulldozers pushed the garbage in waves into the ravines they'd dug, the bright sharp edges of the trash shifting like bits of glass in a kaleidoscope.

"My God, it almost seems alive," Kelly said.

"You've got that right. Alive and growing bigger every day."

We went on to Berkley's and rested on the porch. Kelly had the crew film us there. "This is lovely. Log cabins have always fascinated me."

I laughed. "Not me, I wouldn't want to spend a winter in a place like this. No way you can keep it warm. Belongs to Sarah Rose's brother, Berkley."

"The one who's accused of killing the man . . ."

"Berkley didn't do it." I called to the cameraman: "Come on, we'll get better views farther along the ridge."

"Wait a minute. What makes you say that Berkley is innocent?" Kelly asked.

"I didn't say he was innocent. Anybody who's working in that hellhole isn't innocent. But he didn't kill J.W. He had no reason to—had nothing against him. We all know it was one of Halsey's people. You can talk to the sheriff about it."

We walked the ridge single file, stopping twice for the cameraman to film. "We're going to need some background music for the show. Can you put us in touch with a bluegrass group?" Kelly asked me during one pause.

"This isn't bluegrass country, really."

She seemed surprised. "You know what I'm looking for—mountain music, something to complement the scenery."

"No, I don't know. I like Patsy Cline, Loretta Lynn. Karen McPherson still listens to Bobby Vinton. Saturday afternoons in the store, Sarah Rose tunes in to the egghead station for a dose of opera. Bobby Halsey probably listens to the Grateful Dead. Hell, we aren't the Beverly Hillbillies here."

"I didn't say you were." She fell back with the cameraman and left me alone.

From where we were now, we could see the full reach of the garbage, which poked up through the dirt spread by the bulldozers; the machines were dumping along the borders now, clawing away at the mountain to make more room. The holding pond was full, covered with a rusty scum. Little streams ran from the edges and dug deep gullies in the dirt.

"I don't believe what I'm seeing," Kelly said.

"I keep telling people the same thing, but it doesn't do a damn bit of good," I said. "You recognize anything down there as yours?"

She laughed nervously and looked sideways at me.

"I'm serious. You come here full of good thoughts, about how you're going to tell the world that this landfill is plain wrong, and look at these poor people out in the hills having all this stuff dumped on them. That's fine. But it's nothing new—we've always been pushed around one way or another. We're going to make you a good story, aren't we?"

"That's not why we're here, Reba."

I ignored her. "The funny thing is, it's *your* garbage in that dump—your newspapers and tires and throwaway this and that. So it's just as much your story as ours, isn't it? How about if we use 'New York, New York' for the music?"

"I understand what you're saying. But I also know what will make people sit up and pay attention to what's happening here. And it's not playing opera behind panoramas of this landfill. We're going to do the best job we can, that's what I'm promising you."

Kelly and her boys brought in their equipment before the SOME meeting. The crew ran cables everywhere and fooled with the lights until I told them to move out of the way and be quiet.

Kane sat in the front row. He'd heard about the television crew, so he called me and said he had some information for the group and wondered could he have a few minutes to talk. I told him five and hoped he'd stop at ten.

Karen did the prayer and called for a moment of silence for J.W., then announced that donations would be collected. I stole a look at Kane, who made sure he was filmed putting a twenty-dollar bill in the plate.

Bill gave the treasurer's report. "We need to do another fund-raiser, folks. Chartering the bus to Richmond pretty well wiped us out. Everyone's turning in phone tabs, and since we took on J.W.'s funeral expenses, we're going to have to get some major money in here soon. Anybody have any ideas?"

"How about we plan something for the Fourth of July?" Chance proposed.

"What do you have in mind, honey?" Patty asked. "Fireworks?"

"How are we going to do fireworks, Patty? You have to have a license for that. You don't just walk into the Dollar General and buy the big ones! No, not fireworks. Something else that'll get people out and spending money," Chance said.

"Maybe I could do makeovers, like they do at the malls," Patty suggested.

"Just how many women are going to come around looking for makeovers on the Fourth of July?" Bill said. "It's got to be something to get everyone interested."

"What about a yard sale?" Karen asked. "If we all cleaned out our basements, we could have a heck of a good one."

"That's asking people to donate things they'd sell for themselves," Brenda Campbell complained. "I buy school clothes for Ford with the money I make at my yard sales."

"Isn't Ford the one who wears those fancy sneakers that cost close to a hundred dollars?" Karen said. "Seems like you could sacrifice a little bit, considering."

"Seems like I can live my life any way I please," Brenda shot back.

"Let's settle down! Nobody has to be a part of this who doesn't want to be," I said. The yard-sale idea passed; Brenda refused to vote.

Kane checked his watch, then stood and walked to the front of the room. "Friends, I have another meeting to attend at eight o'clock. I wonder if you would let me speak briefly before I have to leave."

Everyone looked at him. "Go on," I said, and stepped aside.

He smiled. "Thank you. I want to take this opportunity to pass on some items that will be of interest to you all. You're to be commended for your fine sense of civic responsibility."

"Get on with it," someone called from the back.

"First, I spoke with the governor this morning. He asked me to convey his sympathy regarding the recent accident at the shanty."

"It was no accident!" Chance called out. "He knows that as well as we do."

Kane flushed. "The governor also asked me to tell you that he is personally overseeing the investigation. I assure you, the guilty party will be punished."

"You think that makes us feel any better, considering the governor couldn't be bothered to see us when we went to Richmond?" Bill asked.

"I'm not going to tolerate this kind of rudeness." Kane's beefy face shone brick-red in the television lights.

I waved my hands. "Hold on! Let Mr. Kane have his say. It's not going to do any good talking back to him like this."

Kane went on about the phone calls he was making for us and how we were doing a good job keeping the landfill in the newspaper. "Things are happening in Richmond I can't discuss right now, but rest assured that the wheels of justice are rolling."

They're rolling, all right, I thought. *Right across our faces.*

"Thanks, Mr. Kane, for those encouraging words. Now let's get on with the plans for the yard sale," I said.

Kane wasn't quite finished. "Just a couple more things. I'd like to announce that the governor will be making a special trip to the landfill in the next several weeks. He'll be bringing with him the heads of the Department of Solid Waste Management and the Water Control Board." Kane looked pleased with himself as applause broke out around the room.

"And the second thing is this. Since I'm in the middle of my campaign for reelection to the House of Delegates, I won't have time to clean out my basement. But please accept my donation of two hundred and fifty dollars to your treasury." He handed me a check and smiled at the camera.

We were not ones to turn down money, no matter why it was given. "Let's get this in the bank tomorrow, early," I whispered to Bill. "Now that it's on film, he may stop payment on it."

"Either that or it's written in disappearing ink," he answered.

We adjourned early so that everyone could go home to watch the end of the Braves game. Kelly was happy with what the crew got, and I told her this had been a pretty quiet meeting.

"We'll be leaving early tomorrow afternoon, after I spend some time with Mr. Halsey," she said. "I wanted to ask you, do you know anywhere I could pick up some quilts?"

"Pick up?"

"Well, buy. I promised a couple of my coworkers I'd look for quilts while I was here, since . . ." She hesitated.

"Since what? Since all us mountain women sit around down here stitching quilts? You're a real piece of work, you know?" I left Karen to lock the church and went home.

"Quilts," I said out loud. "Hell, I wonder if she'd buy my old electric blanket."

JESSE PAXTON

Hunter woke me. He went up and down the hall, up and down, talking to someone named Eugene, or else he was saying, "You, Gene." Either way, nobody was there. I waited for Sarah Rose to take him back to bed, but she didn't. She must have been used to his wandering, or maybe she was just too tired to get up.

The moon was big outside the west window, and the white light shone on my bed, across my chest and face. I thought about Berkley in jail, about whether the moon was shining in on him, too. We'd gone to see him before supper. He met me in a room with a table and two chairs. The door had a window, and the deputy checked on us more than he needed to.

Berkley looked bad, like a washed-out picture of himself. He said, "I'm almost out of here," and I didn't know what to say back, because it wasn't true, he wasn't getting out of jail anytime soon, so I said, "Maybe."

"There's no maybe about it. I am getting out of here."

"Okay. I didn't mean it that way," I said.

"You doing your schoolwork?" he asked.

"Thursday's the last day. We're having a picnic."

"You need to take something?" He worked his hands together as if he was cold.

"Sarah Rose'll give me food from the store."

"Get five dollars from the cabin and buy something for your teacher."

I felt my face flush. "Nobody does that anymore, Berkley."

Down the hall, two men were yelling at each other. "Turn that shit music off!" one shouted, and the other answered, "It ain't shit, it's Willie Nelson." The deputy disappeared from the window.

"They go at it all the time," Berkley said. "One of them plays only country, the other listens to gospel music all hours."

I made myself laugh. "Sarah Rose brought you some tapes, I don't remember who—"

"It doesn't matter. I'm not going to be here much longer." He took my hands in his. "I'm not."

The deputy brought Sarah Rose in. He watched her unload her bag onto the table: three cassettes, a couple of paperback books, a sack of cookies, clean underwear. The deputy looked at everything and then took me outside to wait.

The hall smelled like coal and sweat and metal. Somebody had started to wash the walls but had quit too soon: they were streaked with black, and you could still make out the bad words, ones I'd seen in the bathroom at school. Inside the room with Berkley, Sarah Rose was crying. I wanted to be finished with the place; I ran for the door, but the deputy caught me and brought me back to wait. He kept his hand on my shoulder until Sarah Rose came out.

Now, lying in bed, I felt the guard's fingers pressing into my skin. Hunter was in the kitchen, rattling the silverware. "Where'd I leave that thing?" I heard him say. Metal against metal. I thought, *Knife, he's after a knife!* and covered my head with the sheet. But it was hot, so I pushed back the bedclothes and opened the door.

There was Hunter, his pajamas half buttoned, holding Sarah Rose's big stirring spoon in his arms. "I just wondered," he said, "where you'd gone to." It made my skin crawl to see him cradling the spoon like it was a baby.

I wasn't going to get any sleep in that house, with Hunter wandering around talking to a spoon. So I locked the bedroom door from the inside and went out the window. I set off toward home.

I passed the store. Hunter's big gray tomcat jumped off the porch and watched me with bright yellow eyes from beside the drainpipe. I caught his musky scent as I walked by the sweet-bush hedge. Sarah Rose's spotlight had burned out around back, and the parking lot was a black hole, shaded as it was from the moon by so many trees.

Along Cedar Creek, the tree frogs were going crazy. Lovestruck, Berkley called them, each one yelling a little louder than his neighbor to attract a mate, like he might die that very night without one. Mosquitoes whined around my head, and when I stopped to tie my shoe, they bit. Clouds crossed the moon, and the scent of rain mixed with the stink of the garbage.

Headlights moved toward me. I thought it might be Sarah Rose, so I hid in the tangled grass and waited for the car to go by. But it turned into Reba's driveway, and right behind it came her truck. She was laughing as she walked to the car and leaned in the front window. I stayed low and went closer, but I couldn't hear what she and the other driver were saying. Then they kissed some.

Crazy Reba Walker making out in a car. With that newspaperman, old enough to be my grandfather. I worked hard to keep from laughing out loud. But then I remembered Amber's hands on my back, and how my skin got tight, and how the only thing I knew then was that heat, flowing from her fingers right into my center.

The newspaperman got out of his car, and he and Reba went up the path to her house holding hands, their shadows stretching behind them until they were swallowed up and all that was left was me in the grass, alone.

Jesse. The wind pushed through the trees, and the grass bent down.

"Who's there?" The moon jumped higher. I started walking. Ahead of me a possum made its way out of a ditch and headed into the dump. Mosquitoes flew in clouds from the creek bottom, and I didn't bother to brush them away.

Jesse.

I crossed the road and climbed the fence into the dump. The ground was soft; it sucked at my shoes and tried to keep me, but I didn't let it. On the porch, Lucy's chair rocked back and forth next to the Coke machine, which burned red in the dark. Wisteria blooms swung above the railing, and I smelled their spicy sweetness above the stink of the garbage.

I tried the front door; it didn't open. I laughed. They locked the door—to keep out who?

Jesse. The parlor window lifted just enough for me to squeeze under, and I went in.

There the smell of garbage was worse, and mixed with workingmen's sweat. But there was also the dusty scent of old people, like the outdated books that never leave library shelves. The tall dump lights shone in the windows and made rectangles on the floor.

The room was empty except for a desk and a metal filing cabinet by the far window. Papers had been tossed all over the floor, and somebody must have been drinking a lot of Coke; the empty cans were stacked in a pyramid by the fireplace. I pulled a couple out of the bottom row, and the noise was wonderful when the tower collapsed.

The rain came hard then, pounding the tin roof and beating against the windows. It came down the chimney and pinged against the cans. I moved into the dining room and went down on the floor, breaking the fall with my hand. When I raised it into the light from the window, I saw dark blood staining my arm. Glass sparkled at my feet—the tiny windows of the china cupboard had been smashed and the mess left there like a trap.

Jesse. I followed my name into the kitchen, but all I found was more dirt, and mouse sounds. I took a rag lying on the counter and wrapped it around my hand. They'd moved the old icebox, and inside I found a McDonald's box holding a few french fries and some Chicken McNuggets, and next to it a baseball cap with a pen clipped to the brim. I took the pen and drew a heart on the kitchen door, with Amber's and my initials inside. Then I scribbled it out and wrote *Ford was here.*

The shower passed as fast as it had come. I went out on the back porch. In the east the clouds crowded together like black sheep; the rest of the sky was swept clear. All above me, the stars pulsed in time with my blood, and the moonlight turned the garbage silvery clean.

Jesse. And then it came to me: The voice I'd been hearing was Lucy's own. I went inside and climbed the stairs to her room.

I saw her outlined in front of the window, sitting square-shouldered in a rocking chair.

"What are you?" I asked.

"Lucy, your Aunt Lucy." It was a whisper, a sigh.

I sat beside her. I felt a gentle stirring of air, only the thought of a touch. My hand stopped bleeding.

"I don't know what to do now," I said. I felt so tired, and I wanted to lay my head in her lap. But I didn't know what she was, and I was afraid.

I walked to the closet. In the very back was an old shoe box coated with dust. I carried it to the window and took off the lid. Inside I found postcards, all addressed to Lucy, all in the same handwriting. I spread them out on the floor and she read them to me, every one. Her voice blanketed me and kept me warm; she made me think of my mother, and I wondered how this Lucy could be what she was. There was no end to what she told me, and she might have been Amber or Sarah Rose or Sharon or even Berkley. The moon went on across the sky and the stars faded. And when the room turned gray, I was alone.

I gathered the postcards into the shoe box and put it back in the closet. My hand ached and throbbed; I followed the spots of dried blood down the stairs, through the dining room into the parlor. I checked the desk drawers, thinking to take something with me in trade for my blood. Everything was locked tight.

The shadow that was Lucy passed before me, and I followed it into the kitchen. I found the desk key hidden in the pie safe.

I left carrying a sackful of papers, Berkley's paycheck stuck in my back pocket. I didn't know exactly what the papers meant, only that they might somehow help Berkley. And they were the only proof that I'd been in Lucy's house; her voice was fresh in my mind, and I didn't want to let go of the night. By the time I reached the store, the sun was showing above the mountain, and I knew Sarah Rose had found my locked room and then my empty bed. Not wanting her to know I'd been in Lucy's house, I worked my way beneath the store porch and pushed the sack into a musty place that I remembered from a long time before. The papers would be safe there until I was ready to let them go, until I decided who needed them the most. Then I ran toward Sarah Rose's, making up a story to tell her as I went.

REBA WALKER

The storms came almost every afternoon, with thunder loud enough to rattle your teeth. It was like the end of the world, dark and shapeless. The corn grew an inch a day, the beans set on early, and the radishes rotted in the ground.

The trucks continued to run one after another, and their tires spun deep in the muddy driveway. The men couldn't keep the garbage covered, but they were trying, since every week or so now a car with government tags pulled up and two men walked around writing on clipboards, looking official. But each time it rained the dirt washed across the road into the cemetery, and the shanty floor stayed slick with mud. Mosquitoes big as hummingbirds hung in the air and left huge welts on our arms and legs.

Berkley sat in the county jail and went soft. I can't say I was that sorry; I knew he hadn't burned the shanty, but I couldn't forget the fact he was working for Halsey.

When I heard who was defending Berkley, I drove up to the store to talk to Sarah Rose. "Why Kane? He's in the middle of all this, as sure as I'm standing here! Why do you think Berkley hasn't had a hearing yet? They know what'll happen if Berkley leaves jail!"

She looked at me with her tired eyes and said that she trusted Kane, that it was the judge who was dragging his feet on it, that Kane was working hard to set a court date. "He's always done our legal work," she told me.

It was the fox guarding the chicken coop, so to speak, and Sarah Rose was too blind or too spent to see beyond Kane's cunning ways. Though it was none of my business, I felt sorry for the boy, Jesse.

George came to Collier now and again, but he was busy in Richmond. There was an election in November, and all the politicians were saying whatever they needed to say to be reelected. George's editor cut back on his time at the landfill, telling him he needed to pay attention to some other stories. I missed him, especially at night, though I didn't tell him that.

The Sunday that Collier was to be featured on *Faces of America,* he drove down for our party. Karen and Bill set up three televisions in their family room and pushed the furniture against the walls. We all brought covered dishes and set them out on the kitchen table.

"Last time I saw a spread like this was at my father-in-law's funeral," Patty said. "What a feast! It almost seemed as if folks were trying to raise Arthur from the dead with all that food. That man surely did enjoy eating." She helped herself to a little of everything.

"Just because it's here doesn't mean you have to eat it all." Chance poked her in the ribs and made her spill her Coke.

"Quit!" Patty took a seat in front of the biggest of the television sets.

"Move, Patty!" Brenda Campbell yelled. "I can't see over your hair."

"Then get yourself some X-ray glasses." Patty started eating, her eyes on the screen.

I spoke up. "Before the show starts, let's have a quick meeting here. The Fourth of July is coming up fast, so what about the yard sale?"

"My basement's full—there's everything from an old commode to a mink jacket," Karen said. "We'll start setting up at seven. That's a.m., in the fire hall parking lot. We're running ads on the radio, and posters are going up tomorrow in all the stores and public buildings. Be sure to sign up for your shift before you leave. The list's on my refrigerator."

"Sounds good. Bill, what about the entertainment?" I asked.

"There'll be music going through the day, and we're bringing a couple of ponies for rides. I'm not sure yet, but we might have a dunking booth—if the Lions will loan us theirs, Chance!" Bill reached over and pretended to twist Chance's arm.

"I'm working on it, but you know Bobby Halsey joined last year. He's not too interested in doing anything for this group," Chance answered.

"Okay, quit the wrestling," I ordered. "This room is too crowded for that. Patty, you have the food arranged?"

"We'll have hot dogs and drinks, and we're waiting

on the Kiwanis to give us word about borrowing their popcorn machine. I need some workers, too."

"Guards are more like it," Chance said.

George spoke up. "Quiet! You folks are going to miss the show."

And there she was, Kelly Holt, standing in front of our town hall in her pink suit. Somebody in the back of the room whistled.

"This is Collier, Virginia, a sleepy little town tucked in the Blue Ridge Mountains."

"Who taught her geography?" Chance said. "Wrong mountains, honey."

Kelly's face took on a serious look. "The people in Collier are used to things staying the same. They go about their business, the way people do in most small towns." The camera switched to Main Street, with cars cruising and a few folks walking. Then they showed Junior Riley and Ray Unger, two of Collier's less reliable citizens, sitting on the courthouse steps. Junior waved his beer can at the camera, and Ray laughed as if it was the funniest thing on earth.

"Like *that's* the only business going on here," I whispered to George.

"But change came in a big way a year ago, when the first tractor-trailers bearing out-of-state garbage drove into the gates of the Buena Vista Landfill." There on the screen was the dump, with Chuck Mitchell at the gates. "Thousands of trucks bearing New York, New Jersey, and Pennsylvania plates have passed through these gates and left behind millions of tons of garbage. And the people of Collier and Ambrose County don't like it one bit."

"Doesn't take a genius to figure that out," Chance said.

"In an effort to stop the flood of garbage," Kelly went on, "people banded together and formed a citizens' action group, which they call SOME, standing for 'Save Our Mountain Environment.' We visited one of their meetings recently."

"There I am!" Patty pointed to the screen. "Lord, I look fat!"

The camera worked its way around the church social hall. Then it settled on Richard Kane, and we got to hear most of his speech all over again.

"These people have been working with their elected officials to close down the landfill," Kelly was saying. "But according to Virginia delegate Richard Kane, it's going to be a long, hard fight. Kane has arranged to have the governor and the heads of the Department of Solid Waste Management and the Water Control Board examine the landfill over the Fourth of July holiday.

"SOME president Reba Walker isn't happy with the response from Richmond. And she isn't shy about saying that her committee isn't getting the attention it deserves." They showed me sitting on Berkley's porch in my old boots and jeans. My voice sounded terrible, as if it had been slowed down. The banjo music playing in the background was very familiar, but I couldn't quite place it. I watched with a sick feeling in my stomach, afraid of what I'd hear next.

And then it struck me—it was the music from *Deliverance,* the dueling-banjos thing. "Typical," I muttered.

There was Rastin the truck driver. When the camera turned his way, he straightened his bandanna and flashed a grin. "Just doing my job," he said, and walked to his truck.

Sarah Rose was beautiful on television, as if someone had painted her on the screen, her cheeks so pink and her green eyes so clear. You could tell they liked her; they let her say her piece without cutting in with questions. I felt the old jealousy burning in my gut.

She stood behind the counter and talked about selling the land, and how she didn't see anything wrong with serving the truck drivers; they had to eat just like everybody else, after all.

"She's got nerve," I said.

George shook his head. "Look at her. She's not telling the truth. It's breaking her heart."

He was right. That was why her eyes were so bright, her cheeks pink. Sarah Rose never could tell a lie, and this one was big enough to smother her.

Then Hunter pushed his head between the curtains and bawled for his wife. The camera hesitated, and swung back to Sarah Rose's face, which was wet with tears. It seemed to stay there forever.

"Bastards," George muttered. "Well, at least you're getting national exposure."

"Who needs this kind of exposure? My God, they're making us look like idiots!" I shouted.

"We haven't heard from Halsey yet," George continued. "He'll be hard-pressed to defend himself."

"Quiet down," Karen said. There was Bobby, sitting with Kelly on Lucy's porch, both of them in rocking chairs. Kelly held a quilt in her lap. Rocking chairs! Quilts! It was shameful.

"What these people don't understand is that our landfill is a scientifically run waste disposal site. This is state-of-the-art." Bobby pointed out the holding pond and pipes.

Kelly didn't set foot off the porch, needless to say. Bobby had given her landfill coveralls, blue to match her eyes, and she looked just as good in them as she did in her street clothes. Bobby ran his gaze over her smooth figure; he always had an eye for women.

And Bobby had answers for everything Kelly asked him. Yes, he and Ferris had a state-issued operating license for the landfill. No, there was no truth to the rumor that Cedar Creek was poisoned. Yes, they had long-range plans for the dump when it reached capacity. No, they weren't at liberty to share the details at this time. Kelly nodded and kept asking questions.

"They should be showing the garbage, dammit," Chance said.

On the screen, Kelly looked at Bobby. "Mr. Halsey, what do you think Lucy McComb would say about this landfill?"

"I don't know as that matters, since she's dead." Bobby was smooth as silk.

"What would she say at seeing that everything she'd worked so hard for had come to . . . garbage?"

"Give him hell, Kelly!" Bill shouted. Everybody clapped.

Bobby sat there for a few seconds, and you could almost hear the wheels turning in his brain. Just when he opened his mouth to respond, there was a commercial.

"Score one for Kelly," George said. "Feel better now, Reba?"

"You think Kelly will let Bobby get away with the lies? The stuff about safety measures and all?"

"Depends on how good her researchers are, and how much time they had to dig." He lit a match for a cigarette and I blew it out.

"Can't smoke here," I told him. "Bill's trying to quit. You should be, too."

Before we could get in a fight, there was Kelly on the screen again. "Now *that's* a sharp-looking pants outfit," Patty commented.

This time Kelly was standing along the road near the shanty. The camera zoomed in on a dead rat in a ditch.

"Recently, the people of Ambrose County began noticing that their rat population was increasing at a faster rate than their human population. And as summer approaches, mosquitoes are swarming in record numbers. Citizens have complained to the state health department, charging that their pest problems were the direct result of unsanitary conditions at the landfill." She swatted at something in front of her face.

"That's a trained mosquito," Chance joked.

"State health officials took those charges seriously, and brought in consultants to evaluate the rodent and insect proliferation. They conducted a survey, going door to door and taking down information to help them pinpoint the root of the problem."

Somebody carrying a clipboard was shown poking around backyards, rattling garbage-can covers, shining flashlights in basements, talking to folks. It all looked real official and serious. The thing was, none of us recognized the people or the houses.

"What'd they do, grab the wrong reel?" Bill said loudly.

"It's probably from their film library," Douglas explained. "Just to show the survey process."

"Process be damned. If they say they talked to us, they should *show* them talking to us," Bill said.

"And they did indeed find a healthy rat and mosquito population here," Kelly continued. "Inspector Mike Wheeler called it a bona fide population explosion. But Wheeler and his men failed to connect the problem to the landfill per se."

"What?" I shouted. George clamped his hand over my mouth.

"Instead, health department officials say that general conditions in the area have encouraged the pests. Things like this open pile of garbage"—there was my compost heap—"penned animals, with their food left outside"—there was the Campbells' run, the dogs going wild—"and unsanitary human-waste disposal."

Bill recognized his old hunt-camp outhouse. "Nobody's used that thing for years!"

"And so the battle proceeds. On one side, the citizens of Ambrose County, trying the best they know how to stop the flow of out-of-state garbage they say is destroying their way of life, the hard proof they need eluding them. On the other, the landfill management, accepting thousands of tons of garbage every week, asserting that theirs is a safe and useful business.

"And the battleground? Well, you have to see it to

appreciate it." The camera took us on a tour of Ambrose County's backside. There was somebody's none-too-clean wash flapping in the wind. The Pentecostal Holiness Church, with snakes painted around the broken-out windows, which had stood empty for years. Snot-nosed kids kicking around an old ball. Everything filmed in dirty gray light, as if there'd been dust on the camera lens.

Then all of a sudden there was J.W., at the statehouse in Richmond, his mouth moving a mile a minute. But they'd tracked Kelly's voice, talking about how he died in the shanty fire, over what he was saying.

The scene shifted to the cemetery, lingering on J.W.'s grave and finally on Lucy's. A tin can stuffed with flowers sat next to her stone, and the light faded into nothing.

For a long time nobody in the room spoke, and then everyone talked at once. A commercial for dog food came on, with big yellow dogs running through fields. "You need to get people's attention and take control," George told me. "This isn't good."

"Shut up, everybody!" I yelled. "George wants to say something."

"Why should we listen to him?" Chance said. "He's no better than they are."

George stood next to me. "I know some of what you saw upset you. Frankly, it was better than I expected. Let me tell you why." He waited for quiet.

"We saw about twelve minutes of television—everything that's gone on here in Collier, presented in twelve minutes. Of course it seemed simpleminded to us. But try to think about watching that report from a New York apartment, say. You've never heard of this landfill. Maybe you've never been south of Washington, D.C."

"Sit down, George!" Chance shouted. "They screwed us, made us look like hillbilly fools. You can't smooth that over!"

"I know, but just listen. I want all of you to close your eyes."

People looked at each other as if they were waiting for a sign.

"Go on, close them, you can concentrate better that way," George said. "Now, think about this. You're New Yorkers, and you've just finished seeing that report. Raise your hand if you know the name of the dump, the names of the people involved, and the fact that it's bad news. And don't raise your hand unless you can point to how you learned it from the show."

Slowly everybody's hand went up.

"Good," George said. "Now, raise your hand if you know that someone died at the landfill."

This time the hands rose right away.

"Okay, so you Yankees learned something. Does what you saw make you mad?"

"Sure as hell does," Bill said. "They're ruining the land and water—"

George cut him off. "So what? You live five hundred miles north of the landfill—what do you care?"

"I care, because people's lives are getting ripped wide open! And somebody's making good money off their misery," Bill answered.

"So it's big business against regular folks, is it? Patty, keep your eyes shut," George said. "Now, Reba, you're a big shot on Wall Street. You don't cook, you eat frozen dinners every night. To keep you company, you read both *The New York Times* and *The Wall Street Journal,* plus about ten magazines a month. What are you doing with the trays and boxes and all those newspapers and magazines?"

"Probably throwing them out in my fancy-ass dumpster—well, not me, I don't go near the thing. I'm paying someone else to do it."

"Right. Now imagine you've just seen this report about the landfill. You've got your coffee table cluttered with stuff, and it's time to straighten up a little. What do you do?"

"Knowing Reba, she'll just toss it out her high-rise window!" Patty called out. Everybody laughed.

I'd had enough of George's game. "You're giving those New York people too much credit. They don't give a damn about us!"

"Listen, everybody. Do you see what I was getting at? Sure, they played on the stereotypes of this place. But I guarantee it's going to stick in people's minds more than some boring technical report about America's garbage problem. And let's face it. Except for the pest-control survey shots, all those pictures came from here."

Nobody denied George's words. "What do you think, Reba?" he asked. "Am I right?"

I smiled. "All I want to know is this: Which one of you sold Kelly that damn quilt?"

JESSE PAXTON

With school finished and Berkley still in jail, I went to work at the store. Being there was better than doing nothing, but it cut into my time at the Castle. I'd set my mind to finish the Cyclorama by July 3, the last day of the Battle of Gettysburg. I believed everything would come together then: the power and wonder of the picture with Amber's shadow cast on it; the weight of all the years turning that power into diamond-hard brightness; the circles that time made around everyone, Sharon and me and our art at the center.

The store stayed busy, with the truckers giving Sarah Rose more business every day. They loved her sandwiches, ordered three or four at a time for the road, and I learned how to use the ripple-edged knife to cut the bread thin and even so it looked like the packaged kind.

I came to know some of the truckers. They'd tell me that I was about the age of their boys, or that they remembered being my age, or that they wished they still were.

One of them, the older man who rode with Rastin, talked to me a lot. "You don't know how lucky you are, growing up out here," he told me. "In Boston, my kids have guards at their school. My boy's best friend got beaten up going home from school last month by some kid wanting his leather jacket. A jacket, for God's sake."

"Sometimes that happens here, too," I said. Out of the corner of my eye I saw Ford Campbell by the candy rack. He stuffed a bag of M&M's in his pocket.

"Yeah, I guess. But you kids have the mountains and nature and all that. My boys have one crummy park to play in, with glass and crap all over it. We're just a couple of blocks off the expressway. The noise and the pollution—y'know, sometimes I think about packing my things and moving to someplace like this." He took a big bite of sandwich and handed me a five-dollar bill. "Keep the change," he said, and winked.

"Why bother moving here, when you can just truck all your trash down instead?" Chance came up behind him with a real dirty look on his face. "Then again, land sure is cheap around here now, with the dump ruining everybody's property and all."

Sarah Rose sent me to check the ice machine on the porch. Somebody had stuffed a bunch of grass up inside the slot. Mud stuck to my hands when I tried to clean it out, and when I pushed the lever, water ran down my arms and made an awful mess.

"Hey, dirtball." I saw Ford's shoes just before he shoved me. My forehead hit the edge of the ice machine and blood ran into my eyes, alongside my nose. "What're you doing to that machine? I sure as hell hope that's not garbage dirt your daddy brought home on his boots."

I wiped my forehead, mixing dirt with the blood. Then I turned back to my work.

"But hey, I forgot. Your daddy's in jail now. That's where he belongs—it's a wonder they waited so long to lock him up. My mother says your daddy's in bed with Halsey and his people. You getting any of that big money, asshole?"

I stood. And discovered that I looked down on him.

It was true. I was taller than Ford, even in his fat-soled, fancy shoes. The sun turned itself up a notch and gave me fire and strength. I pulled back and hit him as hard as I could.

When he fell, the porch shook, and it was a wonderful thing to see him lying there with my blood on his face. Looking at him, I realized this would be the last time I would dare use my fists so; they burned and swelled, and soon enough they'd be the kind of hands that could kill a person. I knew then I would be like Berkley: as big, and as alone. And that seemed all right to me.

Ford's mother came out and saw her boy sitting there, whipped, his head between his knees. Blood dotted the worn porch boards. "Get him some ice!" she shouted. When I paid her no attention, she grabbed the hem of her skirt and pinched it tight against his nose. "Get some ice!" she repeated.

Ford was crying hard. "Wait a minute," his mother said. "Just hold your head back while I get something to stop the bleeding."

She jerked open the screen door and grabbed a bandanna from the rack. Then she tried to get ice out of the machine, but of course it was still jammed up with Ford's trick. She kicked at the machine and beat on it, and finally she got her ice, along with mud and grass, all down the front of her shirt.

I walked into the store. "Ice machine's all right now," I said.

"That wasn't a good thing to do, Jesse." Sarah Rose

stood behind the cash register, and the sun came in the side window and turned her golden. I couldn't keep from staring at her.

"He's been stealing candy from you," I said.

"It was more than that made you knock him down, I hope." A funny look crossed her face. "Jesse, I do believe you're growing an inch a day. You're like a sugar-fed pumpkin vine."

Hunter came through the curtain and moved into the light, throwing a shadow across Sarah Rose's face and taking away her brightness. He looked at me. "Berkley. You have a minute to give me some help with the sheep? I need to move a couple into the lower pasture."

Sarah Rose took his arm. "That's Jesse, Hunter. Berkley's boy. We sold the sheep—they're all gone."

He acted like he didn't hear her. "Dumb as doornails, those two sheep."

Sarah Rose tried to smile. "You've done good work, Jesse. Go on and do what you want the rest of the afternoon."

Before I left, I helped her clean off the porch. Ford's blood left a stain shaped like a fish, which our scrubbing made worse.

"I guess he had it coming, didn't he. I just wish he'd bled in the parking lot," she said.

I waited until no one was around, and pulled out the loose stone in the porch foundation. I slid underneath and made my way into the corner. The dark smelled ancient and foreign. Cats had left their musk in the cool dirt, and along the rock foundation snakes had rubbed free of their skins, leaving them to turn to dust. As I moved my hand around in the dirt, centuries of bones hardened and crumbled, and I touched the center of the earth, hot and violent with energy. Then all of it was gone, and in its place was the sack of papers from Lucy's house.

I carried the papers to Reba Walker's place, meaning to give them to her. But her boyfriend's car was in the driveway, so I put them on the front seat and headed for the Castle. Maybe Amber would be there.

LUCY McCOMB

Of course Berkley did not kill J.W. He pays dearly for someone else's crime. But that is the way of the world. Just as we benefit at one time from another's trials, so must we at other times pay more than our fair share.

The night J.W. died, heat lightning flashed in the sky. He was restless, having sat on the bus for too long, and he thought about leaving Ambrose County. Not to see his cousin in Baltimore—there was no such person—but maybe to go someplace on the ocean, Florida or a sand-beach island. He lay in bed and felt the waves rocking his body, tasted salt on his lips. The heavy air pressed down on him until he rose and left his room, walked out of town toward my house.

He had always been a wanderer, as Mac Avery had been. It is both a blessing and a curse to wander. Like Moses in the wilderness, a wanderer hears God's voice unencumbered by the past, unafraid of the future. But that freedom exacts a cost. For J.W. that night, the price was high.

On his way out of town, he passed the jail, where a man stood by a window, the lightning illuminating his face. It was the same cell that would hold Berkley the next night.

J.W. went on by, thinking about the ocean, and he whistled a lonesome tune. "Hey," the man called out.

"Hey, old guy. What song is that?" When J.W. was well past the jail, the man picked up the tune himself.

J.W. reached Sarah Rose's house. Through the drawn curtains he saw the faint silhouette of Sarah Rose at her dressing table. Hunter came to stand behind her, caressed her shoulders, and Sarah Rose leaned back against him. They could be any couple at all, J.W. thought, any happy man and woman. But he knew better. He walked on. Passing the store, he noticed that the floodlight above the lot had burned out, and he thought to change it for Sarah Rose the next day.

At Reba's house he checked the back door to be sure it was locked. Patsy Cline sat on the window ledge, her tail twitching, and she yowled when she saw him. Hunter's gray tom jumped up on the railing; his eyes shone in the dark and he made hungry growling noises far back in his throat. Patsy Cline rose and arched her back, jumped off the window ledge, and disappeared into the night, the tom in hot pursuit.

J.W. smiled, wondered whether Reba and the newspaperman were sleeping together. It had been a long time since J.W. had been with a woman; the thought of it stirred him. He remembered Marion, his second wife, the one he'd loved the most. They'd married at the start of the war; a year later she had joined the Women's Army Corps as a nurse and gone to London. J.W. had tried to enlist, also; he was told he was too small.

He thought about doing it all over, how if he could have his life back again—that part of it, at least—things would be different. He'd have put his foot down, told Marion she could stay home and work in a factory, as most married women were doing. But when had that ever made a difference with Marion? She would have gone anyway.

Marion had left him for an Englishman, finished her nurse's training and become a London butcher's wife. She'd written him a letter asking for a divorce; he hadn't answered her, had moved to Idaho, to Oregon, Texas, Arkansas.

He wondered if Marion was still alive. By now she'd be an old woman. Maybe it was all for the best; this way he could remember her young and pretty forever. And maybe she dreamed about him once in a while, as he had been then. The man of her dreams. He laughed out loud.

All of this J.W. thought as he walked along the road and into the shanty. Here he found the truck-log notebooks lying empty on the floor. Someone had painted profanities in black all over the ceiling. A hole had been chopped in the rear wall. Pieces of Reba's jacket were scattered in the weeds.

J.W. did not think of the past anymore; there was only the present to consider. He crosses the road and enters the landfill gates, walks up on my porch. In the parlor a light burns, and there is Bobby Halsey with a big man, and J.W. thinks, *It's Berkley, but why?*

When the man turns full-face, J.W. sees it isn't Berkley. But it's too late to leave; they take him and put a bullet through his head. He dies on my front porch, falls across my rocking chair and dies.

Why they moved him into the shanty and burned him beyond recognition—who can know that? Such evil goes beyond understanding. J.W. hadn't the chance to ponder his life as I did; his death was sudden and violent and very wrong. He is unquiet.

What they have done with my land matters less than the utter pain they have caused those I love. In death, if not in life, I will see justice done.

REBA WALKER

Douglas sat at his desk and held out a yellowed newspaper article. "Look at this."

It was the front page of the *Gazette* from December 20, 1959. The headline read "Downtown Burns," in two-inch letters. Dark pictures of what the fire had left behind ran down one side of the page.

"I remember this," I said. "It was awful, right at Christmas and all."

Douglas pointed to the last paragraph. "This is what I want you to see."

I read aloud: " 'Fire investigators suspect that the fire started in Halsey's Drugstore. Russell Halsey was unavailable for comment at the time of this writing.' So? What are you saying?"

"We're putting all the *Gazette*s on microfilm. In the past few months I've gone through them, making sure they're complete. From what I've seen, there never was an answer for that fire, none that was ever reported, anyway."

"Douglas, if I'm late for work again this week I'm going to lose my job. All that fire means to me is bad memories. What are you getting at?"

"Russell Halsey got a brand-new drugstore and wife and son out of that fire."

"You're saying he set that fire?"

"Who knows? I'm just telling you that the whole thing was dropped like a hot potato." He straightened out a paper clip and cleaned his fingernails with it.

"You're thinking about the shanty. Like father, like son? That won't get anywhere in court," I told him.

"It's not easy to fool trained fire investigators," Douglas said. "Whoever lit that fire knew what he was doing. Do you think your newspaperman friend would do a story about it, sort of a follow-up on the shanty burning?"

"I guess I could ask him. But I think you're reaching a little deep here." I stood to leave.

"I'm a librarian," he said. "I'm trained to dig and delve."

"You dig all you want in your newspapers. I've got to go to work."

He looked up at me through his round owl-eye glasses and tapped his head. "Think about it, Reba. Think hard."

What Douglas had said worked on me. We all knew Bobby Halsey was behind the shanty fire and J.W.'s death. Proving it was the hard part. And if the investigation had been dropped thirty years ago, when half the town burned, the same thing would happen again, with only a shack and a drifter gone.

When I arrived at Stoneleigh, Helen Sanders was waiting for me in the hall outside her room. She sat in her wheelchair, a queen on her throne.

"Get your hair done today?" I asked. It was bluer than usual, and fluffed up.

"I did. Believe it or not, Patty came by and took me out."

"There you go. She's not as bad as you make her out to be, is she?" I went into Helen's room and started on the bed. She followed me, bumping my legs with her wheelchair.

"If she wasn't as bad as I make her out to be, I wouldn't be in this place," Helen said. I could tell it was one of her good days.

"We watched the television show Sunday," she went on. "Who'd have thought it, Ambrose County featured on a big news show like that."

"What'd you think?" I straightened up and looked at her.

"Well. Things aren't what they used to be here. I don't mean just the garbage. I mean our town—Collier looked so dirty and run-down."

"The television people filmed what served their purposes. Collier isn't that bad."

"You just don't notice. Patty drove me through the

downtown today, and what did we see? All the flowers the Mountain Garden Club planted in the divider beds downtown are dead, gone to weeds. People don't care anymore about the little things."

"When do we have time to take care of flowers? We're all working, trying to make a living."

"And the stores. Gone. People shopping in malls, letting our stores close and then complaining they can't get what they need here. What's left? A Dollar General, a hunting-and-fishing place, Halsey's Drug—"

"Halsey's. You remember the 1959 Christmas fire, don't you?"

"Of course. Dorothy Halsey was one of our most active parishioners, in spite of Russell. Her dying with that baby was harder on me than losing the church. I still dream about her." Helen's eyes glazed over; she was getting tired.

"Helen, what do you mean about Russell?"

"We always said he was half Jew, keeping her on a tight budget when he was making out well enough in that store. She always apologized for the small money she gave to the church. What she did there more than compensated. All the dishes she washed would fill this room and then some. She—"

"So they didn't get along too well?" I cut in.

"You might say that. Russell Halsey was the kind of man who had a nice word for everyone but his family. None of us was surprised when he married that girl so quickly after Dorothy died, or when Bobby was born just six months later." She turned her wheelchair around and headed for the door. "Dinner smells bad. They burned it again."

I planted myself in front of her. "Do you think Russell Halsey set that fire?"

"Fire? It's just the broccoli they scorched, not a fire." She looked past me into the hall, and I knew I'd lost her.

*

The voice on the lounge phone was so quiet I could hardly hear. Tamyra had turned on the television in the lounge and was hooting it up on the couch, sucking a lollipop.

"Who is this?" I shot Tamyra a dirty look, and she stuck out a bright green tongue.

"It's Sarah Rose. I need to talk to you."

I walked the phone to the window, as far as the cord would go. "What about?"

"Hunter." She stopped, cleared her throat. "Going to Stoneleigh."

"You'll have to work that out with Shirley Carter. I just work here, Sarah Rose," I said.

"I know. I mean, I want to talk to you about what it'd be like for him." Her voice was fading again. "I need to talk to you before I change my mind again, Reba. When are you off work?"

"Not until eleven. Come by the shanty tomorrow morning."

Tamyra laughed again, and I didn't hear what Sarah Rose said before she hung up.

After dinner I grabbed hold of Shirley. "What's our bed situation?" I asked.

"We're full right now. But Edith Halsey may be moving to the hospital, extended care. The doctor thinks she has fluid in her lungs again. He's coming back tomorrow afternoon to check."

"Why don't they just let her go?"

Down the hall, Cleveland Lee was cheating at gin rummy; Grover played on, whining about his hand.

Shirley looked at me as if I'd lost my mind. "You've been here longer than I have, Reba. You know the answer to that. They all approach death differently. Bobby says, 'Do whatever you have to for her,' and as long as he's paying the bills, that's what we're obligated to do. Which includes a daily bath, if you don't mind."

Edith's skin was hot and dry beneath my hands as I took off her gown. She breathed fast, then slow, and her mouth was loose, spit dribbling from the corners. She was pitifully thin, her body shrunken and grooved by the years. What did she dream of, lying here? People from her childhood, sweethearts, ice wagons and buggies and trains rolling around in her head like marbles?

"Edith," I whispered. "Do you hear me?"

Nothing.

"What's in there, Edith?" Her eyelids twitched, and a thick sound came from far back in her throat.

I washed her pale belly and her thin legs. Goose bumps rose on her skin, and I covered her with a sheet.

She'd been at Stoneleigh, dreaming, for six years. And now Hunter McComb might come and take her bed. The thought of it pained me beyond words. Whether the hurt was for Hunter or for myself, I wasn't at all sure.

SARAH ROSE McCOMB

I waited on Reba's porch for more than an hour. I kept thinking that each approaching car was hers, slowing as it crested the hill, then going on. Reba's big black cat rubbed against my legs and made sparks. In the yard, fireflies hovered about the bushes, tracking the night with their phosphorescence.

Just before midnight she pulled into the driveway, her windows open, the radio on. "Reba," I called out. "It's Sarah Rose. I didn't want to scare you."

She walked up the steps and leaned against the railing. Neither of us said anything. "This couldn't have waited until tomorrow?" she finally asked.

I shook my head.

Reba stretched and rubbed her back. "Come on in the house, then."

I shook my head again. "Can we talk out here on the porch? I'm inside all day—"

"Wherever you want." She switched on the bug zapper and sat on the swing; I took the rocker. We sat facing each other, silent. It was still and hot; moths circled our heads and fluttered around the porch lamps. Shiny brown June bugs moved across the porch as if they had somewhere important to go.

"I was thinking about what you said a while ago, about getting some help with Hunter," I told her.

"Uh-huh." Reba wasn't going to make it easy for me.

The blue light of the bug zapper crackled and the porch lights dimmed. I shuddered. "Turn that thing off!"

Reba laughed. "Sure, Sarah Rose."

"So what do you think about putting Hunter in Stoneleigh?" I looked at my hands, folded tightly together so they wouldn't shake.

"What does it matter what I think? He's not my husband," she answered.

"He's gotten worse. He hardly sleeps. I don't sleep, either. I've done about all I can think of to keep him with me. I can't continue like this." I stopped before my voice broke.

"Stoneleigh isn't cheap," she said quietly. "And he's not going to get better there."

"If I had any hope of Hunter getting better, I wouldn't be sitting here talking to you. I know what I have to look forward to."

"How you'd pay for it is none of my business—"

"There's the money from Lucy's place. I haven't touched it."

I followed Reba into the front yard. We stood side by side, covered by dark. Up the road, the landfill lights shone orange; Halsey's crews were bulldozing dirt over the garbage late at night now, then opening the gates at six every morning for more. The landfill was alive and hungry, eating up everything in sight.

"It's taken over our lives, hasn't it, Sarah Rose? This stopped being my personal battle a long time ago, fighting to keep my property value, my mother's gravestone upright and neat. It's about more than Lucy's place, Cedar Creek, or Ambrose County. What they say about us on television or in the paper, that doesn't matter. I think what we're fighting for is our stories, and our past. Yours and Hunter's and Jesse's, and everyone's at the shanty."

She turned toward me. "You want my advice? Put Hunter in Stoneleigh and get on with whatever you need to do." Then she walked into the house and shut the door.

JESSE PAXTON

The middle of June, Sarah Rose took Hunter to the nursing home. She asked me to go with her. I said no, let me stay and take care of the store, but Amber's mother was doing that, and Sarah Rose said she needed my help.

We put Hunter in the backseat of Sarah Rose's car, and I sat up front. She gripped the steering wheel so hard her knuckles were white. "It's too hot back here," Hunter said. "Roll down your windows." He'd lowered both of the rear windows, and Sarah Rose's hair blew forward like the car was going in reverse.

Hunter was quiet. I watched him in my visor mirror and could tell that he knew he wouldn't be coming home again. Sarah Rose took some deep breaths and pushed her hair off her forehead. We came to the bridge and faced a line of trucks on the other side.

"I can't drive. I can't do this." Sarah Rose steered the car to the side of the road and turned off the ignition.

"What's the matter—why are we stopping? We're not anywhere," Hunter said.

Trucks rolled across the bridge and past the car. Sarah Rose's face was empty like a mask. "We can't stay here," I told her.

"I'm sorry," she repeated. "I just can't do this."

I stepped out of the car. In the bright heat the gunmetal stink of the dump blended with the noise of working trucks. At my feet, chicory bloomed in the tangled grass, still damp with dew.

"Let's get going, it's too hot to sit here," Hunter said. "Let's go home."

Sarah Rose looked at me, waiting. There was an edge of smoke in the air, like time had jumped and it was October, some other part of my life. A cool wind rose up from the grass and worked its way beneath my shirt, which suddenly felt very small.

I opened Sarah Rose's door. "Move over. I'll drive."

She gave me the keys, and I started the engine the way Hunter had taught me two summers before, when we drove the back roads in his old Chevy truck. I started across the bridge and prayed it would stay clear of trucks until we reached the other side.

Sarah Rose closed her eyes. "I'll need some help here," I reminded her.

"You're doing fine. Just go slow and watch out for other people." Her voice came from someplace far away that had nothing to do with me.

"Are you old enough to be driving?" Hunter asked. "Let me."

"You aren't allowed to anymore," Sarah Rose told him.

"Who's going to know? Pull over." Hunter stuck his head between the seats. "He's too young to drive this car."

Sarah Rose and I looked at each other. Hunter was making too much sense; did he really belong in Stoneleigh?

"Go on, Jesse. You're doing just fine," she said.

"But you're not old enough, are you?" he asked again.

"I guess I am—I'm doing it, right?" I roared onto the road, my foot heavy on the gas.

Hunter stared out the window. "We'll need to cut hay this afternoon. Can't let this weather get by us."

Sarah Rose didn't answer right away. "We won't cut hay, Hunter. There's no need, we sold the animals."

"That's all right. It's something to do. Somebody will use the hay," he said. Sarah Rose started to cry.

Driving that car wasn't the hardest thing I'd ever done. The road was straight, and I took my time. After a couple of miles I got brave and went a little faster. Sarah Rose didn't pay any attention.

Hunter pointed out things on the car that I didn't need to know about, but I listened the best I could and cruised on toward Stoneleigh Nursing Home.

"What I'm sort of worried about is running into Sheriff Anstett," I told Sarah Rose.

"There's no one else to drive this car. He's got my brother in jail," she said.

Hunter had gotten quiet again in the back, so I turned on the radio and found some music. Bruce Springsteen was playing and I started thinking that maybe I'd be a rock star and make good music until I died. I rolled my window down the rest of the way and hung my elbow out.

Down the road, a blue car took the curve and moved over the center line. I steered to the right and hoped for the best. "Go a little slower," Sarah Rose said.

It was Mrs. Campbell, with Ford in front with her. I waved and smiled at Ford as our cars passed, imagining what he'd tell Ricky when he saw him.

"Watch the road. We're almost there." She turned off the radio.

A big woman in a uniform and nurse's hat stood by the door waiting for us when we got to Stoneleigh. Hunter looked at her, at the building, then at Sarah Rose.

Her cheeks were shiny with tears. As they went up the walk, Hunter looked small and pitiful, and I wasn't proud of the part I'd played bringing him to this place. The woman took Hunter's free arm and the three of them moved through the doors.

The sun bubbled the tar patches in the driveway and bounced off the flat roof in waves. I wondered if Berkley was hot in his cell. I wanted to tell my father I'd driven a car, and when he got out of jail I'd take him to the Castle and show him what I'd done there.

Berkley in the Castle—only half of him would fit inside. Even I had to move carefully there now; my head bumped the roof when I stood up too quickly. The day Amber found me working, the small space closed in on us more and more the longer we stayed.

Through the window I saw Sarah Rose and Hunter sitting side by side in an office. Across the desk, the nurse was talking at them, her hands moving through the air like caged birds. The overhead light made them all look too pale. Sarah Rose signed some papers and then sat up straight, with her jaw set tight. I knew she'd taken herself out of the room so she wouldn't have to watch herself doing what had to be done. It was a trick I'd learned a long time ago.

Two little kids on bikes pedaled into the driveway and rode around the circle. Ricky's father went past me, probably on his way to the liquor store. Birds picked food from the lawn. Things went on the way they always had, even though I'd driven a car for the first time and Berkley was in jail, even though Hunter was never going home again.

Sarah Rose came out the side door. "Let's go."

I started the car and drove to the main road. "Where to?"

"The store," she said. And then, "Oh, what am I thinking? I've got to drive now." We changed places, and Sarah Rose drove straight to the store without a wrong turn, using the right signals, obeying the speed limit. But she didn't answer any of my questions; I don't think she even knew I was still in the car with her.

After the lunch rush, I walked to the Castle to work on my picture. But it was hot, and I was tired. I bunched up my shirt for a pillow and lay down in a square of sun, waiting for things to come alive.

I looked at the first wall I'd drawn on. It had been cold the day I started; I remembered the stiffness of my fingers, and how hard I had had to work to put heat in the air. I'd left the trees bare, shivered as I'd drawn the boy sitting by the creek with his shirt off. I'd planned to color in the trees a thick green later, so they'd look like July trees. But I hadn't. How could I have let that go? Things were wrong here, things I'd not seen before. I'd never be able to fix it all.

And I didn't much care anymore. Why had I thought I needed to copy a painting that already had a life of its own somewhere else? Sharon wasn't coming back here, no matter how good my picture was. Berkley knew it all along; that's why he'd kept me up on the mountain and stayed to himself for those years, just getting by until he took the job at the dump and went on with things the best he could.

What was I to my mother but a tiny piece of herself mixed together with a little piece of Berkley? Now I was growing as big as my father, and all I carried of Sharon were my hands, my pictures. Our lives were as separate as they could possibly be; I belonged here and she didn't, and it was all right.

I rolled over on my stomach and looked out. Amber hung on the fence watching Sunny graze, her strong legs wrapped around the post and her hair hanging loose. When her mother drove up, Amber walked toward the house. Just before she went inside, she turned and waved at me.

4

THE MIDDEN

LUCY McCOMB

Here it is, almost the Fourth of July. Do you wonder if time goes slowly for the dead? It does not, because there are no calendars and clocks to remind us of it. Time stops when the heart stops.

Edith Halsey lies in a hospital, ready now to let go of time. But doctors have put her on a machine, and her heart cannot quit. She fights for death, but they will not let her have it. Light shines day and night over her bed, surrounding her with a hard electric shell.

At Stoneleigh, Hunter sits up in bed and wonders what has happened to the rhythms of his life. His hands lie empty in his lap; he stares, trying to remember what he used to hold in them. The windows will not open, and his senses wither with disuse.

Berkley becomes stooped in his small cell. The walls press in on him; he wakes from his sleep crying out for release. The sheriff tells him that it won't be much longer; that things are fitting together and he will be free soon. Sarah Rose comes, brings Jesse, brings with her whiffs of the outside that fill Berkley with regret. His son changes before his eyes, grows distant, and Berkley knows things have gone on in his absence that can never be reclaimed.

Atop the mountain, squirrels have moved into Berkley's cabin. They make nests in the eaves and sit like statues on the table. They creep beneath the bed and wonder at the chest of memories they find there, curious enough to gnaw within. The paints and brushes skitter among the dust and disappear. On the roof, shingles curl like dry leaves in the hot sun; the wind pries them loose.

Sarah Rose does not sleep. She reaches out for her husband but finds only empty silence. She cannot bring herself to visit Hunter; she drives to the nursing home, sits in the parking lot crying, then drives home. She calls the head nurse, intending to arrange to take her husband home, and hangs up before anyone answers. She works in the store days, bakes nights. Only Jesse makes her smile.

Jesse. He stretches toward the sun like corn after a soaking rain. He has lost the haunted, scared look about his eyes. His voice deepens; his shoulders broaden. No longer does he wander at night, climbing the mountain seeking solace, his mother. He has taken root, thrives, brings joy.

Reba goes to work with great trepidation. She asks to be transferred to the new wing, away from Hunter. The head nurse refuses, asking why, after so many years of walking the worn hardwood floors of the main building, Reba would ask such a thing. Reba will not talk about it; she gets the young aide to shave Hunter and give him baths.

But tonight Tamyra calls in an excuse, and doesn't come to work. Reba is shorthanded. Hunter sits in his chair, looking out the window, waiting.

REBA WALKER

I told Shirley that I needed a substitute for Tamyra, that I couldn't do it all by myself, and she said, "You've done it plenty of times before. I can't find anyone to come in on such short notice. All I got were answering machines when I tried."

I dug in my heels. It had been a busy day at the shanty, with more trucks than ever, ninety-two of them through the landfill gates by three-thirty. And George was back; I'd left him in my garden pulling weeds. "Either you bring someone from the other wing to work over here, or I'll go home," I demanded.

Shirley glared at me. "You'll get comp time, as usual, Reba. We're short one girl on the north wing, too. I heard there's a big concert in Richmond tonight, that's where everyone's gone. If they'd just *tell* me these things when I'm doing the schedule—"

"I'll quit," I said.

"I'm going to pretend I didn't hear that." She turned her back on me and walked away, knowing I couldn't afford to carry through with my threat.

I saved Hunter for last, half hoping Sarah Rose would come by and care for him. But she didn't—Helen Sanders told me nobody but Chance and Patty had been in to see him—and when I passed his door he looked into the hall as if he was expecting company.

I put the Lee brothers to bed and went to shut off Helen's light. Her medicine was working just enough to confuse her, not enough to put her to sleep. "You're late coming in. I suppose you were with the McComb boy across the hall."

"It's only nine-fifteen. I'm not that late," I said.

"Uh-huh, that's what my Chance says when he comes in from being with that Patty. I can smell the sex on him, and he says, 'We were sitting on her porch talking and didn't know the time.' Him with a perfectly fine watch on his wrist!"

"Okay, Helen. Nighty-night."

"This isn't my bed—it smells wrong," she complained.

"You've got that right." I walked into the hall.

I stood at the medications cart and rearranged things,

thinking that if I spent enough time puttering, Hunter might fall asleep and I could leave him for the night shift. Shirley had gone home, and she wouldn't know the difference if I just checked off his room on the duties list. The pencil made the mark, and that was the end of it.

I called home and let the phone ring twelve times, then hung up and dialed again. Finally George answered; he said he'd been typing in the back bedroom and hadn't heard the phone the first time. His voice sounded faraway and blurry.

"What did you call for?" he asked.

"I just wondered if you were there."

"Where else would I be this time of night in this godforsaken place? There's no place to go for a drink if I wanted to!"

I pictured him in the kitchen, rumpled-looking in the bad light. He was probably putting out his cigarette in my aloe plant and wishing I'd hang up. "All right, go on back to work." I slammed the receiver and hoped the sound hurt his ear.

Men could be so moody. It was plain wrong that women were accused of being nasty and hormonal, when most of the time they didn't have a whole lot to be happy about, thanks to men. Maybe I'd move my things into the other bedroom.

The phone rang and I picked it up fast, so it wouldn't wake the residents.

"Hello?" Nothing. "Stoneleigh. Hello?"

"Reba?" It was Sarah Rose.

"Yes, it's Reba."

"I couldn't sleep," she said.

"He's all right." How could I tell her that, when I was afraid to go into his room?

"Is he sleeping? He wouldn't sleep at home." She was crying now.

"He's resting," I said.

"I just wondered . . . if you could check on him."

"If I have time, sure." I waited for something more, but she was gone.

Grover Lee came out into the hall, laughing like crazy. "My boys have done it again—they whipped the Yankees good! Not even close. What a game!"

"Go back to bed," I told him. "You can let Cleveland know in the morning. If you get up again, I'll take your radio."

"Just try it, Miss Priss," he said. "You think you own this place. You just work here—you're not the boss."

I led him into his room and tuned his radio to the egghead public station, thinking it would bore him either to sleep or to death, whichever came first. The Lee brothers wore thin fast, especially when I had other things on my mind.

On my way up the hall I stopped outside Hunter's room. He'd been quiet all night; I was sure he was asleep. I peeked in the door and saw an empty bed.

I switched on the overhead light and looked in the bathroom, in the closet, behind the heavy drapes—nothing. Of all the people in Stoneleigh, why Hunter? Why me? I hurried to the nurses' station and phoned the other wing for help, then called Shirley and told her to get herself to Stoneleigh right away.

We turned the building upside down: no Hunter. I grabbed a flashlight and ran out the back door into the night, scaring up rabbits on the lawn and pushing away fireflies as I shone the light into the trees. "Hunter!" I called. There was no answer.

Pausing to catch my breath, I stared into the darkness. I thought about the nights I'd driven around with Danny, pressed tight against him, hoping I'd catch a glimpse of Hunter. Sometimes I did—but he was always with Sarah Rose and never looked my way. How could it be that forty years later I was still searching for Hunter?

Not because I loved him. Because I was in charge of him. He had become my job; I was his keeper. God, I thought, you surely do play some freak tricks on us.

Shirley found him about a mile up the road, walking toward home. "We're going to have to use restraints if he leaves again," she said. "Especially the nights we're shorthanded. I'll talk to Mrs. McComb about it in the morning." She moved an aide over from the other wing and went home.

When the night shift came on, I sat in Hunter's room for a few minutes before leaving. He'd had medicine and he slept heavily, his breathing slow and mechanical.

How often as a girl had I dreamed about sleeping beside him? I remembered his young face, smooth and square, his raven's-wing hair: were they hidden beneath the old-man mask in front of me? I couldn't stand thinking it was gone, just gone.

And I remembered all the time I'd spent hating Sarah Rose for what she had. It wasn't her fault that I'd loved someone who loved her instead. Here we were, suddenly old, more alone than we had ever dreamed we'd be. I shivered in the air-conditioning, and tucked the sheets around Hunter, kissed his cheek, and left.

George had gone out and bought a bottle of wine at Kroger. "Sorry I was so short on the phone," he said. "I get that way when I'm stuck on something."

"Sure, George. I mean, sure, I know how that goes." I was glad I'd caught myself.

We poured some wine, and he talked about the big article he was writing about the landfill, how it had changed so many lives as well as polluted our land. "Can I read you what I'm saying about you?" he asked.

"Let's go outside on the porch. I don't want you to see my face in case it makes me mad." We went out and got comfortable. "Give me some more wine before you start."

George filled my glass and cleared his throat. "Well, this is just a rough draft. It'll be different when it goes to my editor—"

"Just read it."

" 'Reba Walker was elected president of SOME, and her life will never be the same.' "

"Says who?" I asked.

"You have to listen straight through. I'm not going to read this if you cut in on every sentence."

" 'Walker, who works as an aide at Stoneleigh Nursing Home, lives a quarter-mile from the landfill. The fifty-nine-year-old Ambrose County native spends eight hours a day at a rough shanty, logging the trucks as they come loaded and leave empty.' "

"Fifty-eight," I said. "I'm fifty-eight until September."

" 'She's seen one of her fellow protesters killed and the shanty burned to the ground. She's had cans and insults thrown at her, and Richmond officials have refused repeatedly to talk to her. But Ms. Walker persists. Why?' "

He stopped reading. "Why?" he repeated.

"Hell, George, don't you know?"

"Do you?"

I looked out into the darkness. "I'd damn well better know. It's a question of right and wrong—people dumping their garbage where they think it doesn't count."

"No, I don't mean why the fight. I mean, why are *you* giving your life to it, every bit of your energy? You, Reba—not people, not *we*."

"They shouldn't be able to ruin our lives—it's not right."

"It happens all the time. What you told me about your husband, your kids . . ."

"You can't help what one person does to another. You've just got to go on and live with that the best you can. Over time it'll most likely work itself out. But this? It'll never go away."

"You've been working two full-time jobs for months.

You're tired. Couldn't someone else take over for a while?"

"You don't have to tell me how hard I'm working." I pushed my chair back and walked into the yard. George followed me. I told him about Hunter, how I'd felt sitting beside his bed, after all the years I'd dreamed about him. "I don't have a whole lot else except for this place. That's why I 'persist,' as you call it. It's my life."

I started to cry, not tight little tears but wild, loud howling. My body ached all over, nowhere worse than in the center of my heart. I forgot George was there, and I cried for my kids and for Sarah Rose and Hunter, for Berkley and Jesse, for J.W., for everyone in Stoneleigh who'd been set aside and forgotten, for all the hurt we put on each other.

George hugged me tight against his chest, and his warm, round body comforted me beyond words. We stood in the yard, our backs to the dump, and listened to the night sounds. By the creek, peepers still whistled. The McPhersons' barn owl flew overhead and lit in a cedar at the edge of the garden, making its hollow noises. Patsy Cline stalked through the grass and jumped onto the porch, a black shape dangling from her sharp teeth. Muffled voices floated from the far side of the creek, then went on past George and me into the darkness. Was the McPherson girl old enough already for that?

The moon had horns, as my mother used to say, and looked out of focus in the hazy sky. We lay down together in the grass and loved each other. We forgot we were old people: our bodies cooperated without complaining much. George's hands were smooth and smart as they moved over my body. When I lay with him, all the pieces fit together warmly, just right, my skin and bones becoming his, and his mine. The damp grass made tangled marks on my backside, and I thought I heard someone singing deep beneath me. It was a good song, and George and I sang it together.

When we stood up we felt what we'd done, and we

limped inside and fell into bed. There were no dreams left for either of us that night. We slept nestled like spoons in a drawer, without moving.

JESSE PAXTON

The first couple of days after Hunter left, Sarah Rose didn't talk much. At night I'd wake up and hear noises in the dark house, and think Hunter was back and roaming. But in the morning Sarah Rose would be pale, with black circles around her eyes, and I'd know she'd been the wanderer. She'd make it through days at the store and then come home and lie on the sofa near the telephone, waiting for a call. I wondered what difference there was having Hunter at Stoneleigh; Sarah Rose seemed just as unhappy as she was before.

Then, one night after supper, she was resting on the sofa, and Amber's mother walked right in the front door. "You two come on," she told us. "We're going to Stoneleigh to do some visiting."

I checked out the window, and there was Amber sitting in the back of the McPhersons' car. She had headphones on and was keeping the rhythm of the music with her sneakers, which were pressed against the back of the driver's seat.

"I'm tired—I'm just not feeling up to it tonight," Sarah Rose said. "Go on without us, Karen."

Mrs. McPherson pulled Sarah Rose to a sitting position. "You're never going to sleep right until you spend some time with Hunter."

"I guess that's my business." Sarah Rose lay back down and turned away from her.

Amber's mother moved a chair next to Sarah Rose

and held her hand. "Reba tells me you haven't been to see Hunter since you took him to Stoneleigh. I thought you might need some company the first time."

Amber was outside the car now, looking at the wasps' nest under the porch eaves. She found a stick and poked at it.

"I'll get there, maybe tomorrow," Sarah Rose said.

"Tonight—now. Before it gets any later," Amber's mother told her.

Sarah Rose was crying again, which is how I figured things would end up.

"Jesse, you run on and keep Amber company," Mrs. McPherson ordered. "We'll be right out."

I went outside. Amber had climbed onto the porch railing for a closer look at the nest. "I don't think there's anything in here," she said.

She was sunburned, and standing next to her I felt the heat from her skin. "They're in there, for sure. I saw a couple go inside a little bit ago. You're going to get stung."

"Bees don't care about me. I've never been stung in my life. So, are you coming with us? I hate Stoneleigh. It stinks. That's why I always take along some music. I sort of block out what's around me that way."

"Amber, you'd better drop the stick. Those are wasps, the ones with white stripes on the legs."

"Is it true you drove your aunt's car the other day?" She dug the tip of the stick in the cells of the nest and rattled it around. I moved away.

"I guess it is."

"How was it?" She poked some more.

"Okay. I mean, no big deal. I've been driving for a while."

"That's a lie." A couple of wasps crawled out and circled the nest, their striped legs dangling.

"Maybe," I said. "Listen. You'd better quit on that nest." A few more wasps came out.

"You haven't been working on your picture," Amber said. "I checked yesterday, and it didn't look like you'd been there in a while."

"I've been busy. At the store and all. Anyway, I don't care much about finishing it. I'm thinking about maybe drawing some things I could sell on the Fourth."

She held the stick like a tightrope walker's pole and started around the porch railing. "You're good enough. You could make plenty of money, I bet." She lost her balance, and the stick hit the nest broadside.

I heard Sarah Rose say, "Let me put on some shoes," and then the wasps were everywhere and Amber and I were running fast for the car.

They let Berkley out of jail the Friday before the Fourth. The sheriff came by the store early in the morning and told Sarah Rose they'd gotten word the fire was accidental.

"The hell it was, John Anstett." Sarah Rose stared at him until he looked away.

"Watch that talk," he said. "You're going to get yourself in trouble."

"You accuse my brother of burning somebody up and leave him in jail for a month waiting for a hearing—and then decide the whole thing was an accident? That's asinine, John!"

He looked in his wallet for cigarette money. "I just did what I was told. You can come by and get him anytime."

"No, *you* can bring him by here anytime—like right now." She grabbed his wrist and squeezed.

"I'm not in the taxi business," he told her. "Let go of me, Sarah Rose. I thought you knew better than to act this way. You're being like Reba now!"

"Maybe I am. Bring my brother back here now, or there'll be hell to pay." Her eyes glittered like green ice, and she dug her nails into his skin.

"You threatening me?"

"I don't have to threaten you, John." She let him go and took his money, kept the change. "Think about what you've done to Berkley, and go get him out of jail. Now."

He came into the store, blinking like he'd walked into a bright, sunny day, instead of the opposite. "Hey," he said.

I walked around the counter, and his eyes ran over me from top to bottom. Then he hugged me hard against him. All around us, people went about their business, and I told the little part of me that was embarrassed to be quiet.

"Go on to the house," Sarah Rose told us. "Stay for dinner, at least."

We walked down the road, and I held my father's hand tight. Trucks went past us, and some of the drivers honked and waved at Berkley. He looked straight ahead and ignored them. Ricky drove by with his father and pointed at me and laughed. I didn't care.

The dump stink was all around us in the afternoon sun. When we came to the shanty, Berkley's grip tightened. Reba stood by the road holding her notebook. She looked tired and hot, and didn't notice us until we were even with her. Then she stared at Berkley like he was a ghost.

"You by yourself today?" Berkley broke the silence.

"For a while." She watched a truck leaving the landfill and wrote down something as it shifted gears.

I went into the shanty and sat. Somebody had drawn a funny picture of rats on the wall. They were dancing in a line, wearing shirts with "Buena Vista Landfill" in big black letters. Closer to the floor, there was a picture of the rats lying on their backs with their feet in the air. "R.I.P.," it said underneath. I found a marker and added vultures. Up in the corner I drew two small figures—Amber and me—walking into the sky.

When Berkley and Reba came inside, I gave Reba my chair and sat on the floor. She asked Berkley questions about being in jail, and then, "What you going to do for a job?"

He was quiet, shook his head. "I won't work for Halsey."

"I didn't expect you would."

"I could help out here, until I find something."

Reba looked hard at him.

"It's what I want to do. If you'll have me."

"There's no reason I wouldn't." She showed him the bag of papers I'd left in the newspaperman's car. "I was wondering if you knew anything about this."

Berkley flipped through the papers. "It's Halsey's writing. How'd you get hold of all these?"

"That's sort of a mystery. Look real close, Berkley. There are two figures for each entry, one double the other. I'm guessing these numbers show what they're collecting. Which set is right?"

Berkley studied them awhile, then pointed to the second column. "It's these. They're getting forty-three dollars a ton."

"And reporting half." Reba turned to me. "I've been wondering how these papers got in George's car. Do you know, Jesse?"

I kept on doodling.

"Jesse," Berkley said. "Reba's talking to you."

"I might know a little something about that stuff," I said.

"Thank you," Reba said. "However you got hold of them."

Berkley and I left the shanty and started up the mountain. In the weeks we'd been off the path, weeds had worked through the hard dirt, and now thorny vines stretched from one side to the other. Poison ivy tilted in close to our ankles.

Somebody had been in the cabin. The door hung open and two of the windows were broken. Inside, whoever it was had helped himself to our food, then left what he didn't want scattered on the floor and table. The jar of money we kept in the back of the dish cupboard was missing. Sheets and blankets off the beds had been burned out back. I found Ford's big, fancy sneaker prints pressed into the dust all around.

Berkley and I packed some clothes. I gathered up Sharon's stuff that was spread under Berkley's bed and put it in a grocery bag along with my sketches. Berkley pretended not to notice. But on the way down the mountain he said, "I saw the pictures you did of the dump. They're good."

"I did them the night you were looking for the baby."

Berkley nodded and put his hand on my shoulder.

The sun came through the trees and made yellow patterns in the woods. A breeze carried the garbage smell away from us. Wood violets and jack-in-the-pulpits, waterleaf and mountain laurel grew thick in the tree shade. With my father, I felt happier than I had in a very long time.

SARAH ROSE McCOMB

I sat by Hunter's bed and watched him sleep. His chest rose and fell in rhythm with my own. I felt his cheek; someone had shaved him. In the dim light from the corner of the room, Hunter looked calm and smooth, as if he might sleep there for a hundred years and never change.

I spread our wedding quilt across the foot of the bed, then took down the picture hanging near the door and replaced it with one Sharon had done, a sketch of Hunter in the barn kneeling beside a laboring ewe. Then I eased onto the bed and wrapped my arms around my husband.

I blocked out the hall noises and the medicine smell of the sheets and imagined that we were home, that Hunter had fallen asleep exhausted from a hard day's work rather than from a pill.

It was shameful of me to have stayed away so long. I had let Hunter sit at Stoneleigh, waiting, because I hadn't had the courage to face him. I'd never been a strong woman, not like Reba, or Lucy in her time. But guilt had no place lying between Hunter and me; he'd always been one to talk me out of my worries. I could hear his sweet voice: "None of us knows why we do what we do. And it's a mistake to waste time trying to figure it out," he'd say. "Just live true to yourself." I hugged Hunter tight to me and knew he'd always done that the best he knew how.

I heard Reba's voice: "You're here."

I sat up and smoothed my skirt. "I'm here."

"He asked for you last night. Well, every night."

"It's hard. I just . . ."

She raised her hands to stop me. "I figured you'd come when you were ready." She showed me how to work the bed, told me about the medicine Hunter was taking to help him see things clearer. "We work with him, remind him of who he is and all."

"You're taking good care of him," I said. "Shaving him, keeping him clean."

She flushed. "Not me. Not his baths, I—"

"Thank you." I took her hands, not trusting my voice to say more.

"It's my job. It's nothing special." She picked up the water pitcher and left the room.

Hunter slept on, moving his legs now and again. I wondered what he was dreaming of, hoped his sleep was rich with warmth and love, and free of pain. I hoped he dreamed of fertile fields and strong lambs, dry hay sweet with clover and timothy. I hoped he dreamed of simple rhythms and love. I hoped he dreamed of me.

REBA WALKER

The Fourth started with showers. Patty called me just after sunrise, wanting to know what we would do if the rain kept up.

"The sky's supposed to clear," I told her. "My God, Patty, it's only six o'clock. Go back to sleep."

George rolled over and coughed.

"Am I disturbing you?" Patty asked.

"Yes, you are. Wait until seven and call me again if the rain is still coming down." I hung up, dozed.

I dreamed about Hunter as a young man. He stood on the banks of the Jackson River. The light reflected off the moving water and marked his face with shadow. Huge fish rose to the surface and dove under again, their mouths moving silently.

In my dream, Hunter looked into the water and grabbed bare-handed at the fish, their backs arched and golden. They leaped and twisted and slid through his fingers. I leaned over and tried to help, scooping water so cold it numbed my fingers. He raised his hands, and blood ran down his wrists. As the river turned red with it, his face paled and fell in on itself. He was old. I knew I was, also, by the shaking of my hands.

Fighting to wake, I sat straight up in bed and pressed my hands to my face: they were damp, and a fishy, metallic smell clung to them.

Feeling restless, I went out on the porch. The rain had turned to fine mist, settling low in the hollows, where the sun would burn it dry by mid-morning. In the east, over the landfill, the sky shone red like a new scar. For an instant I thought, *Berkley's cabin—it's on fire.* But the red wasn't hot: it was a cool warning, a sailor's red sky.

I walked around the side of the house to the bedroom window and knocked on the glass, then watched, laughing, as George jumped out of bed and ran stark naked for his pants. I waved, then went in the back door and put on the coffee to make amends.

"Scaring a man like that can give him a heart attack!" he shouted from the bathroom.

I went to get dressed. The yellow shirt George had brought me from Richmond fit perfectly, and the nubby cloth was surprisingly soft against my skin. "It suits you," he said when we sat down for breakfast.

"You're the first man who ever bought me clothes." I told him about my dream, how I'd wakened and smelled the river on my skin, a scent like something broken open.

"I don't dream," he said.

"Never? You don't ever dream?"

"I wake up knowing things, but I don't dream to learn them. They're just there when I wake up."

"Maybe from the newspaper."

He shook his head. "I've always been that way. I don't make a lot of it."

"So what did you wake up knowing this morning?" I asked.

"It doesn't need to be talked about." No amount of coaxing would get him to say what the day held for us.

By ten o'clock the fire hall parking lot was full of booths, and we had a good crowd shopping at what we jokingly called the Ambrose County Secondhand Mall. We'd all cleaned out closets and attics and found parts of ourselves we'd thought were gone forever.

Patty and Chance had a rack of Helen's clothes from forty years back. I imagined Helen wearing them, tall and slender and in charge of her household. The wasp-waisted jackets and slender skirts caught Amber McPherson's eye. "Out of your closet, into mine," Karen said, handing Patty her money.

Brenda Campbell had given in and set up a table. She was selling Ford's baseball-card collection, which he said he didn't care about anymore, and George's photographer paid fifty dollars for it. "That's my money," Ford said, and his mother said all right, but I happened to overhear them and made Ford hand over half the money for the treasury. He fussed for a while, then left with a friend of his, an extra five dollars from his mother in his pocket.

George came up behind the ticket table and whispered in my ear: "Andrews is on his way. His guard dogs are buying out the hot dog stand." He pointed to a group of dark-suited men, walkie-talkies hanging from their belts.

"I don't believe it. Not after all these months."

"I do. He's not going to miss an opportunity like this. He's got his eye on higher things than being governor, and he's out to make some friends," George said. "Over there—that's John Garber from *The Washington Post*. Shana O'Dell from *The Baltimore Sun* is here, too. There are TV crews from all over the state filming. They're expecting something good. Andrews won't disappoint them."

I handed out SOME T-shirts free to all the reporters, making sure they knew that donations were appreciated. By eleven o'clock we had a dozen shirts on them and seventy dollars more in our treasury. I sent Jesse around with cups of ice water for everybody, but when Amber McPherson showed up he went with her to run the pony rides.

Berkley came down the mountain around noon, carrying a box. He found a table in the shade and spread out a couple dozen pictures. I got Karen to watch my booth and walked over.

"I'm glad you're here," I said. "Just so you know, I want you to keep what you make from selling these."

He shook his head. "I'm not doing this for the money."

Most of the pictures were pretty enough watercolors that Sharon had done; they'd sell fine. But the sketches of the dump, Jesse's work, took my breath away. How did someone so young know how to make sound and scent rise up from pencil marks on paper? There was a sharpness to them, angles and grit, that thickened the air and gave it life.

Jesse had made space disappear in his pictures. That power could scare you to death, spark the kind of fear that pulled you from happy dreams late at night. The landfill nightmare was right there on paper.

I knew Berkley felt the strength of the pictures, too. Selling them was his way of saying what needed to be said. Berkley had paid a higher price for his job at the landfill than any of us would ever understand.

I found George and brought him to look at Jesse's work. He bought four of the pictures and paid more than the asking price. "I think I can talk my editor into running a few of these with my story," he told Berkley. "Maybe with a color wash."

"No color," Berkley said. "They're better without."

Over in the dunking booth, Chance Sanders was dripping wet. The Jackson School baseball players had lined up and were spending lots of money giving their coach a bath. Chance laughed and egged the boys on. With his hair plastered to his forehead, he looked like a boy himself; how could it have been more than forty years since he'd pitched for Jackson? Patty got someone to watch her food booth and took her turn; after missing him twice she found her mark.

By noon the sun had burned away the haze. The air was humid and still. Bill McPherson drove to Rogers Funeral Home and brought back a couple of gravesite canopies. We crowded together in the shade and fanned ourselves with whatever we could find. We were making a fortune selling drinks, but the candy melted in the heat. Nobody was hungry: the popcorn machine fell quiet, and Patty turned off the fire beneath the hot dogs. "Anyone who wants one can cook it on this pavement," she said. Only Chance stayed cool, on his perch over the water tank, badgering passersby until they dunked him just so he'd be quiet.

We'd taken in more than three hundred dollars in admission fees when Governor Andrews dropped a fifty in the jar. He walked through the parking lot surrounded by his people, looking at each table and talking with everyone as if he'd known us all for years. I marveled at his cool neatness; I was feeling sweat trickle down my back and between my breasts.

Then came Angela Finnerty and her Water Control people, followed by a man George said was Attorney General Lanier. They sampled a little of everything and wiped their fingers on their clean white handkerchiefs. Reporters and cameras followed them around everywhere.

Richard Kane showed up to shake hands and hung tight by the governor. I left my table and caught up with them by the drink machine. "Reba Walker." I took the governor's hand.

"Ms. Walker is the head of the citizens' group I was telling you about," Kane said.

"I'm the one you couldn't see last month when we came to Richmond," I reminded the governor.

He let go of my hand. "Yes, I remember that. I'm sorry you had to leave before Monday."

"Me, too. See, one of our group got killed. And our shanty burned down."

Andrews looked at Kane, startled.

"The investigation showed the fire started from natural causes," Kane told him.

"Fire is always natural. Doesn't always get used naturally, though. So, maybe we can talk a little bit now."

"We'll be making a major announcement at the landfill soon. I think you'll be happy with what I have to say, Mrs. . . ."

"Walker, Ms. Walker. I sure hope we will be, because we're awfully tired of the bullshit running out of Richmond." I poured myself a lemonade and went back to my table.

I was having a good time watching the government people avoid the manure Amber's pony had left behind, when George sneaked up behind me and told me the governor was making his way to the landfill for his speech. "He's promising big news. You mind your manners."

"Sure, George. I've been minding them," I said.

We closed up all the booths and drove to the landfill. We'd let the day go at the shanty, it being the Fourth, but the trucks came one after the other, lined up at the gates, and threw diesel fumes and garbage stink into the heavy afternoon heat.

"Anybody seen Bobby Halsey today?" I asked Bill. We put chairs outside the shanty and used umbrellas to keep off the sun.

He shook his head. "I heard over the radio his grandmother died this morning, just before sunrise. They've been looking for him."

"My Lord, Edith's gone?" I said. "The poor soul deserves her rest." Beneath my feet the earth quivered and rumbled. I looked at Bill.

He went on as if nothing had happened. "Karen says the trucks have been backed up awful all day—took her over twenty minutes to get the pony back home. From what I can see, there's only about three men working inside."

"Lucy's house looks pretty deserted," I said. There was smoke in the still air, burning my eyes and nose.

"Don't get your hopes up. Bobby probably went to Virginia Beach for the weekend. Watch, he'll be back Monday with a good tan."

"Or not at all." For the first time, I thought about what would happen if Halsey and his people walked away from here: left the garbage half covered, stinking; the leachate running beneath the road into Cedar Creek and then into the Jackson River; the mountain washing away behind the garbage. Even if we got the government to close the place down, that was just the beginning. We would be living with what they left behind for the rest of our lives.

*

The governor's men closed the gates, and sent the loaded trucks back to the interstate so Andrews could give his speech. "These guys are something, aren't they?" Patty said. "Don't they look funny, out there in white shirts and ties, walking around those trucks?"

We stood in a long line across the road, watching the men set up a portable microphone. In the heat, time stopped. I heard voices: Lucy, explaining life to thousands of Ambrose County children; Sarah Rose, young, behind the counter of the store; Hunter, with his wonderful laugh; J.W.; my long-gone children; my mother. They all talked at once, and their voices made strange music.

I looked around me. Did the others hear it, too? I covered my ears to block the sound, but the words went on, hovering above me like a cloud.

Sheltered between Sarah Rose and Berkley, Jesse smiled at me, and I knew that the boy had been hearing the voices for a very long time, and had made peace with them.

The governor stood in the shade of Lucy's walnut tree and began to speak. "We're honored to be here this beautiful Fourth of July. You know, hidden away in Richmond as we too often are, we forget just how beautiful the western part of our state is. You live in God's country, and I pledge to you that we're going to do everything we can to keep it that way.

"After closely following the events at this landfill for the past months, consulting regularly with my Water Control staff and my Solid Waste Management people, I must tell you that I am vitally concerned about the situation here."

"Where were you three months ago?" Chance Sanders asked.

"Believe me, we've been on top of the problem from the beginning," the governor continued. "My staff and

I have been exploring every possible remedy to the problem, so that Virginia will never again fall prey to a similar indignity. The time has come to put down our legislative foot, to say no to out-of-state garbage."

He paused, and there was scattered applause. The cameras rolled; he smiled.

"My God, he's going to close the dump!" Patty said. "It's going to happen."

"So I've chosen today, Independence Day, to publicly declare that I plan to issue an executive order banning any future out-of-state-garbage dumping in the state of Virginia."

"You can't do that! Interstate commerce is protected by the Constitution!" Chance shouted.

The governor ignored him. "Never again will Virginia be a dumping ground for the cities of the Northeast!"

"But what about *this* dump? When are you going to close it?" I called out.

He went on. "I am standing here today to promise you that the State will continue to monitor this operation to assure your health safety."

"Hey! Shut this hellhole down!" Patty screamed.

The governor's people looked worried. Andrews raised his hands. "We're working on several scenarios that may make that possible in the near future."

Four empty trucks idled behind the landfill gates, the drivers leaning out of their cabs to listen to the speech. One of them was Rastin, the young man I'd tangled with at Sarah Rose's nearly three months back, three months that might as well have been three years.

Beyond the trucks, Lucy's house stood alone in the bare dirt. Like Lucy herself: solitary, firm, a little battered finally, but everlasting. As the governor went on and on for the cameras, about how our land was our future, I thought, *Thank God that Lucy was a good Christian and had heaven to look forward to, rather than this hell.*

Then a breeze moved the curtains in the windows of

her house, and Lucy's shadow moved with them in a comforting rhythm, like the slow nodding of a head, or the gentle rocking of a cradle.

I looked down the line of our people, folks I'd fought with and worked with my whole life, their faces marked with pain and happiness. At the end, Sarah Rose held Berkley's arm tight and hugged Jesse to her breast. I knew beyond doubt that Lucy was there for her, too. Jesse reached out to Lucy's house as if he could touch it, and her within.

"You should be proud of your efforts in monitoring the landfill," Governor Andrews was saying. "Citizens like you are what makes Virginia great, people who are not afraid to take action and work with us in Richmond to assure our common safety. Thank you for being here today. I consider it a real privilege to serve you, and I hope you'll reelect Delegate Kane as part of our team." The governor stepped aside and began talking to reporters.

We were stunned and silent. Lucy's presence was strong among us, and when the trucks came back and the landfill gates swung open, we knew what to do.

All fifty-five of us moved across the road toward the fence. The right gate had banged against the walnut tree, cutting deep into the bark. Chance took one side and I took the other; together we shut the gates. Sarah Rose tied them closed with her scarf.

Three deep, we planted our feet in the dirt and stood before the gates. Our children—Jesse and Amber and the others—we put in the center, and we linked arms tightly, standing in the way of the trucks.

They could neither enter nor leave with us there. We felt the thunder of their engines, breathed their poisonous fumes. The drivers beat their horns and gunned their engines. The first in line crept forward to within a couple inches of Chance and Patty. But we would not be moved.

John Anstett pulled up in his cruiser. "You can't do this, folks. You're obstructing traffic. Until this dump is legally closed, you'll have to let these trucks do their business."

"No more," I said. "We won't wait for these gates to be legally locked."

"I'll have to arrest you all."

"So be it, John. You do what you feel is right," I said.

"Go on home!" someone called to the sheriff. "Just turn your back and don't see."

George raised his fist in the air, and the spiraled metal binding of his notebook caught the sunlight and threw brightness into the air.

The trucks pulled in closer, making us pack together tighter.

"Reba! Somebody's going to get killed!" Karen screamed.

"Somebody already has!" I answered.

Centuries of Ambrose County bones strengthened our own. We stood fast. We did it for Lucy and J.W., beneath our feet, and Edith Halsey, soon to be. For Hunter, living out confused days and nights in his lonely world. We did it to ease Berkley's pain. And I looked at Jesse and Amber, and knew that this was for them, finally.

One of the drivers jumped out of his truck, pushed among us and tried to tear open the gates, but Chance stopped him. Berkley put himself solidly in front of the knotted scarf and stood like a rock.

"Go home," he said. "This dump is closed."

LUCY McCOMB

It is dusk. The trucks have all gone, leaving in their wake an odd silence. The landfill gates are chained, and Reba has adorned them with fat black bows. Berkley has torn the electric wires loose from the poles planted in my garden; no longer will lights shine all night into my bedroom window.

Bobby Halsey has disappeared, taken his altered files and money and gone somewhere far away with Wesley Ferris, who is practiced at disappearance. Bobby left without knowing his grandmother was dead; she will have a quiet burial without him.

Reba holds her lover's hand, knowing they have done their jobs well. What lies between them does not lend itself to words: it goes well beyond the politics of trash and will endure long separation and distance.

Berkley and Jesse stand at the mountain's edge, amazed by the quiet that has been returned to them. As darkness deepens, house lights begin to dot the valley spread out below. Jesse leans against his father; Berkley remains still, afraid that this moment will pass too quickly to be remembered.

A burst of small explosions startles them both. Bright-colored stars appear over the McPhersons' farm. "Fireworks," Jesse says, and looks at his father. Berkley nods, and Jesse starts down the mountain toward Amber's house. Hesitantly, Berkley follows.

At Stoneleigh, Sarah Rose waits in shadows for Hunter to waken. His calm sleep drifts into the heart of night. She removes her shoes and unbuttons her dress to lie with him, and whispers of the day's events. She knows her husband will never come home again, but she will give him the peace of hearing that my land will no longer be trespassed upon.

My house sits strong and dark in a wasteland. In time, the land will be smoothed over, and grass will grow on the gentle contours of garbage. People will come to marvel at the neat surface of things. Many of them will forget what lies beneath.

What is left behind? Millions of tons of thrown-away lives, pieces that don't seem to matter separately but that come together now on my land to take on new life. Some of it will return to the air, and some to the earth, wells of methane waiting for fiery transformation.

But it is the water that will change forever. From deep inside the mountain it comes, pushing downhill. Springs run fresh to the far edge of my land, then slow at the presence of tires, batteries, furniture, twisted playthings, newspaper, shards of metal. The water persists, works its way through the remnants of city lives, picking up a romance of elements: cadmium, chromium, selenium, copper, mercury, arsenic, lead.

The altered water pours, pools, goes on. It rolls darkly into rivers and transmutes all it touches. We cannot contain it; like sin, it will be with us forever.